Anonymous

**The Life, Campaigns, and Public Services of General McClellan**

The hero of western Virginia! South Mountain! and Antietam!

Anonymous

**The Life, Campaigns, and Public Services of General McClellan**
*The hero of western Virginia! South Mountain! and Antietam!*

ISBN/EAN: 9783337213497

Printed in Europe, USA, Canada, Australia, Japan

Cover: Foto ©Raphael Reischuk / pixelio.de

More available books at **www.hansebooks.com**

MAJOR-GENERAL GEORGE B. McCLELLAN.

# THE LIFE, CAMPAIGNS,

### AND

# PUBLIC SERVICES

### OF

# GENERAL McCLELLAN.
### (GEORGE B. McCLELLAN.)

### THE

# HERO OF WESTERN VIRGINIA! SOUTH MOUNTAIN! AND ANTIETAM!

With a full history of all his Campaigns and Battles; as well as his Reports and Correspondence with the War Department and the President in relation to them, from the time he first took the field in this war, until he was finally relieved from command after the Battle of Antietam, with his various Speeches to Soldiers, etc., made by him up to the present time.

PHILADELPHIA:
## T. B. PETERSON & BROTHERS,
### 306 CHESTNUT STREET.

# CONTENTS.

# LIFE AND PUBLIC SERVICES

OF

# GENERAL GEORGE B. McCLELLAN.

To PEN a Biographical Sketch of a distinguished man, in whatever sphere of life he may have been eminent, is always a pleasing task, but how much is that gratification enhanced when the sketch is to give, in detail, the various incidents which comprise the varied career of one who as a citizen is beloved, as a soldier is regarded with esteem and confidence, as a military commander is viewed with veneration and devotion, and by military critics is considered probably the best strategist of his time.

## HIS EARLY LIFE.

General McClellan was born in the city of Philadelphia, on the third day of December, 1826. His father, Dr. George McClellan, was a distinguished physician and surgeon, and was for a long time one of the Professors in the Jefferson Medical College in that city. The son, for a brief period, was a student at the University of Pennsylvania, which venerable institution he left at the age of sixteen, to enter West Point. He graduated in 1846, second in his class, and July first, of that year, entered the army as Brevet Second-Lieutenant of Engineers.

## HIS SERVICES IN MEXICO.

He was ordered to Mexico immediately thereafter, where, as Lieutenant of Sappers, Miners and Pontoniers, he performed valuable service, and for the first time was afforded the opportunity of displaying upon the field of battle those military talents which have since made him so esteemed.    For gallantry at Vera Cruz, where he was attached to General Worth's Division, he was highly commended in official reports; at Cerro Gordo, and the city of Mexico, he was connected with General Twiggs's Division, and was specially commended for gallant conduct; at Contreras and Cherubusco he won the brevet of First-Lieutenant, and at Molino del Rey was offered the additional brevet of Captain, which he declined.    The offer, however, being subsequently tendered for "gallant and meritorious conduct at Chepultepec," was accepted, and in May, 1848, he assumed command of the company, in which he had previously been a subordinate officer.

Among other incidents which occurred during his service in Mexico is one which created no little amusement at the time.    When about twelve miles from Puebla, the young Lieutenant was out reconnoitering unattended, when he observed a tall Engineer officer of the Mexican army near by.    The discovery was, however, not made a moment too soon, as the Mexican had espied the Lieutenant and was advancing towards him.    A mutual demand for surrender was made, and a hand-to-hand scuffle commenced, resulting in McClellan collaring his more gigantic opponent, and taking him into camp.

## HIS SUBSEQUENT MILITARY CAREER.

After the declaration of peace, he was ordered to West Point as director of field labors and instructor of the bayonet exercise.    While thus employed at the Academy,

he translated from the French a "Manual of Bayonet Exercise," which became the text-book of the service. In
1851 he was ordered to Fort Delaware to superintend its
construction, and the following year he accompanied Capt.
R. B. Marcy (now his father-in-law) on an expedition to
explore the Red river. In September of the same year
he was assigned to accompany General Persifer F. Smith
to Texas, as Senior Engineer to survey the rivers and har-
bors of that State. In the following spring he was ordered
to report to Governor Isaac I. Stevens, of Washington
Territory, who had been placed in charge of the survey of
a Northern route for a railroad to the Pacific, and was
subsequently detailed by that officer for the examination
of the Western part of the proposed line. Starting from
Steilacoom, he explored the Yakima pass and other portions of the Cascade range, and the most direct route to
Puget Sound, and the report of his observations, written
in a highly interesting style, formed the first volume of
the "Pacific Railroad Surveys." He was subsequently
complimented by the Secretary of War for the superior
manner in which he had performed the important duty.

## IMPORTANT MISSIONS ENTRUSTED TO HIM.

Soon afterwards he was detailed to visit the principal
lines of railway in the United States, and to thoroughly
investigate the railroad system of the country, with a view
of obtaining such information relative to construction,
equipment and management as might be of service in the
successful operation of the Pacific railroad. A full report
of his investigations was published in November, 1854.

A secret mission to the West Indies was the next important duty entrusted to him by the Government. Leaving
the United States in the frigate Columbia, he proceeded
to San Domingo, and from there to some of the other
islands, returning with a vast amount of information important at the time to the administration, and a large

number of maps and sketches of the country he had visited.

## IS SENT TO EUROPE—REPORT OF HIS OBSERVATIONS IN THE CRIMEA.

In July, 1853, he was commissioned as First Lieutenant, and in March, 1855, he was promoted to a Captaincy in the First Cavalry. One year later, he was sent to Europe with Majors Delafield and Mordecai, to observe the operations in the Crimea, and to study the organization of the opposing armies.

The report of his observations was printed by order of Congress, and subsequently republished in Philadelphia. It is full and complete, and will be found invaluable to officers of the army. Although the youngest officer of the commission, his labor in preparing a statement of what he had seen and heard in military circles and in the scenes of strife, was by no means less arduous than that of his companions. Although more attention was probably paid to the Engineer and Cavalry branches of the service, the military student of the other departments can find a vast amount of interesting and instructive matter within its pages. He may not have been able, from circumstances over which he had no control, to practically carry out, during the present rebellion, much of what he recommends theoretically in this voluminous work, but that does not detract in the least from the merits of his suggestions.

## RESIGNS THE SERVICE AND BECOMES A RAILROAD PRESIDENT.

On the sixteenth of January, 1857, he resigned from the army, and removing to Chicago, filled for three years the responsible position of Vice-President and Engineer of the Illinois Central railroad, at the end of which time he resigned and became General Superintendent of the Ohio and Mississippi railroad, and, two months later, President of the Eastern Division of the same road, with his residence at Cincinnati, and with a salary of ten thousand dollars a year—a post he held and an income he enjoyed when the rebellion commenced.

## "LITTLE MAC" APPOINTED MAJOR-GENERAL.

With the patriotic motive and unselfish nature which have always actuated him, he immediately offered his services in whatever capacity he might be useful. Governor Curtin expressed his desire to have him command the troops organized in Pennsylvania for active service, but before the unanimous sentiment of the authorities and the people of the Keystone State could be gratified, General McClellan received a commission as Major-General from the Governor of Ohio, and proceeded to organize the nine months' troops from that State.

## ASSUMES COMMAND OF THE DEPARTMENT OF THE OHIO.

On the tenth of May, 1861, the States of Ohio, Indiana and Illinois were formed into a Department, to be known as the "Department of the Ohio," and "Major-General McClellan, Ohio Volunteers," was assigned to the command, with his head-quarters at Cincinnati. Four days later he was appointed Major-General in the regular army.

On the twenty-sixth of the same month, he received information that two bridges on the Baltimore and Ohio railroad, near Farmington, had been burned, and that others were threatened. The intelligence induced the General, who had been making arrangements to move on Grafton, to hasten his movements ; and returning to Cincinnati, he directed one column of his command to move from Wheeling and Bellaire, and another from Marietta on Parkersburg. Simultaneously with the advance, the following proclamation to the people of Western Virginia, and address to his troops, were issued :

"To the People of Western Virginia.

"Head-quarters, Department of the Ohio,
"Cincinnati, *May 26th*, 1861.

*"To the Union Men of Western Virginia:*

"Virginians :—The General Government has long endured the machinations of a few fractious rebels in your midst. Armed traitors have in vain endeavored to deter you from expressing your loyalty at the polls ; having failed in this infamous attempt to deprive you of the exercise of your dearest rights, they now seek to inaugurate a reign of terror, and thus force you to yield to their schemes, and submit to the yoke of the traitorous conspiracy, dignified by the name of Southern Confederacy. They are destroying the property of citizens of your State, and ruining your magnificent railways. The General Government has heretofore carefully abstained from sending troops across the Ohio, or even from posting them along its banks, although frequently urged by many of your prominent citizens to do so. It determined to await the result of the late election, desirous that no one might be able to say that the slightest effort had been made from this side to influence the free expression of your opinion, although the many agencies brought to bear upon you by the rebels were well known. You have now shown, under the most adverse circumstances, that the great mass of the people of Western Virginia are true and loyal to that beneficent Government under which we and our fathers have lived so long. As soon as the result of the election was known, the traitors commenced their work of destruction. The General Government cannot close its ears to the demands you have made for assistance. I have ordered troops to cross the river. They come as your friends and your brothers—as enemies only to the armed rebels who are preying upon you. Your homes, your families, and your property are safe under our protection. All your rights shall be religiously respected.

"Notwithstanding all that has been said by the traitors to induce you to believe that our advent among you will be signalized by interference with your slaves, understand one thing clearly— not only will we abstain from all such interference, but we will, on the contrary, with an iron hand, crush any attempt at insurrection on their part. Now, that we are in your midst, I call upon you to fly to arms and support the General Government. Sever the connection that binds you to traitors ; proclaim to the world that the faith and loyalty so long boasted by the Old Dominion, are still preserved in Western Virginia, and that you remain true to the Stars and Stripes.

"George B. McClellan,
*"Major-General Commanding."*

"ADDRESS TO THE VOLUNTEER ARMY.

"HEAD-QUARTERS, DEPARTMENT OF THE OHIO,
"CINCINNATI, *May* 26*th*, 1861.

"SOLDIERS :—You are ordered to cross the frontier and enter upon the soil of Virginia. Your mission is to restore peace and confidence, to protect the majesty of the law, and to rescue our brethren from the grasp of armed traitors. You are to act in concert with the Virginia troops and to support their advance.

"I place under the safeguard of your honor the persons and property of the Virginians. I know that you will respect their feelings and all their rights. Preserve the strictest discipline ; remember that each one of you holds in his keeping the honor of Ohio and of the Union.

"If you are called upon to overcome armed opposition, I know that your courage is equal to the task ; but remember that your only foes are the armed traitors,—and show mercy even to them when they are in your power, for many of them are misguided. When, under your protection, the loyal men of Western Virginia have been enabled to organize and arm, they can protect themselves, and you can then return to your homes, with the proud satisfaction of having preserved a gallant people from destruction.          "GEORGE B. McCLELLAN,
*"Major-General Commanding."*

## THE FIGHT AT PHILIPPI.

On the thirtieth of May, Colonel B. F. Kelley's command occupied Grafton, the rebels evacuating the town without firing a gun. On the second of June, a large Union force left Grafton, and at an early hour on the following morning approached Philippi. At five o'clock they encountered the enemy, who had advanced to meet them ; but after a short and sharp engagement, the rebels fled in the wildest disorder. In the fight Colonel Kelley was badly wounded. On the twelfth of June a resolution was unanimously adopted by the Western Virginia Convention, thanking General McClellan for sending troops to Western Virginia ; commending the gallant troops at Philippi, and complimenting Colonel Kelley's bravery.

## HE TAKES THE FIELD IN PERSON.

On the eighteenth of June, the " Young Napoleon" left Cincinnati to take personal command of his troops in the field, a change which had been ardently desired by the officers and men, and urged by the loyal citizens of the section in which the military operations had been progressing. His arrival upon the field was the signal for renewed activity, and on all sides could be heard the note of preparation for the important campaign which the able and energetic commander had planned for immediate prosecution.

## ASSUMES COMMAND IN WESTERN VIRGINIA.

On the twentieth of June, 1861, General McClellan assumed command of the Union forces in Western Virginia, and made immediate arrangements to increase his command to a numerical strength equal to the emergency. His extended fame and personal popularity soon accomplished the desired object. On the twenty-third, he issued from his head-quarters at Grafton the following proclamations:

"HEAD-QUARTERS. DEPARTMENT OF THE OHIO,
"GRAFTON, (VA.,) *June 23d*, 1861.

"*To the Inhabitants of Western Virginia:*

"The army of this department. headed by Virginia troops, is rapidly occupying all Western Virginia. This is done in co-operation with and in support of such civil authorities of the State as are faithful to the Constitution and laws of the United States. The proclamation issued by me, under date of May 26th, 1861, will be strictly maintained. Your houses, families, property, and all your rights will be religiously respected. We are enemies to none but armed rebels, and those voluntarily giving them aid. All officers of this army will be held responsible for the most prompt and vigorous action in repressing disorder and punishing aggression by those under their command.

"To my great regret I find that the enemies of the United States continue to carry on a system of hostilities prohibited by the laws of war among belligerent nations, and of course far more wicked and intolerable when directed against loyal citizens engaged in the defence of the common Government of all. Individuals and marauding parties are pursuing a guerilla warfare, firing upon sentinels and pickets, burning bridges, insulting and even killing citizens because of their Union sentiments, and committing many kindred acts.

"I do now, therefore, make proclamation, and warn all persons, that individuals or parties engaged in this species of warfare, irregular in every view that can be taken of it, thus attacking sentries, pickets, or other soldiers, destroying public or private property, or committing injuries against any of the inhabitants because of Union sentiments or conduct, will be dealt with in their persons and property according to the severest rules of military law.

"All persons giving information or aid to the public enemies will be arrested and kept in close custody; and all persons found bearing arms, unless of known loyalty, will be arrested and held for examination. "GEORGE B. McCLELLAN,
"*Major-General, U. S. A., Commanding Department.*"

"*To the Soldiers of the Army of the West:*

"You are here to support the Government of your country, and to protect the lives and liberties of your brethren, threatened by a rebellious and traitorous foe. No higher or nobler duty could devolve on you, and I expect you to bring to its performance the highest and noblest qualities of soldiers, discipline, courage, and mercy.

"I call upon the officers of every grade to enforce the highest discipline, and I know that those of all grades, privates and officers, will display in battle cool heroic courage, and will know how to show mercy to a disarmed enemy. Bear in mind that you are in the country of friends, not of enemies—that you are here to protect, not to destroy. Take nothing, destroy nothing, unless you are ordered to do so by your general officers. Remember that I have pledged my word to the people of Western Virginia that their rights in person and property shall be respected. I ask every one of you to make good this promise in its broadest sense.

"We have come here to save, not to upturn. I do not appeal to the fear of punishment, but to your appreciation of the sacredness of the cause in which we are engaged. Carry into battle the conviction that you are right and that God is on our side. Your enemies have violated every moral law; neither God nor man can sustain them. They have without cause rebelled against a mild and paternal Government; they have seized upon public and private property; they have outraged the persons of Northern men, merely because they came from the North, and of Southern Union men, merely because they loved the Union; they have placed themselves beneath contempt unless they can retrieve some honor on the field of battle.

"You will pursue a different course; you will be honest, brave, and merciful; you will respect the right of private opinion; you will punish no man for opinion's sake. Show to the world that you differ from our enemies in these points of honor, honesty, and respect for private opinion, and that we inaugurate no reign of terror wherever we go.

"Soldiers, I have heard that there was danger here. I have come to place myself at your head and share it with you. I fear now but one thing, that you will not find foemen worthy of your steel. I know that I can rely upon you.

"GEORGE B. McCLELLAN,
"*Major-General Commanding.*"

## THE BATTLE OF RICH MOUNTAIN—DESTROYS THE REBEL ARMY.

On the eleventh of July was fought the battle of Rich Mountain, a gap in the Laurel Hill range, where the Staunton and Weston turnpike crosses it between Buckhannon and Beverly, and about two miles east of Roaring Run. The enemy, numbering about two thousand men under Colonel Pegram, were strongly intrenched, a portion of the works being surrounded by dense woods. At an early hour of the morning the General commanding sent General Roscerans, with his brigade, along the summit of the eminence with a view of surrounding the enemy. After a long and tedious march the intrenchments were reached, and after a short engagement a charge was made and the works carried, the rebels fleeing in the greatest confusion, leaving all their guns, camp equipage and several prisoners. The same night Pegram withdrew from a position he had taken near Beverly, leaving behind him six guns, a large number of horses, wagons and his camp equipage, but finding that the gallant Union commander was following him closely, his men flushed with victory, he on the morning of the twelfth sent a flag of truce announcing his desire to surrender his men and himself as prisoners of war. The request was worded in the following language:

'NEAR TYGART'S VALLEY RIVER, SIX MILES
"FROM BEVERLY, *July* 12th, 1861.

"*To Commanding Officer of Northern Forces, Beverly, Va.:*

"SIR: I write to state to you that I have, in consequence of the retreat of General Garnett, and the jaded and reduced condition of my command, most of them having been without

food for two days, concluded, with the concurrence of a majority
of my captains and field officers, to surrender my command to
you to-morrow, as *prisoners of war.* I have only to add, I
trust they will only receive at your hands such treatment as
has been invariably shown to the Northern prisoners by the
South.            " I am, sir, your obedient servant,

"JOHN PEGRAM,
"*Lieutenant-Colonel P. A. C. S., Commanding.*"

To this General McClellan replied as follows :

"HEAD-QUARTERS, DEPARTMENT OF THE OHIO,
" BEVERLY, Va., *July* 13th, 1861.
"JOHN PEGRAM, ESQ., *styling himself Lieutenant-Colonel,*
"*P. A. C. S.:*

"SIR : Your communication dated yesterday, proposing the
surrender as prisoners of war of the force assembled under your
command, has been delivered to me.   As commander of this department, I will receive you and them with the kindness due
to prisoners of war, but it is not in my power to relieve you or
them from any liabilities incurred by taking arms against the
United States.
" I am, very respectfully, your obedient servant,
" GEORGE B. McCLELLAN,
"*Major-General U. S. A., Commanding Department.*"

General McClellan then sent to General Scott the
following report :

" HEAD-QUARTERS, BEVERLY, Va., *July* 13th, 1861.
"COL. E. D. TOWNSEND, *Washington, D. C.:*

" I have received from Col. Pegram propositions for the surrender, with his officers and remnant of his command—say six
hundred men.   They are said to be extremely penitent, and determined never again to take up arms against the General
Government.   I shall have near nine hundred or one thousand
prisoners to take care of when Col. Pegram comes in.   The
latest accounts make the loss of the rebels in killed some one
hundred and fifty.            " GEORGE B. McCLELLAN,
"*Major-General Department of Ohio.*"

Colonel Pegram, finding it impossible to elude the vigilance of his opponent, and to extricate himself from his
position, acceded to the terms of surrender, and with his
entire force, having been disarmed, was sent to Beverly.
Among the prisoners was a company of students, with a

Professor from Hampden Sidney College. On the fourteenth, General Morris overtook at Carrick's Ford, the rebel forces under General Robert S. Garnett, who were retreating from Laurel Hill, and after a severe fight routed them and killed their commander, who was shot in the spine while rallying his men. General McClellan's official despatches give the following brief history of this important campaign, which, by the complete destruction of the rebel army in Western Virginia, relieved the suffering Union people of that section from the presence of the implacable rebels, who had devastated their property and slaughtered at will the defenceless objects of their enmity:

"HEAD-QUARTERS, DEPARTMENT OF THE OHIO,
  "RICH MOUNTAIN, Va., 9 A.M., *July 12th*, 1861.

"COL. E. D. TOWNSEND: We are in possession of all the enemy's works up to a point in the right of Beverly. I have taken all his guns, a very large amount of wagons, tents, etc.—every thing he had—a large number of prisoners, many of whom were wounded, and several officers prisoners. They lost many killed. We have lost, in all, perhaps twenty killed and fifty wounded, of whom all but two or three were in the column under Rosecrans, which turned the position. The mass of the enemy escaped through the woods, entirely disorganized. Among the prisoners is Dr. Taylor, formerly of the army. Col. Pegram was in command.

"Col. Rosecrans's column left camp yesterday morning, and marched some eight miles through the mountains, reaching the turnpike some two or three miles in rear of the enemy, defeating an advanced post, and taking a couple of guns. I had a position ready for twelve guns near the main camp, and as guns were moving up, I ascertained that the enemy had retreated. I am now pushing on to Beverly, a part of Colonel Rosecrans's troops being now within three miles of it.

"Our success is complete, and almost bloodless. I doubt whether Wise and Johnson will unite and overpower me. The behavior of the troops in the action and toward the prisoners was admirable          "GEORGE B. McCLELLAN,
              "*Major-General Commanding.*"

              "BEVERLY, *July 12th*, 1861.
"COL. E. D. TOWNSEND, *Washington, D. C.:*
  "The success of to-day is all that I could desire. We cap-

tured six brass cannons, of which one is rifled, all the enemy's camp equipage and transportation, even to his cups. The number of tents will probably reach two hundred, and more than sixty wagons. Their killed and wounded will amount to fully one hundred and fifty, with one hundred prisoners, and more coming in constantly. I know already of ten officers killed and prisoners. Their retreat is complete.

'"I occupied Beverly by a rapid march. Garnett abandoned his camp early in the morning, leaving much of his equipage. He came within a few miles of Beverly, but our rapid march turned him back in great confusion, and he is now retreating on the road to St. George. I have ordered General Morris to follow him up closely. .

"I have telegraphed for the two Pennsylvania regiments at Cumberland to join General Hill at Rowlesburg. The General is concentrating all his troops at Rowlesburg, and he will cut off Garnett's retreat near West Union, or, if possible, at St. George.

"I may say that we have driven out some ten thousand troops, strongly intrenched, with the loss of eleven killed and thirty-five wounded. The provision returns here show Garnett's force to have been ten thousand men. They were Eastern Virginians, Tennesseeans, Georgians, and, I think, Carolinians. To-morrow I can give full details, as to prisoners, etc.

"I trust that General Cox has, by this time, driven Wise out of the Kanawha Valley. In that case, I shall have accomplished the object of liberating Western Virginia.

"I hope the General-in-Chief will approve of my operations.

"GEORGE B. McCLELLAN,

"*Major-General Com'dg the Dep. of Ohio.*"

## GENERAL McCLELLAN'S REPORT.

"HUNTONSVILLE, VA., *July 14th*, 1861.

"COL. E. D. TOWNSEND, *Assistant Adjutant-General:*

"General Garnett and his forces have been routed and his baggage and one gun taken. His army is completely demoralized. General Garnett was killed while attempting to rally his forces at Carrackford, near St. George.

"We have completely annihilated the enemy in Western Virginia.

"Our loss is but thirteen killed and not more than forty wounded, while the enemy's loss is not far from two hundred killed, and the number of prisoners we have taken will amount to at least one thousand. We have captured seven of the enemy's guns in all. .

"A portion of Garnett's forces retreated, but I look for their capture by General Hill, who is in hot pursuit.

2

" The troops that Garnett had under his command are said to be the crack regiments of Eastern Virginia, aided by Georgians, Tennesseeans, and Carolinians.

" Our success is complete, and I firmly believe that secession is killed in this section of the country.

" GEORGE B. McCLELLAN.
" *Major-General U. S. A.*"

The victories thus accomplished were not unappreciated by the millions of freemen, who had anxiously awaited tidings from the department over which the young patriot had taken command. They knew his ability and prophesied success. They were not disappointed, and from Maine to the Mississippi, peans of praise were sung to the conqueror, while the States upon the Pacific coast joined in the chorus. Congress unanimously adopted a joint resolution thanking him with his officers and soldiers for the victories, and the press was loud in its eulogy. Thousands of extracts might be given from the newspapers of the day, to prove the unanimous sentiment that prevailed, but one will be sufficient. The Louisville *Journal* remarked :

" It is a finished piece of work. It stands before us perfect and entire, wanting nothing ; like a statue or picture just leaving the creative hand of the artist, and embodying his whole idea. McClellan set out to accomplish a certain definite object. With that precise object in view he gathers his forces and plans his campaign. Onward he moves, and neither wood, mountain, nor stream checks his march. He presses forward from skirmish to skirmish, but nothing decoys or diverts or forces him from the trail of the enemy. Outpost after outpost, camp after camp, gives way ; the main body falls back, and is at last put to an ignominious and disgraceful retreat. He remains master of the field, and reports that he has accomplished his mission. There is something extremely satisfactory in contemplating what might be called a piece of finished military workmanship by a master hand. It is one thing *done*. It is, besides, a poetic retribution, for it commemorates the quarter day after the bombardment of Sumter.

" Thus shall we go on from one step to another. Eastern Virginia will next be *McClellanized* in the same finished style. The triumphant columns of the Grand Army of the United

States will soon begin to move Southward from North, East, and West, headed by the old victor-chief now coming as the conquering liberator of his native State. Then will the pseudo-Government at Richmond either repeat the flight at Harper's Ferry, Philippi, Martinsburg, and Beverly, or, if it stands its ground, fall as surely before the concentrating hosts of the Republic as if it were meshed and crushed in the folds of some entangling and overwhelming fate."

On the nineteenth of July he issued the following address to his gallant men :

"HEAD-QUARTERS, ARMY OF OCCUPATION, WESTERN
"VIRGINIA, BEVERLY, VA., *July 19th*, 1861.

"*Soldiers of the Army of the West :*

"I am more than satisfied with you. You have annihilated two armies, commanded by educated and experienced soldiers, intrenched in mountain fastnesses and fortified at their leisure. You have taken five guns, twelve colors, fifteen hundred stand of arms, one thousand prisoners, including more than forty officers. One of the second commanders of the rebels is a prisoner, the other lost his life on the field of battle. You have killed more than two hundred and fifty of the enemy, who has lost all his baggage and camp equipage. All this has been accomplished with the loss of twenty brave men killed and sixty wounded on your part.

"You have proved that Union men, fighting for the preservation of our Government, are more than a match for our misguided and erring brothers. More than this, you have shown mercy to the vanquished. You have made long and arduous marches, with insufficient food, frequently exposed to the inclemency of the weather. I have not hesitated to demand this of you, feeling that I could rely on your endurance, patriotism, and courage. In the future I may have still greater demands to make upon you, still greater sacrifices for you to offer. It shall be my care to provide for you to the extent of my ability ; but I know now that, by your valor and endurance, you will accomplish all that is asked.

"Soldiers ! I have confidence in you, and I trust you have learned to confide in me. Remember that discipline and subordination are qualities of equal value with courage. I am proud to say that you have gained the highest reward that American troops can receive—the thanks of Congress and the applause of your fellow-citizens.

"GEORGE B. McCLELLAN,
"*Major-General.*"

## HE IS ORDERED TO WASHINGTON—ENTHUSI-
## ASTIC RECEPTION IN PHILADELPHIA.

While engaged at Beverly in preparing for a campaign
in the Upper Kanawha Valley, he received information
of the disaster at Bull Run, and later on the same day,
the twenty-first of July, received an order from Washington directing him to move into East Virginia, and while
hastily making arrangements to conform to the instructions, received another despatch ordering him to turn
over his command to General Rosecrans, and report
immediately at Washington.    He immediately issued an
order relinquishing the command of the army of occupation of Western Virginia, and the Department of Ohio,
and hastened to conform to the urgent order for his immediate presence at the Capital.    On the twenty-fifth he
reached Philadelphia, and was received at the depot by
an immense concourse of persons, who escorted him to
the residence of a relative, thronging the streets, making
the air echo and re-echo with their enthusiastic cheers.
His order to report at Washington had been caused in a
great measure by the unanimous call which had been made
after the battle of Bull Run, by the people of the North
and West for the young hero, and it was fitting that the
residents of the city of his birth should give him a public
reception as he passed through their midst, to assume the
duties of a more exalted position.    In response to the
numerous demands for his presence on the balcony, he
came forward and said :

" My friends and old townsmen, I thank you for your reception, and might reply, if this were not a time for action and not
for speech.    Your applause, as I take it, is intended for my
brave soldiers in Western Virginia.    I am going to fulfil new
duties, and I trust that your kindness will give me courage and
strength.    Good-bye."

## TAKES COMMAND IN WASHINGTON—HIS PLANS.

On the 25th of July, the War Department announced that the "Department of Washington and the Department of Northeastern Virginia will constitute a geographical division under General McClellan, United States Army, head-quarters Washington." Five days later he issued the following order, the provisions of which were immediately enforced by the Provost-Marshal, much to the advantage of the service :

"HEAD-QUARTERS, DIVISION OF THE POTOMAC,
"WASHINGTON, *July 30th*, 1861.

"The General commanding the Division has, with much regret, observed that large numbers of officers and men stationed in the vicinity of Washington are in the habit of frequenting the streets and hotels of the city. This practice is eminently prejudicial to good order and military discipline, and must at once be discontinued.

"The time and services of all persons connected with this division should be devoted to their appropriate duties with their respective commands. It is therefore directed that hereafter no officer or soldier be allowed to absent himself from his camp and visit Washington, except for the performance of some public duty, or the transaction of important private business, for which purposes written permits will be given by the commanders of brigades. The permit will state the object of the visit. Brigade commanders will be held responsible for the strict execution of this order.

"Col. Andrew Porter, of the 16th U. S. Infantry, is detailed for temporary duty as Provost Marshal in Washington, and will be obeyed and respected accordingly. Col. Porter will report in person at these head-quarters for instructions.

"By command of        "Maj.-Gen. McCLELLAN.
"S. WILLIAMS, *Assistant Adjutant-General.*"

On the 4th of August, 1861, he laid before the President his scheme of the war, in which he showed that our best, if not our only hope of a speedy and lasting peace lay in convincing the disloyal populations, at the outset of hostilities, that resistance to the Government must prove impracticable.

Virginia having been made the battle-field, it became necessary to fight there; but, in order to success in the campaign against Virginia, General McClellan pointed out the importance of opening the Mississippi, of pacifying Missouri, and of advancing through Kentucky into Eastern Tennessee, for the purpose of assisting the Union men of that region, and of seizing the railway leading from the Mississippi to the East.

The importance of availing ourselves, as far as possible, in every case, of water transportation, was strongly urged, as well as of the naval diversions against the leading cities of the Southern coast. The importance of these points was shown to be much enhanced by the existence of the great railway system of the South, which would enable the enemy to concentrate rapidly upon interior lines; and the inference was drawn, that the operations of the main army ought to be strictly connected with all subsidiary operations, wherever undertaken.

One of these subsidiary operations, through Nebraska and Kansas into Western Texas, in connection with a movement to the same end from the Pacific through Arizona and New Mexico, was especially designated for its importance; and it was suggested that an intimate alliance with Mexico might be effected, which would materially facilitate the results of such a combined movement.

To effect these objects, General McClellan estimated would require an army of about 300,000 men. With this force, acting under the control of a policy strictly protective of private property, and merciful to private soldiers taken in arms, he was of the opinion that the organized strength of the rebellion might be overwhelmed, and the populations of the South compelled to recognize the folly of persisting in an attempt to resist the Government.

General McClellan found the army at Washington at this time, thus constituted:

| | |
|---|---:|
| Infantry | 50,000 |
| Cavalry | 1,000 |
| Artillery | 650 |
| Total | 51,650 |

With nine imperfect field-batteries of thirty guns.

This force was scattered in and around the city with no general organization. The city was defended by a few insignificant earthworks, and there was nothing to prevent its being shelled from heights within easy range, which could be occupied by a hostile column almost without resistance. The *morale* of the army was miserable, and desertions were the general order of the day.

Steps were at once taken to restore order in the city of Washington. Camps of instruction were located and filled with the new levies, and fortifications were pushed forward under a systematic plan.

## TAKES COMMAND OF THE ARMY OF THE POTOMAC.

On the 20th of August, 1861, he issued an order assuming command of the Army of the Potomac, comprising the troops serving in the former Department of Washington and Northeastern Virginia, in the valley of the Shenandoah, and in the States of Maryland and Delaware, and announcing his staff.

The better organization of the army was begun as soon as practicable after taking command, and on the fourth of August, 1861, the Brigade organization was effected; on the fifteenth of October, the Divisions; and on the eighth of March, 1862, by order of the President, the Army Corps.

Early in October, 1861, General McClellan addressed a letter to Secretary Cameron, in which he showed that the force under his orders was greatly inferior to that asked for by him in August for the prosecution of a vigorous and successful invasion of the South. He urged the concentration of the national forces on Virginia for the purpose of "striking the rebellion at the heart." He showed that for the defence of Washington there would be required—

| | |
|---|---:|
| Of the engineers and artillery | 35,000 |
| For Baltimore and the Potomac | 15,000 |
| For operations against the enemy | 150,000 |
| For Lower Potomac | 8,000 |
| Total effectives required | 208,000 |

The actual effective strength at his disposal he then showed to be, including all points held, 147,695, with 228 field guns—some of the batteries being unfit for active service, and the whole force being 200 guns less than was estimated on all hands as necessary.

General McClellan recommended a complete and vigorous concentration of all the forces not required for defensive purposes upon the active campaign in Virginia. "Unity in councils, the utmost vigor and energy in action," he added, "are indispensable. The entire military field should be grasped as a whole and not in detached parts." * * * "The rebels," he continued, "have displayed energy, unanimity and wisdom worthy the most desperate days of the French revolution. Should we do less?" Were such a concentration as he proposed to be effected, General McClellan expressed his conviction that the rebel organization might still, by a well-planned and well-executed movement, be overthrown before the winter should set in.

## BALL'S BLUFF.

While these propositions were under consideration, the disaster of Ball's Bluff took place. Of this, General McClellan states that the movement of General Stone was ordered by him, as a demonstration which he thought it possible might induce the enemy to abandon Leesburg— being made, as it was, cotemporaneously with reconnoissances in force toward Drainesville under General McCall. General Stone having accomplished, on the morning of October 20th, all that he was expected to accomplish, General McCall was recalled from Drainesville to his camp at Langley. The fact that General Stone's troops were in action on the Virginia side, was telegraphed to General McClellan on the 21st, and reaching the ground the next day, he learned the full extent of the disaster which had followed from this movement, and by 4 A.M. of the 24th had caused the whole command to recross the Potomac in safety.

## RETIREMENT OF GENERAL SCOTT—"LITTLE MAC" SUCCEEDS HIM IN COMMAND OF THE ARMY.

On the last day of October, 1861, Lieutenant-General Winfield Scott addressed a letter to the Secretary of War, in which he stated that, being admonished by his increasing infirmities that repose of mind and body, with the appliances of surgery and medicine, were necessary, he was compelled to ask that his name might be placed on the list of officers retired from active service. The subject was considered at a special Cabinet council held on the following day, and the request of the veteran having been granted, General McClellan was, with the unanimous consent of the Cabinet, and to the great gratification of the people of the loyal States, called to the command of the army of the Union, with his head-quarters at Washington. As soon as advised of the honor conferred upon him, he issued the following order :

"*General Order No.* 19.

"HEAD-QUARTERS OF THE ARMY,
"WASHINGTON, D. C., *Nov. 1st,* 1861.

"In accordance with General Order No. 94, from the War Department, I hereby assume command of the armies of the United States.

"In the midst of the difficulties which encompass and divide the nation, hesitation and self-distrust may well accompany the assumption of so vast a responsibility; but confiding, as I do, in the loyalty, discipline, and courage of our troops, and believing, as I do, that Providence will favor ours as the just cause, I cannot doubt that success will crown our efforts and sacrifices.

"The army will unite with me in the feeling of regret that the weight of many years, and the effect of increasing infirmities, contracted and intensified in his country's service, should just now remove from our head the great soldier of our nation—the hero who, in his youth, raised high the reputation of his country in the fields of Canada, which he sanctified with his blood; who, in more mature years, proved to the world that American skill and valor could repeat, if not eclipse, the exploits of Cortez in the land of the Montezumas; whose whole life has been devoted to the service of his country; whose whole efforts have been directed to uphold our honor at the smallest sacrifice of life;—a warrior who scorned the selfish glories of the battle-field, when his great qualities as a statesman could be employed more profitably for his country; a citizen who, in his declining years, has given to the world the most shining instances of loyalty in disregarding all ties of birth, and clinging to the cause of truth and honor. Such has been the career of Winfield Scott, whom it has long been the delight of the nation to honor as a man and a soldier.

"While we regret his loss, there is one thing we cannot regret —the bright example he has left for our emulation. Let us all hope and pray that his declining years may be passed in peace and happiness, and that they may be cheered by the success of the country and the cause he has fought for and loved so well. Beyond all that, let us do nothing that can cause him to blush for us. Let no defeat of the army he has so long commanded embitter his last years, but let our victories illuminate the close of a life so grand.      "GEO. B. McCLELLAN,

"*Major-General Commanding U. S. A.*"

## PRESENTATION OF A SWORD BY THE CITY OF PHILADELPHIA.

On the following day, General McClellan was presented with a costly sword by the City Councils of Philadelphia, a deputation of which body had proceeded to Washington to make the presentation. In responding to the complimentary remarks of the donors, he said:

"I ask you, sir, to give my warmest and deep thanks to the honorable body you represent for this entirely unmerited compliment. I could thank you better if I thought that I deserved it, but I do not feel that I do. Nothing that I have yet accomplished would warrant this high compliment. It is for the future to determine whether I shall realize the expectations and hopes that have been centred in me. I trust and feel that the day is not far distant when I shall return to the place dearest of all others to me, there to spend the balance of my life among the people from whom I have received this beautiful gift. *The war cannot last long. It may be desperate.* I ask in the future, forbearance, patience, and confidence. With these we can accomplish all; and while I know that, in the great drama which may have our hearts' blood, Pennsylvania will not play the least, I trust that, on the other hand, she will play the highest and noblest part.

"I again thank you, and ask you to convey to the Councils my most sincere thanks for the sword. Say to them that it will be my ambition to deserve it hereafter. I know I do not now."

## AN UNUSUAL HONOR.

On the twelfth of November one of the most signal manifestations of the esteem in which "Little Mac" was held by the officers and soldiers of the Army of the Potomac was witnessed—General Blenker's Division that night having marched from their camping-ground to General McClellan's residence in Washington, and tendered him a most delightful serenade. The line of the procession was illuminated throughout its length by thousands of torches; and while the offering was in every way creditable to the participants, and complimentary to the distinguished man they honored, it was one of the most enthusiastic displays ever witnessed at the Capital.

## THE OBSERVANCE OF THE SABBATH.

On the twenty-seventh of November, General McClellan issued an additional order in regard to the observance of the Sabbath by the army. Fighting in a holy cause, he believed it to be the duty of his men to deserve the favor of the Almighty by resting from their labors and, whenever practicable, attending Divine service. One day's rest in a week he considered necessary for man and animal, and, to use his own language, "The observance of the holy day of the God of mercy and of battles is our sacred duty." To facilitate the chaplains in their Sunday duties, the hour of company inspections was changed, and officers were notified to see that all persons connected with their commands, when not engaged on important service, should have the opportunity to attend the religious services. Respectful deportment towards the chaplains and a hearty co-operation with them was also enjoined.

## MILITARY MOVEMENTS PROJECTED.

An organization of troops for occupying the coast line of the South on the middle Atlantic, which had been suggested by General McClellan in September, 1861, took shape in January, 1862, as an expedition under General Burnside, designed to facilitate the movements of the main body in Eastern Virginia by an occupation of the coast line of North Carolina, General Burnside being ordered, when he should have seized Newbern, to occupy and destroy the Weldon and Wilmington railroad as far west as Goldsboro', and should circumstances favor, to push as far as Raleigh, Wilmington being, however, his ultimate objective point.

At the same time letters were sent to General Halleck, (appointed to the command of the Department of Missouri), to General Buell (in command of the Department of the Ohio), to General Sherman (commanding in South Carolina and Georgia), and to General Butler (commanding the Department of the Gulf). General Halleck was charged with the duty of "reducing chaos to order." In respect to military operations, he was ordered to hold the State by fortified posts and concentrate his force on the Mississippi, in readiness for ulterior operations.

General Buell was instructed as to the vast importance of the military occupation of Eastern Kentucky and Tennessee. In Kentucky itself he was advised, "the conduct of our political affairs is perhaps more important than that of our military operations," and he was urged to bear in mind "that we shall most readily suppress this rebellion and restore the authority of the government by religiously respecting the constitutional rights of all." In accordance "with the feelings and opinion of the President," General McClellan requested General Buell to assure "the people of Kentucky, that their domestic institutions will in no manner be interfered with;" and "to allow nothing but the dictates of military necessity," to cause him to "depart from the spirit of his instructions." In respect to Tennessee, General Buell was ordered to throw the mass of his troops "by rapid marches, by Cumberland or Walker's gap, on Knoxville, in order to occupy the railroad at that point," and "cut the communication between Eastern Virginia and the Mississippi." General Buell was further counselled to avoid "widening the breach existing between us and the rebels," by "causeless arrests and persecutions of individuals." "I have always found," adds General McClellan, "that it is the tendency of subordinates to make vexatious arrests on mere suspicion."

General Sherman was advised that the favorable moment for a *coup de main* against Savannah had been lost, and that the best course before him would be to "isolate and reduce Fort Pulaski." But the "reduction of Charleston and its defences," was held up as the great moral advantage to be sought for, and this was stated to be an object for which General McClellan was actively maturing his combinations. General Butler was instructed as to the obstacles to be encountered in reducing New Orleans, and was ordered, as soon as possible after the fall of that city, to "seize all the approaches leading to it from the east," and particularly "Jackson, in Mississippi," with an ultimate view, as well to the capture of Mobile, as to the opening of the Mississippi.

The instructions thus issued to the Generals named,

comprehend the entire scope of the plans of General
McClellan, of which plans the movement of the Army
of the Potomac under his own orders was the central
feature.   It was considered by him necessary to the success of these plans, that they should be carried out simultaneously, or as nearly so as possible, and the advance of the
Potomac army upon Richmond by the lower Rappahannock was kept in hand by him, to be delivered as the
decisive blow, in conjunction with all the rest of the
general movement.

## "ON TO RICHMOND."

On the 27th of January, 1862, President Lincoln
assumed command of all the armies prepared and preparing for these general movements.   He issued on that
day his "War Order No. 1," prescribing that on the 22d
of February, 1862, a general movement of all the land
and naval forces of the United States should be made
against the insurgent forces.   This order was followed
four days after by a second order, commanding the Army
of the Potomac to occupy a point "southwestward of
Manassas Junction."

On the 3d of February, General McClellan received a
note from the President, reasoning with him on the choice
he had made of a route to Richmond.   General McClellan replied substantially, in a letter to Secretary Stanton,
reciting what had been done with the Army of the Potomac, and what remained to be done with that and with all
the other armies of the Republic; stating his reluctance
to "waste life in useless battles," and his desire "to strike
at the heart;" and pointing out the military reasons for
preferring the base of the lower Chesapeake, to that of
Washington, for operations against the army intrenched
at Manassas.

"For many long months," he said, "I have labored to

prepare the Army of the Potomac to play its part in the programme; I have exerted myself to place all the other armies in such a condition, that they too, could perform their alloted duties." "I know," he concludes, "that his excellency the President, you, and I, all agree in our wishes, and that those wishes are to bring this war to a close as promptly as the means in our power will permit. I believe that the mass of the people have entire confidence in us. Let us then look only to the great result to be accomplished, and disregard every thing else."

The President, subsequently, forbore to urge his war orders. Conferences were held, the base of the lower Chesapeake was finally selected for the movement against Richmond, and steps were taken to prepare the necessary transports, under the exclusive direction of the Assistant-Secretary of War.

The Navy Department had been invited as early as August 12, 1861, by General McClellan, to take steps for protecting the navigation of the Lower Potomac. Nothing had been done, however, and General Barnard, chief of engineers, reported that it would be "impossible" for the army to prevent the erection by the enemy, of batteries at "High Point, and thence down to Chopa-wampsic." As the navy took no steps to prevent the erection of batteries on the Virginia shore, nothing was left but to manœuvre so as to compel the enemy to evacuate.

On the 8th of March, the President renewed his objections to the Chesapeake movement, but after a full conversation again withdrew them, and the plans of General McClellan being laid by him the same day before a council of division generals, they were by the majority approved: and on the same 8th of March, the President issued two orders: one constituting the army into army corps; the other limiting the army of operations to fifty thousand men, in the event of certain contingencies. He also fixed a date for the commencement of operations, and ordered a combined land and naval assault on the Potomac batteries.

The appearance of the Merrimac modified the Peninsular campaign in the respect, that it made the York, and not the James river, the line of the army's communications with Fortress Monroe; but the evacuation of Manassas by the enemy prepared the way for the full success of his plan of operations.

With the hope of harassing their rear, and the certainty of employing the troops usefully in the interval before their embarkation for the Peninsula, General McClellan ordered an advance upon Manassas, as soon as he learned that the enemy were moving. This advance began on the 9th of March.

At that time the force of the enemy, as reported by the chief of the secret service corps, was as follows:

| | |
|---|---:|
| At Manassas and vicinity | 80,000 |
| At Lower Occoquan and vicinity | 18,000 |
| Leesburg | 4,500 |
| Shenandoah Valley | 13,000 |
| | 115,500 |

With about 300 field guns and 30 siege guns.

On the eleventh of March, an order from the President announced, that as General McClellan had personally taken the field, he was relieved from the command of the other military departments, and would retain command of the Department of the Potomac.

On March thirteenth, a council of Generals commanding army corps decided in favor of the Peninsular campaign. The President, renewing his entreaties that Washington might be kept perfectly safe, gave his assent to this movement. A few days afterward, Blenker's division was ordered to join General Fremont, and General McClellan was thus deprived of 10,000 of the troops upon which he had counted.

On the fourteenth he issued the following address to his troops :

"HEAD-QUARTERS, ARMY OF THE POTOMAC,
"FAIRFAX COURT-HOUSE, Va., *March 14th*, 1862.

*"Soldiers of the Army of the Potomac :*

" For a long time I have kept you inactive, but not without a purpose. You were to be disciplined, armed and instructed ; the formidable artillery you now have had to be created ; other armies were to move and accomplish certain results. I have held you back that you might give the death-blow to the rebellion that has distracted our once happy country. The patience you have shown, and your confidence in your General, are worth a dozen victories. These preliminary results are now accomplished. I feel that the patient labors of many months have produced their fruit ; the Army of the Potomac is now a real army—magnificent in material, admirable in discipline and instruction, excellently equipped and armed—your commanders are all that I could wish. The moment for action has arrived, and I know that I can trust in you to save our country. As I ride through your ranks, I see in your faces the sure presage of victory ; I feel that you will do whatever I ask of you. The period of inaction has passed. I will bring you now face to face with the rebels, and only pray that God may defend the right. In whatever direction you may move, however strange my actions may appear to you, ever bear in mind that my fate is linked with yours, and that all I do is to bring you, where I know you wish to be—on the decisive battle-field. It is my business to place you there. I am to watch over you as a parent over his children ; and you know that your General loves you from the depths of his heart. It shall be my care, as it has ever been, to gain success with the least possible loss ; but I know that, if it is necessary, you will willingly follow me to our graves, for our righteous cause. God smiles upon us, victory attends us, yet I would not have you think that our aim is to be attained without a manly struggle. I will not disguise it from you ; you have brave foes to encounter, foemen well worthy of the steel that you will use so well. I shall demand of you great, heroic exertions, rapid and long marches, desperate combats, privations, perhaps. We will share all these together ; and when this sad war is over, we will return to our homes, and feel that we can ask no higher honor than the proud consciousness that we belonged to the Army of the Potomac.           " GEO. B. McCLELLAN,
            *"Major-General Commanding."*

3

## THE PENINSULAR CAMPAIGN.

On the first of April, General McClellan estimated the troops he had left in and near Washington, including those in the Shenandoah Valley, after embarking the main portion of his army for Fortress Monroe, at about seventy-three thousand five hundred men, with one hundred and nine light guns. General Barry, Chief of Artillery, states that thirty-two field pieces were left at Washington.

Unavoidable delays, not to be ascribed to any inattention or delinquency on his part, the inability of the naval vessels at the Fortress to cooperate with him in the prosecution of his plans; the withdrawal of an important part of his command ; and other causes, combined to make a remodeling of the campaign necessary. On the fourth of April, the Army of the Potomac took up its line of march from the camping ground near Hampton for Yorktown. At Big Bethel the enemy's pickets were encountered, but they fell back to Howard's creek, to which point they were followed by the main body of the army. The next morning the column again advanced, and in a few hours was in front of the enemy's works at Yorktown.

## CORRESPONDENCE BETWEEN GEN. McCLELLAN AND THE GOVERNMENT.

General McClellan, immediately upon his arrival at Yorktown, commenced the stupendous preparations he deemed necessary to reduce the formidable fortifications which confronted him on every side, and as a part of the history of that siege, we publish the following despatches which passed between the President and General McClellan in the early part of April.

At eight o'clock, on the evening of the sixth of April, the President sent the following despatch :

"Yours of 11 A. M., to-day, received. Secretary of War informs me that the forwarding of transportation, ammunition and Woodbury's brigade, under your orders, is not, and will not be, interfered with. You now have over one hundred thousand troops with you, independent of General Wool's command. I think you better break the enemy's line from Yorktown to Warwick river at once. This will, probably, use time as advantageously as you can."

On the following day, General McClellan sent the following answer :

"Your telegram of yesterday is received. In reply, I have the honor to state that my entire force for duty amounts to only about (85,000) eighty-five thousand men. General Wool's command, as you will observe from the accompanying order, has been taken out of my control, although he has most cheerfully co-operated with me. The only use that can be made of his command is to protect my communications in rear of this point. At this time, only fifty-three thousand men have joined me, but they are coming up as rapidly as my means of transportation will permit. Please refer to my despatch to the Secretary of War to-night, for the details of our present situation."

He also sent the following to the Secretary of War :

"IN FRONT OF YORKTOWN, *April 7th*—7 P.M.—Your telegram, of yesterday, arrived here while I was absent examining the enemy's right, which I did pretty closely. The whole line of the Warwick, which really heads within a mile of Yorktown, is strongly defended by detached redoubts, and other fortifications, armed with heavy and light guns. The approaches, except at Yorktown, are covered by the Warwick, over which there is but one, or, at most, two passages, both of which are covered by strong batteries. It will be necessary to resort to the use of heavy guns, and some siege operations before we assault.

"All the prisoners state that General J. E. Johnston arrived at Yorktown yesterday with strong reinforcements. It seems clear that I shall have the whole force of the enemy on my hands—probably not less than (100,000) one hundred thousand men, and probably more. In consequence of the loss of Blenker's division and the First Corps, my force is possibly less than that of the enemy, while they have all the advantage of position.

"I am under great obligations to you for the offer that the whole force and material of the Government will be as fully and as speedily under my command as heretofore, or as if the new Department had not been created.

"Since my arrangements were made for this campaign, at least (50,000) fifty thousand men have been taken from my command. Since my despatch of the 5th instant, five divisions have been in close observation of the enemy, and frequently exchanging shots. When my present command all joins, I shall have about (85,000) eighty-five thousand men for duty, from which a large force must be taken for guards, scouts, etc. With this army, I could assault the enemy's works, and perhaps carry them; but were I in possession of their intrenchments, and assailed by double my numbers, I should have no fears as to the result.

"Under the circumstances that have been developed since we arrived here, I feel fully impressed with the conviction that here is to be fought the great battle that is to decide the existing contest. I shall of course commence the attack as soon as I can get up my siege train, and shall do all in my power to carry the enemy's works; but to do this with a reasonable degree of certainty, requires, in my judgment, that I should, if possible, have at least the whole of the First Corps to land upon the Severn river and attack Gloucester in the rear.

"My present strength will not admit of a detachment sufficient for this purpose, without materially impairing the efficiency of this column. Flag-officer Goldsborough thinks the works too strong for his available vessels, unless I can turn Gloucester. I send by mail copies of his letter, and one of the commander of the gunboats here."

On the ninth, the President thus addressed General McClellan:

"Your despatches complaining that you are not properly sustained, while they do not offend me, do pain me very much. Blenker's division was withdrawn from you before you left here, and you know the pressure under which I did it, and as I thought, acquiesced in it—certainly, not without reluctance. After you left, I ascertained that less than twenty thousand unorganized men, without a single field-battery, were all you designed to be left for the defence of Washington and Manassas Junction, and part of this even was to go to General Hooker's old position. General Banks' Corps, once designed for Manassas Junction, was diverted, and tied up on the line of Winchester and Strasburgh, and could not leave it without again exposing the Upper Potomac and the Baltimore and Ohio railroad. This presented (or would present, when McDowell and Sumner should be gone) a great temptation to the enemy to turn back from the Rappahannock, and sack Washington. My implicit order that Washington should, by the judgment of all the commanders of army corps, be left entirely secure, had been neglected. It was precisely this that drove me to detain McDowell.

"I do not forget that I was satisfied with your arrangement to leave Banks at Manassas Junction, but when that arrangement was broken up, and nothing was substituted for it, of course I was constrained to substitute something for it myself, and allow me to ask: Do you really think I should permit the line from Richmond via Manassas Junction to this city to be entirely open, except what resistance could be presented by less than twenty thousand unorganized troops? This is a question which the country will not allow me to evade.

"There is a curious mystery about the number of troops now with you. When I telegraphed you on the 6th, saying you had over a hundred thousand with you, I had just obtained from the Secretary of War a statement taken, as he said, from your own return, making 108,000 then with you, and *en route* to you. You now say you will have but 85,000 when all *en route* to you shall have reached you. How can the discrepancy of 23,000 be accounted for?

"As to General Wool's command, I understand it is doing for you precisely what a like number of your own would have to do if that command was away.

"I suppose the whole force which has gone forward to you, is with you by this time, and if so, I think it is the precise time for you to strike a blow. By delay the enemy will relatively gain upon you; that is, he will gain faster by fortifications and reinforcements than you can by reinforcements alone. And once more let me tell you, it is indispensable to *you* that you strike a blow. *I* am powerless to help this. You will do me the justice to remember I always insisted that going down the Bay in search of a field, instead of fighting at or near Manassas, was only shifting, and not surmounting a difficulty; that we would find the same enemy and the same or equal intrenchments, at either place. The country will not fail to note—is now noting, that the present hesitation to move upon an intrenched enemy is but the story of Manassas repeated.

"I beg to assure you that I have never written you, or spoken to you, in greater kindness of feeling than now, nor with a fuller purpose to sustain you, so far as in my most anxious judgment I consistently can. But you must act."


## EVACUATION OF YORKTOWN.

On the first of May, our siege batteries opened fire on the rebel works, and during the night of the third, the rebels evacuated Yorktown, leaving their guns and ammunition. The following despatches were sent to Washington in reference to the capture:

"HEAD-QUARTERS OF THE ARMY OF THE POTOMAC,
"*May 4th*, 9 A.M.

"To Hon. EDWIN M. STANTON, *Secretary of War:*

"We have the ramparts. Have guns, ammunition, camp equipage, etc. We hold the entire line of his works, which the engineers report as being very strong. I have thrown all my cavalry and horse-artillery in pursuit, supported by infantry. I move Franklin's division, and as much more as I can transport by water, up to West Point to-day. No time shall be lost. The gunboats have gone up York river. I omitted to state that Gloucester is also in our possession. I shall push the enemy to the wall. "GEORGE B. McCLELLAN,
"*Major-General.*"

"HEAD-QUARTERS OF THE ARMY OF THE POTOMAC,
"MONDAY, *May 5th*, 11.30 A.M.

"To Hon. E. M. STANTON, *Secretary of War:*

"An inspection just made shows that the rebels abandoned, in their works at Yorktown, two three-inch rifled cannon, two four-and-a-half-inch rifled cannon, sixteen thirty-two-pounders, six forty-two-pounders, nineteen eight-inch columbiads, four nine-inch Dahlgrens, one ten-inch columbiad, one ten-inch mortar, and one eight-inch siege howitzer, with carriages and implements complete, each piece supplied with seventy-six rounds of ammunition. On the ramparts there are also four magazines, which have not yet been examined. This does not include the guns left at Gloucester Point and their other works to our left. "GEORGE B. McCLELLAN,
"*Major-General.*"

## THE BATTLE OF WILLIAMSBURG.

Immediately upon receiving information that the works had been abandoned, General McClellan ordered his whole available cavalry force, with four batteries of horse artillery under General Stoneman, into pursuit by the Yorktown and Williamsburg road, Generals Heintzelman, Hooker and Smith being moved forward to support Stoneman. These were afterwards followed up by the divisions of Kearney, Couch, and Casey. General Sumner, second in command of the army, was then sent to the front to take charge of the operations. About two miles east of Williamsburg, General Stoneman came upon the enemy's works, four miles in extent, nearly three-fourths of their front being covered by the tributaries of Queen's creek and College creek. The main works were a large fortification called Fort Magruder and twelve other redoubts and epaulements for field guns. The woods in the fort were felled, and the open ground dotted with rifle-pits. From this position the enemy opened fire upon General Stoneman as his advance-guard debouched from the woods. General Stoneman, having no infantry, was forced to retire, but held the enemy in check, until the arrival of General Sumner, with part of General Smith's division, at half-past five P.M. The cross movement of this division, made necessary by the impassable character of the road on which it had been moving, had delayed the movement of General Hooker's column between three and four hours; but Heintzelman and Keyes reached Sumner during the afternoon. Early in the morning of the 5th, Hooker came up. General Hooker began the attack on the enemy's works at $7\frac{1}{2}$ o'clock in the morning of the 6th, and for a time silenced Fort Magruder. But the enemy being heavily reinforced attacked in his turn. Hooker lost seriously in men, five of his guns were taken, and between 3 and 4 P.M., when his ammunition was giving out and his men with it, Kearney came up, after pushing through the deep mud and dense forest; and saved Hooker. About 1 P.M., of the 7th, General McClellan, who had remained at Yorktown to move forward the whole army, received information for the first time that a serious conflict was going on in front of Williamsburg. He at once pushed forward to the front, about fourteen miles, through a most difficult country, and reached the front about half-past 4 P.M., and took a rapid survey of the field. He learned that there was no direct communication between the centre and the left under Heintzelman, and, hearing heavy firing in the direction of Hancock's command, he moved the centre forward, attempted to open communication with Heintzelman, and sent Smith and Naglee to the support of Hancock. Before these generals reached Hancock, however, the latter general, finding himself confronted by a superior force, had feigned a retreat, awaited their onset, and then turning upon them fiercely, had driven back the whole force at the point of the bayonet, routing them utterly, with a total loss to them of between five or six hundred men, he himself losing but fifty-one. The total loss of the army is put down at 2,228 men. The troops were so much exhausted by the marches and conflict which resulted in the victory at Williamsburg, as to render an immediate pursuit of the enemy impossible in the then condition of the country.

On the seventh, General Franklin's division, then landing, had a most creditable affair with the enemy under General Whiting.

## THANKS BY CONGRESS.

On the ninth of May, the United States House of Representatives adopted a resolution tendering its thanks to General McClellan " for the display of those high military qualities which secure important results with but little sacrifice of human life."

## THE EXCITEMENT IN RICHMOND.

As the Army of the Potomac advanced up the Peninsula, the greatest excitement prevailed in Richmond. The people were well aware of the determined force, which, within a few days, would probably be knocking at the gates of the rebel capital, and they had long known and recognized the skill and valor of General McClellan, the Union commander. The General Assembly of Virginia adopted a joint resolution desiring that Richmond might

be defended to the last extremity, and assuring Jefferson
Davis that any destruction or loss of property would be
cheerfully submitted to ; the rebel President assured the
Assembly that it would be the effort of his life to defend
the soil of Virginia and to cover her capital, but even if
the capital should fall, the war could be still successfully
maintained in Virginia for twenty years ; Governor Letcher
declared " the capital must not be surrendered," and the
press of the city were urgent in their appeals to the citizens to come forward and organize for active service. The
following from one of the journals is a sample of the edi-
torials with which the columns of the papers of Richmond
teemed at that exciting time :

> "The next few days may decide the fate of Richmond. It is
> either to remain the capital of the Confederacy, or to be turned
> over to the Federal government as a Yankee conquest. The
> capital is either to be secured or lost—it may be feared not tem-
> porarily—and with it Virginia. Then, if there is blood to be
> shed, let it be shed here ; no soil of the Confederacy could drink
> it up more acceptably, and none would hold it more gratefully.
> Wife, family and friends are nothing. Leave them all for one
> glorious hour to be devoted to the Republic. Life, death and
> wounds are nothing, if we only be saved from the fate of a cap-
> tured capital and a humiliated Confederacy. Let the govern-
> ment act ; let the people act. There is time yet. If fate
> comes to its worst, let the ruins of Richmond be its most last-
> ing monument."

## REINFORCEMENTS URGED.

On the tenth of May, head-quarters were established
beyond Williamsburg, and communications established
between the forces moving by land and by water. The
following despatch was then sent by General McClellan to
Secretary Stanton :

> "CAMP AT EWELL'S FARM,
> "THREE MILES BEYOND WILLIAMSBURG,
> "*May* 10*th*—5 A.M.

> "From the information reaching me from every source, I re-
> gard it as certain that the enemy will meet us with all his force
> on or near the Chickahominy. They can concentrate many

more men than I have, and are collecting troops from all quarters, especially well disciplined troops from the South. Casualties, sickness, garrisons and guards have much reduced our numbers, and will continue to do so. I shall fight the rebel army with whatever force I may have; but duty requires me to urge that every effort be made to reinforce me, without delay, with all the disposable troops in Eastern Virginia, and that we concentrate all our forces, as far as possible, to fight the great battle now impending, and to make it decisive.

"It is possible that the enemy may abandon Richmond without a serious struggle, but I do not believe he will; and it would be unwise to count upon any thing but a stubborn and desperate defence—a life and death contest. I see no other hope for him than to fight this battle, and we must win it. I shall fight them, whatever their force may be; but I ask for every man that the department can send me. No troops should now be left unemployed. Those who entertain the opinion that the rebels will abandon Richmond without a struggle are, in my judgment, badly advised, and do not comprehend their situation, which is one requiring desperate measures.

"I beg that the President and Secretary will maturely weigh what I say, and leave nothing undone to comply with my request. If I am not reinforced, it is probable that I will be obliged to fight nearly double my numbers strongly intrenched. I do not think it will be at all possible for me to bring more than (70,000) seventy thousand men upon the field of battle."

Four days later he sent the following despatch from his camp at Cumberland, to the President:

"I have more than twice telegraphed to the Secretary of War, stating that in my opinion the enemy were concentrating all their available force to fight this army in front of Richmond, and that such ought to be their policy. I have received no reply whatever to any of these telegrams. I beg leave to repeat their substance to your Excellency, and to ask that kind consideration which you have ever accorded to my representations and views. All my information, from every source accessible to me, establishes the fixed purpose of the rebels to defend Richmond against this army, by offering us battle with all the troops they can collect from the East, West and South, and my own opinion is confirmed by that of all my commanders whom I have been able to consult.

"Casualties, sickness, garrisons and guards have much weakened my force, and will continue to do so. I cannot bring into actual battle against the enemy more than eighty thousand men at the utmost, and with them I must attack in position, probably intrenched, a much larger force—perhaps double my number. It is possible that Richmond may be abandoned without a serious struggle; but the enemy are actually in great strength between here and there, and it would be unwise, and even insane, for me to calculate upon any thing but a stubborn and desperate resistance.   If they should abandon Richmond, it may well be that it is done with the purpose of making the stand at some place in Virginia south or west of there, and we should be in condition to press them without delay.  The Confederate leaders must employ their utmost efforts against this army in Virginia, and they will be supported by the whole body of their military officers, among whom there may be said to be no Union feeling, as there is also very little among the higher class of citizens in the seceding States.

"I have found no fighting men left in this Peninsula; are all in the ranks of the opposing foe.

"Even if more troops than I now have should prove unnecessary for purposes of military occupation, our greatest display of imposing force in the capital of the rebel government will have the best moral effect.   I most respectfully and earnestly urge upon your Excellency that the opportunity has come for striking a fatal blow at the enemies of the Constitution, and I beg that you will cause this army to be reinforced without delay by all the disposable troops of the Government.   I ask for every man that the War Department can send me.   Any commander of the reinforcements whom your Excellency may designate will be acceptable to me, whatever expression I may have heretofore addressed to you on that subject.

"I will fight the enemy, whatever their force may be, with whatever force I may have, and I firmly believe that we shall beat them; but our triumph should be made decisive and complete.   The soldiers of this army love their Government, and will fight well in its support.   You may rely upon them.   They have confidence in me as their General, and in you as their President.   Strong reinforcements will at least save the lives of many of them.   The greater our force, the more perfect will be our combinations, and the less our loss.

"For obvious reasons I beg you to give immediate consideration to this communication, and to inform me fully at the earliest moment of your final determination."

## THE ADVANCE CONTINUED.

On the fifteenth and sixteenth, Generals Franklin, Smith and Porter reached White House, the roads being so bad that one train occupied thirty-six hours in passing over the short distance of five miles.  About this time two Provisional Army Corps were organized—the one under Fitz John Porter, the other under Franklin.  Head-quarters reached White House on the sixteenth, and a permanent depot was at once organized there.

On the seventeenth, the advance-guard reached the Chickahominy River at Bottom's Bridge, but its further march was obstructed by the rebels who had burned the bridge.

On the following day, Secretary Stanton sent the following despatch to General McClellan :

### SECRETARY STANTON TO GENERAL McCLELLAN.

"*May* 18*th.*—Your despatch to the President, asking reinforcements, has been received and carefully considered :

" The President is not willing to uncover the capital entirely, and it is believed that, even if this were prudent, it would require more time to effect a junction between your army and that of the Rappahannock, by the way of the Potomac and York rivers, than by a land march. In order, therefore, to increase the strength of the attack upon Richmond, at the earliest moment, General McDowell has been ordered to march upon Richmond by the shortest route. He is ordered, keeping himself always in position to save the capital from all possible attack, so to operate as to put his left wing in communication with your right wing; and you are instructed to co-operate so as to establish this communication as soon as possible, by extending your right wing to the north of Richmond. It is believed that this communication can be safely established either north or south of the Pamunky river. In any event, you will be able to prevent the main body of the enemy's forces from leaving Richmond, and falling in overwhelming force upon General McDowell. He will move with between thirty-five (35,000) and forty thousand (40,000) men. A copy of the instructions to General McDowell are with this. The specific task assigned to his command has been to provide against any danger to the capital of the nation. At your earnest call for reinforcements, he is sent forward to co-operate in the reduction of Richmond ; but charged, in attempting this, not to uncover the city of Washington. And you will give no order, either before or after your junction, which can put him out of position to cover this city. You and he will communicate with each other by telegraph, or otherwise, as frequently as may be necessary for sufficient co-operation. When General McDowell is in position on your right, his supplies must be drawn from West Point, and you will instruct your staff officers to be prepared to supply him by that route.

" The President desires that General McDowell retain the command of the Department of the Rappahannock, and of the forces with which he moves forward."

## POSITION OF THE CORPS—SEVERE SKIR-
## MISHING.

On the nineteenth, General Stoneman's Brigade of Cavalry left their camping ground near White House, and
pushed on towards the Chickahominy.   The head-quarters
and the corps of Generals Porter and Franklin also moved
to Tunstall's Station.   On the twenty-first, the position of
the troops were as follows: Stoneman's advance-guard
one mile from New Bridge ; Franklin's corps three miles
from New Bridge, with Porter's corps in advancing distance in its rear ; Sumner's corps on the railroad, about
three miles from the Chickahominy, connecting the right
with the left ; Keyes' corps on New Kent road, near Bottom's Bridge, with Heintzelman's corps at supporting
distance in its rear.   The ford at Bottom's Bridge was in
our possession, and the rebuilding of the bridge was commenced.

On the twenty-second, head-quarters were removed to
Coal Harbor, and on the twenty-fourth three important
skirmishes took place.   General Naglee made a reconnoissance in force for the purpose of ascertaining the strength
of the enemy in the vicinity of the " Pines," some eight
miles from Richmond, and while engaged in that important duty was fired upon by two batteries, both of which,
however, were soon silenced.   Another and a much smaller
portion of the army became engaged near Coal Harbor,
and after a spirited engagement for two hours, drove their
assailants from the field.   In the third skirmish the brigades of Generals Stoneman and Davidson were engaged,
and their gallantry compelled the rebels to hastily evacuate Mechanicsville, and repair to a position where they
would be more secure from the unerring aim of our artil-
lerists.   General Stoneman also sent a portion of his
cavalry three miles up the river, and destroyed the bridge

of the Richmond and Fredericksburg railroad at that point.

On that day and the next, the following despatches passed between the President and General McClellan :

### THE PRESIDENT TO GENERAL McCLELLAN.

"*May 24th*, 1862.—After giving an account of matters at Front Royal, Mr. Lincoln says:

"If, in conjunction with McDowell's movement against Anderson, you could send a force from your right to cut off the enemy's supplies from Richmond, preserve the railroad bridges across the two forks of the Pamunky, and intercept the enemy's retreat, you will prevent the army now opposed to you from receiving an accession of numbers of nearly fifteen thousand men ; and if you succeed in saving the bridges, you will secure a line of railroad for supplies, in addition to the one you now have. Can you not do this almost as well as not, while you are building the Chickahominy bridges ? McDowell and Shields both say they can, and positively will, move Monday morning. I wish you to move cautiously and safely. You will have command of McDowell after he joins you, precisely as you indicated in your long despatch to us."

"*May 24th*.—In consequence of General Banks' critical position, I have been compelled to suspend General McDowell's movement to join you. The enemy are making a desperate push upon Harper's Ferry, and we are trying to throw General Fremont's force, and part of General McDowell's, in their rear."

### THE PRESIDENT TO GENERAL McCLELLAN.

"*May 25th*, 1862—2 P.M.—The enemy is moving north in sufficient force to drive General Banks before him ; precisely in what force we cannot tell. He is also threatening Leesburg and Geary on the Manassas Gap Railroad, from both north and south ; in precisely what force we cannot tell. I think the movement is a general and concerted one—such as would not be if he was acting upon the purpose of a very desperate defence of Richmond. I think the time is near when you must either attack Richmond or give up the job, and come to the defence of Washington. Let me hear from you instantly."

### GENERAL McCLELLAN TO THE PRESIDENT.

"COAL HARBOR, *May 25th*.—Telegram received. Independently of it, the time is very near when I shall attack Richmond. The object of the movement is probably to prevent reinforcements being sent to me. All the information obtained from balloons, deserters, prisoners, and contrabands, agree in the statement that the mass of the rebel troops are still in the immediate vicinity of Richmond, ready to defend it.  I have no knowledge of Banks' position and force, nor what there is at Manassas; therefore cannot form a definite opinion as to the force against him.  I have two corps across Chickahominy, within six miles of Richmond; the others on this side at other crossings, within same distance, and ready to cross when bridges are completed.

## ORDERS FOR CROSSING THE CHICKAHOMINY.

On the same day, the railroad being in operation as far as the Chickahominy, and the railroad bridge across that stream nearly completed, the Commanding General issued the following order to his troops:

"HEAD-QUARTERS, ARMY OF THE POTOMAC,
"CAMP NEAR COAL HARBOR, VA., *May 25th*, 1862.

"1.  Upon advancing beyond the Chickahominy the troops will go prepared for battle at a moment's notice, and will be entirely unencumbered, with the exception of ambulances.  All vehicles will be left on the eastern side of the Chickahominy, and carefully packed.  The men will leave their knapsacks, packed, with the wagons, and will carry three days rations.  The arms will be put in perfect order before the troops march, and a careful inspection made of them, as well as of the cartridge-boxes, which in all cases will contain at least forty rounds; twenty additional rounds will be carried by the men in their pockets.  Commanders of batteries will see that their limber and caisson-boxes are filled to their utmost capacity.

"Commanders of army corps will devote their personal attention to the fulfilment of these orders, and will personally see that the proper arrangements are made for packing and properly guarding the trains and surplus baggage, taking all the steps necessary to insure their being brought promptly to the front when needed; they will also take steps to prevent the ambulances from interfering with the movements of any troops.  Sufficient guards and staff-officers will be detailed to carry out these orders.

"The ammunition-wagons will be in readiness to march to their respective brigades and batteries at a moment's warning, but will not cross the Chickahominy until they are sent for.  All quartermasters and ordnance officers are to remain with their trains.

"II.  In the approaching battle the General Commanding trusts that the troops will preserve the discipline which he has been so anxious to enforce, and which they have so generally observed.  He calls upon all the officers and soldiers to obey promptly and intelligently all orders they may receive; let them bear in mind that the Army of the Potomac has never yet been checked, and let them preserve in battle perfect coolness and confidence, the sure forerunners of success. They must keep well together, throw away no shots, but aim carefully and low, and, above all things, rely upon the bayonet. Commanders of regiments are reminded of the great responsibility that rests upon them; upon their coolness, judgment and discretion the destinies of their regiments and success of the day will depend.

"By command of "Major-General McCLELLAN.

"S. WILLIAMS, *Assistant Adjutant-General.*"

## BATTLE OF HANOVER COURT-HOUSE.

On the twenty-seventh was fought the battle of Hanover Court-House. The enemy for some days had been throwing forces upon our right flank and threatening our communications with the river. To dispose of this force, and also to cut the Virginia Central and Richmond and Fredericksburg railroads, a portion of Fitz-John Porter's Corps was detailed. The work was well done. The railroad communication was cut, and after two severe engagements, the enemy retreated, leaving behind them several hundred prisoners, their cannon and camp-equipage. General McClellan came up the next morning, and was enthusiastically welcomed.

On the same day the following despatch was sent to the Secretary of War by the Commanding General:

"CAMP NEAR NEW BRIDGE, *May 28th.*—Porter has gained two complete victories over superior forces. Yet I feel obliged to move in the morning with reinforcements, to secure the complete destruction of the rebels in that quarter. In doing so I run some risk here, but I cannot help it. The enemy are even in greater force than I had supposed. I will do all that quick movements can accomplish, but you must send me all the troops you can, and leave me to full latitude as to choice of commanders. It is absolutely necessary to destroy the rebels near Hanover Court-House before I can advance."

To which he received the following from the President:

"*May 28th.*—I am very glad of General F. J. Porter's victory. Still, if it was a total rout of the enemy, I am puzzled to know why the Richmond and Fredericksburg railroad was not seized again, as you say you have all the railroads but the Richmond and Fredericksburg. I am puzzled to see how, lacking that, you can have any, except the scrap from Richmond to West Point, the scrap of the Virginia Central from Richmond to Hanover Junction; without more, it is simply nothing. That the whole of the enemy is concentrating on Richmond, I think cannot be certainly known to you or me. Saxton, at Harper's Ferry, informs us that large forces, supposed to be Jackson's and Ewell's, forced his advance from Charlestown to-day. General King telegraphed us from Fredericksburg that contrabands give certain information that 15,000 left Hanover Junction on Monday morning to reinforce Jackson. I am painfully impressed with the importance of the struggle before you, and shall aid you all I can consistently with my view of due regard to all points."

Two days later, General McClellan telegraphed to the Secretary:

"*May 30th*, 1862.— From the tone of your despatches and the President's, I do not think that you at all appreciate the value and magnitude of Porter's victory. It has entirely relieved my right flank, which was seriously threatened, routed and demoralized a considerable portion of the rebel forces, taken over seven hundred and fifty prisoners, killed and wounded large numbers; one gun, many small arms, and much baggage taken. It was one of the handsomest things in the war, both in itself and in its results. Porter has returned, and my army is again well in hand. Another day will make the probable field of battle passable for artillery. It is quite certain that there is nothing in front of McDowell at Fredericksburg. I regard the burning of South Anna Bridges as the least important result of Porter's movement."

## BATTLE OF FAIR OAKS.

On the thirty-first of May, the enemy, taking advantage of a terrible storm of rain which had flooded the valley, attacked our troops, comprising the corps of Generals Sumner, Heintzelman and Keyes, in position on the right bank of the Chickahominy. The battle commenced about one o'clock in the afternoon, and after three hours of desperate fighting, Casey's Division, which occupied the first line, was compelled to fall back, and in considerable disorder, upon the second line. This caused a temporary confusion, but Generals Heintzelman and Kearney rapidly advanced their troops and checked the enemy, who were pouring down in immense force. Sumner, Keyes, - Couch, Sedgwick and the other commanders also labored

4

valiantly to retrieve the injury effected by the unfortunate retirement of Casey's command.    It was after eight o'clock in the evening before the battle of Fair Oaks terminated for the day, and the enemy fell back to their defensive line. During that night our lines were newly formed, and artil- . lery placed in position, and at an early hour of the following morning the rebels again attacked.    As rapidly as their ranks were broken by the shot and shell from our pieces, and the balls from the muskets of our infantry, were they filled with fresh troops.    Both armies fought with determination and gallantry, until victory again rewarded General McClellan's brave men.

The rebel loss was enormous, while our own summed up in killed, wounded and missing, nearly seven thousand. A correspondent, describing the battle, says, "General McClellan was where his duty called him.    I saw him in the field during the Sunday fight, and afterwards he rode along the entire battle-front.    During his progress he was greeted with great enthusiasm.    It was a splendid ovation."

## ADDRESS TO THE ARMY—FURTHER DESPATCHES.

On the evening of the third of June, the victorious commander issued the following address, which was read the same evening at dress-parade, and was received with the most enthusiastic cheering from every regiment:

"HEAD-QUARTERS, ARMY OF THE POTOMAC,
"CAMP NEAR NEW-BRIDGE, VA., *June 2d*, 1862.

"Soldiers of the Army of the Potomac! I have fulfilled at least a part of my promise to you.    You are now face to face with the rebels, who are held at bay in front of their capital. The final and decisive battle is at hand.    Unless you belie your past history, the result cannot be for a moment doubtful.    If the troops who labored so faithfully and fought so gallantly at Yorktown, and who so bravely won the hard fights at Williamsburgh, West Point, Hanover Court-House, and Fair Oaks, now prove themselves worthy of their antecedents, the victory is surely ours.

"The events of every day prove your superiority. Wherever you have met the enemy you have beaten him. Wherever you have used the bayonet he has given way in panic and disorder. I ask of you now one last crowning effort. The enemy has staked his all on the issue of the coming battle. Let us meet him, crush him here, in the very centre of the rebellion.

"Soldiers! I will be with you in this battle, and share its dangers with you. Our confidence in each other is now founded upon the past. Let us strike the blow which is to restore peace and union to this distracted land. Upon your valor, discipline, and mutual confidence, the result depends.

"GEORGE B. McCLELLAN,
"*Major-General Commanding.*"

## On the same day the following despatches passed:

### FROM THE PRESIDENT.

"*June 3d.*—With these continuous rains, I am very anxious about the Chickahominy, so close in your rear, and crossing your line of communication. Please look to it."

### TO THE PRESIDENT.

"NEW-BRIDGE, *June 3d.*—Your despatch of 5 P.M. just received. As the Chickahominy has been almost the only obstacle in my way for several days, your Excellency may rest assured that it has not been overlooked. Every effort has been made, and will continue to be, to perfect the communications across it. Nothing of importance, except that it is again raining."

And on the next day he sent the following to the Secretary of War:

"NEW-BRIDGE, *June 4th.*—Please inform me at once what reinforcements, if any, I can count upon having at Fortress Monroe or White House, within the next three days, and when each regiment may be expected to arrive. It is of the utmost importance that I should know this immediately.

"The losses in the battle of the 31st and 1st will amount to (7,000) seven thousand. Regard this as confidential for the present.

"If I can have (5) five new regiments for Fortress Monroe and its dependencies, I can draw (3) three more old regiments from there safely. I can well dispose of (4) four more raw regiments on my communications. I can well dispose of from (15) fifteen to (20) twenty well-drilled regiments among the old brigades, in bringing them up to their original effective strength. Recruits are especially necessary for the regular and volunteer batteries of artillery, as well as for the regular and volunteer regiments of infantry.

"After the losses in our last battle, I trust that I will no longer be regarded as an alarmist. I believe we have at least one more desperate battle to fight."

On the fifth, the rebel artillery opened upon our forces at New-Bridge, from five different points, to prevent them from rebuilding the bridge, but after an engagement of two hours, the rebels were compelled to cease their fire.

From this time until the Battle of Oak Grove, numerous important reconnoissances were made, and several skirmishes of greater or less importance occurred, and during the same interval the following communications passed between the authorities at Washington and the gallant leader of the Union forces :

### FROM THE SECRETARY OF WAR.

"*June 5th.*—I will send you (5) five new regiments as fast as transportation can take them, the first to start to-morrow from Baltimore. I intend sending you a part of McDowell's force as soon as it can return from its trip to Front Royal, probably as many as you want. The order to ship the new regiments to Fortress Monroe has already been given. I suppose that they may be sent directly to the Fort. Please advise me if this be as you desire."

### TO THE SECRETARY OF WAR.

"*June 7th.*—In reply to your despatch of 2 P.M., to-day, I have the honor to state that the Chickahominy river has risen so as to flood the entire bottoms to the depth of three and four feet ; I am pushing forward the bridges in spite of this, and the men are working, night and day, up to their waists in water, to complete them. The whole face of the country is a perfect bog, entirely impassable for artillery, or even cavalry, except directly in the narrow roads, which renders any general movement, either of this or the rebel army, entirely out of the question until we have more favorable weather. I am glad to learn that you are pressing forward reinforcements so vigorously. I shall be in perfect readiness to move forward and take Richmond the moment McCall reaches here, and the ground will admit the passage of artillery. I have advanced my pickets about a mile to-day, driving off the rebel pickets, and securing a very advantageous position. The rebels have several batteries established, commanding the debouches from two of our bridges, and fire upon our working parties continually ; but as yet they have killed but very few of our men."

## To the Secretary.

"*June 10th.*—I have again information that Beauregard has arrived, and that some of his troops are to follow him. No great reliance, perhaps none whatever, can be attached to this; but it is possible, and ought to be their policy. I am completely checked by the weather. The roads and fields are literally impassable for artillery—almost so for infantry. The Chickahominy is in a dreadful state. We have another rain storm on our hands. I shall attack as soon as the weather and ground will permit, but there will be a delay, the extent of which no one can foresee, for the season is altogether abnormal. In view of these circumstances, I present for your consideration the propriety of detaching largely from Halleck's army, to strengthen this; for it would seem that Halleck has now no large organized force in front of him, while we have. If this cannot be done, or even in connection with it, allow me to suggest the movement of a heavy column from Dalton upon Atlanta. If but the one can be done, it would better conform to military principles to strengthen this army. And even although the reinforcements might not arrive in season to take part in the attack upon Richmond, the moral effect would be great, and they would furnish valuable assistance in ulterior movements. I wish to be distinctly understood that whenever the weather permits I will attack with whatever force I may have, although a larger force would enable me to gain much more decisive results. I would be glad to have McCall's infantry sent forward by water at once, without waiting for his artillery and cavalry. If General Prim returns via Washington, please converse with him as to the condition of affairs here."

## From the Secretary.

"*June 11th.*—Your despatch of 3.30 P.M. yesterday has been received. I am fully impressed with the difficulties mentioned, and which no art or skill can avoid, but only endure; and am striving to the uttermost to render you every aid in the power of the Government. Your suggestions will be immediately communicated to General Halleck, with a request that he shall conform to them. At last advice he contemplated sending a column to operate with Mitchel against Chattanooga, and thence upon East Tennessee. Buell reports Kentucky and Tennessee to be in a critical condition, demanding immediate attention. Halleck says the main body of Beauregard's force is with him at Oakolona. McCall's force was reported, yesterday, as having embarked, and on its way to join you. It is intended to send the residue of McDowell's force also to join you as speedily as possible. Fremont had a hard fight, day before yesterday, with Jackson's force at Union Church, eight miles from Harrisonburg. He claims the victory, but was pretty badly handled. It is clear that a strong force is operating with Jackson, for the purpose of detaining the forces here from you. I am urging as fast as possible the new levies. Be assured, General, that there never has been a moment when my desire has been otherwise than to aid you with my whole heart, mind, and strength, since the hour we first met; and whatever others may say for their own purposes, you have never had, and never can have, any one more truly your friend, or more anxious to support you, or more joyful than I shall be at the success which I have no doubt will soon be achieved by your arms."

On the twelfth and thirteenth, General McCall's division arrived. On the thirteenth of June, two squadrons of the Fifth United States Cavalry, under the command of Captain Royall, stationed near Hanover Old Church, were attacked and overpowered by a force of the enemy's cavalry, numbering about 1500 men, with four guns. They pushed on towards our depots, but at some distance from our main body; and, though pursued, made the circuit of the army, repassing the Chickahominy at Long Bridge. The burning of two schooners laden with forage, and fourteen Government wagons; the destruction of some sutler's stores; the killing of several of the guard and teamsters; some little damage done to Tunstall's Station, and a little *eclat*, were the results of the expedition.

### To the Secretary.

"Camp Lincoln, *June 14th, midnight.*—All quiet in every direction. The stampede of last night has passed away. Weather now very favorable. I hope two days more will make the ground practicable. I shall advance as soon as the bridges are completed, and the ground fit for artillery to move. At the same time, I would be glad to have whatever troops can be sent to me. I can use several new regiments to advantage. It ought to be distinctly understood that McDowell and his troops are completely under my control. I received a telegram from him, requesting that McCall's division might be placed so as to join him immediately on his arrival. That request does not breathe the proper spirit. Whatever troops come to me must be disposed of so as to do the most good. I do not feel, that in such circumstances as those in which I am now placed, General McDowell should wish the general interests to be sacrificed for the purpose of increasing his command. If I cannot fully control all his troops, I want none of them, but would prefer to fight the battle with what I have, and let others be responsible for the result. The department lines should not be allowed to interfere with me; but General McDowell's and all other troops sent to me, should be placed completely at my disposal to do with them as I think best, in no other way can they be of assistance to me. I therefore request that I may have entire and full control. The stake at issue is too great to allow personal considerations to be entertained. You know that I have none. The indications are, from our balloon reconnoissances, and from all other sources, that the enemy are intrenching, daily increasing in numbers, and determined to fight desperately."

### TO THE PRESIDENT.

"CAMP LINCOLN, *January* 20*th*, 2 P.M.—Your Excellency's despatch of 11 A.M. received; also that of General Sigel. I have no doubt that Jackson has been reinforced from here. There is reason to believe that General R. S. Ripley has recently joined Lee's army with a brigade or division from Charleston. Troops have arrived recently from Goldsboro'. There is not the slightest reason to suppose that the enemy intends evacuating Richmond. He is daily increasing his defences. I find him everywhere in force, and every reconnoissance costs many lives. Yet I am obliged to feel my way—foot by foot, at whatever cost—so great are the difficulties of the country. By to-morrow night, the defensive works covering our position on this side of the Chickahominy should be completed. I am forced to this by my inferiority of numbers, so that I may bring the greatest possible numbers into action, and secure the army against the consequences of unforeseen disaster. I would be glad to have permission to lay before your Excellency, by letter or telegraph, my views as to the present state of military affairs throughout the whole country. In the meantime, I would be pleased to learn the disposition, as to numbers and position, of the troops not under my command, in Virginia and elsewhere."

### THE PRESIDENT'S REPLY.

"*June* 21*st*.—If it would not divert too much of your time and attention from the army under your immediate command, I would be glad to have your views as to the present state of military affairs throughout the whole country, as you say you would be glad to give them. I would rather it should be by letter than by telegraph, because of the better chance of secrecy. As to the numbers and positions of the troops not under your command, in Virginia and elsewhere, even if I could give it with accuracy, which I cannot, I would rather not transmit either by telegraph or letter, because of the chances of its reaching the enemy. I would be very glad to talk with you; but you cannot leave your camp, and I cannot well leave here."

### GENERAL McCLELLAN'S REJOINDER.

"CAMP LINCOLN, *June 22d.*—Under the circumstances, as stated in your despatch, I perceive that it will be better, at least, to defer for the present the communication I desired to make."

### TO THE SECRETARY.

"*June 24th*, 12 P.M.—A very peculiar case of desertion has occurred from the enemy. The party states that he left Jackson, Whiting, and Ewell (fifteen brigades) at Gordonsville on the 21st; that they were moving to Frederickshall, and that it was intended to attack my rear on the 28th. I would be glad to learn at your earliest convenience the most exact information you have as to the position and movements of Jackson, as well as the sources from which your information is derived, that I may the better compare it with what I have."

### FROM THE SECRETARY.

"*June 25th.*—We have no definite information as to the numbers or position of Jackson's force. General King yesterday reported a deserter's statement, that Jackson's force was, nine days ago, forty thousand men. Some reports place ten thousand rebels under Jackson at Gordonsville; others that his force is at Port Republic, Harrisonburgh, and Luray. Fremont yesterday reported rumors that Western Virginia was threatened, and General Kelley, that Ewell was advancing to New Creek, where Fremont has his depots. The last telegram from Fremont contradicts this rumor. The last telegram from Banks says the enemy's pickets are strong in advance at Luray. The people decline to give any information of his whereabouts. Within the last two days the evidence is strong, that for some purpose the enemy is circulating rumors of Jackson's advance in various directions, with a view to conceal the real point of attack. Neither McDowell, who is at Manassas, nor Banks and Fremont, who are at Middletown, appear to have any accurate knowledge of the subject.

"A letter transmitted to the department yesterday, purporting to be dated Gordonsville, on the 14th instant, stated that the actual attack was designed for Washington and Baltimore, as soon as you attacked Richmond; but that the report was to be circulated that Jackson had gone to Richmond, in order to mislead. This letter looked very much like a blind, and induces me to suspect that Jackson's real movement now is towards Richmond. It came from Alexandria, and is certainly designed, like the numerous rumors put afloat, to mislead. I think, therefore, that, while the warning of the deserter to you may also be a blind, that it could not safely be disregarded. I will transmit to you any further information on this subject that may be received here."

## THE BATTLE OF OAK GROVE.

On the twenty-fifth of June, occurred the battle of Oak Grove. General Hooker's Division had been ordered to occupy a new and important position, and were advancing with that view through dense thickets and almost impassable swamps, when they were suddenly attacked and the battle commenced. Our gallant men gradually pushed the foe back, until at length he was driven to his rifle-pits. Then, eager for the fray, they were rapidly following, when an order came to cease the pursuit. About noon, General McClellan, who had remained at head-quarters to communicate with the left wing, rode upon the field, and to the joy of his soldiers ordered them to again advance. The order was cheerfully obeyed, and after renewed desperate fighting, at sunset the day was ours. During the afternoon, General McClellan occupied a seat on the parapet of a redoubt in front of General Hooker's intrenchments, regardless of the shells which were falling around him, and in opposition to the requests of the commanding officers and others, who appreciated the perilous position of their beloved superior.

## THE SEVEN DAYS' BATTLES — DESPATCHES AND REPORTS OF GENERAL McCLELLAN.

Of the celebrated "Seven Days' Fights," no better account can be given than that to be derived from the reports and despatches of the great commander who fought them. They give the correct history—the record of a succession of bloody contests, and of a subsequent retreat, which has but few, if any, equals, in the superior and successful manner in which it was conducted, in the annals of warfare. General McClellan was always to be found where the duties and responsibilities of his position required him to be. Day and night his great mind was taxed to its utmost tension, but difficulties, which to others would have been deemed insurmountable, were grappled and easily overcome, generally without consultation with his subordinate commanders. The despatches sent on the twenty-fifth and twenty-sixth were as follows:

### To the Secretary.

"Camp Lincoln, *June 25th*—6.15 p.m.—I have just returned from the field, and find your despatch in regard to Jackson. Several contrabands just in, give information confirming the supposition that Jackson's advance is at or near Hanover Court House, and that Beauregard arrived, with strong reinforcements, in Richmond yesterday. I incline to think that Jackson will attack my right and rear. The rebel force is stated at (200,000) two hundred thousand, including Jackson and Beauregard. I shall have to contend against vastly superior odds if these reports be true. But this army will do all in the power of men to hold their position and repulse any attack. I regret my great inferiority in numbers, but feel that I am in no way responsible for it, as I have not failed to represent, repeatedly, the necessity of reinforcements; that this was the decisive point, and that all the available means of the Government should be concentrated here. I will do all that a general can do with the splendid army I have the honor to command, and if it is destroyed by overwhelming numbers, can at least die with it and share its fate. But if the result of the action, which will probably occur to-morrow, or within a short time, is a disaster, the responsibility cannot be thrown on my shoulders: it must rest where it belongs. Since I commenced this, I have received additional intelligence, confirming the supposition in regard to Jackson's movements and Beauregard's arrival. I shall probably be attacked to-morrow, and now go to the other side of the Chickahominy to arrange for the defence on that side. I feel that there is no use in again asking for reinforcements.

"The report of the Chief of the Secret Service Corps, herewith forwarded and dated the 26th of June, shows the estimated strength of the enemy at the time of the evacuation of Yorktown to have been from 100,000 to 120,000 men. The same report put his numbers on the 26th of June at about 180,000, and the specific information obtained regarding their organization warrants the belief that this estimate did not exceed his actual strength. It will be observed that the evidence contained in the report shows the following organizations, viz: 200 regiments of infantry and cavalry, including the forces of Jackson and Ewell, just arrived; eight battalions of independent troops; five battalions of artillery; twelve companies of infantry and independent cavalry, besides forty-six companies of artillery, amounting in all to from forty to fifty brigades. There were, undoubtedly, many others whose designations we did not learn. The report also shows that numerous and heavy earthworks had been completed for the defence of Richmond, and that in thirty-six of these were mounted some two hundred guns."

### From the Secretary.

"*June 25th*—11.20 P.M.—Your telegram of 6.15 has just been received. The circumstances that have hitherto rendered it impossible for the Government to send you any more reinforcements than has been done, have been so distinctly stated to you by the President, that it is needless for me to repeat them. Every effort has been made by the President and myself to strengthen you. King's division has reached Falmouth. Shields's and Ricketts's divisions are at Manassas. The President designs to send a part of that force to aid you as speedily as it can be done.",

### To the Secretary.

"Camp Lincoln, *June 26th*—12 M.—I have just heard that our advanced cavalry pickets, on the left bank of Chickahominy, are being driven in. It is probably Jackson's advance guard. If this be true, you may not hear from me for some days, as my communications will probably be cut off. The case is, perhaps, a difficult one; but I shall resort to desperate measures, and will do my best to outmanœuvre, outwit, and outfight the enemy. Do not believe reports of disaster, and do not be discouraged if you learn that my communications are cut off, and even Yorktown in possession of the enemy. Hope for the best, and I will not deceive the hopes you formerly placed in me."

### To the Secretary.

"Camp Lincoln, *June 26th*—2.30 P.M.—Your despatch and that of the President received. Jackson is driving in my pickets, etc., on the other side of Chickahominy. It is impossible to tell where reinforcements ought to go, as I am yet unable to predict result of approaching battle. It will probably be better that they should go to Fortress Monroe, and thence according to state of affairs when they arrive. It is not probable that I can maintain telegraphic communication more than an hour or two longer."

### From the Secretary.

"*June 26th*—6 P.M.—Arrangements are being made as rapidly as possible to send you 5,000 men as fast as they can be brought from Manassas to Alexandria and embarked, which can be done sooner than to wait for transportation at Fredericksburgh. They will be followed by more if needed. McDowell, Banks, and Fremont's force will be consolidated as the Army of Virginia, and will operate promptly in your aid by land. Nothing will be spared to sustain you, and I have undoubting faith in your success. Keep me advised fully of your condition."

From the report of General McClellan, we extract the following details.    General McClellan says:

"Up to the 26th of June, the operations against Richmond had been conducted along the roads leading to it from the east and northeast.  The reason (the President's anxiety about covering Washington from Fredericksburg, McDowell's promised co-operation, partial advance, and immediate withdrawal) which compelled the choice of this line of approach, and our continuance upon it, have been attended to above."

### PREPARATIONS TO CHANGE BASE.

"The superiority of the James River route, as a line of attack and supply, is too obvious to need exposition.  My own opinion on that subject had been early given, and need not be repeated here.  The dissipation of all hope of the co-operation by land of General McDowell's forces, deemed to be occupied in the defence of Washington, their inability to hold or defeat Jackson, disclosed an opportunity to the enemy and a new danger to my right, and to the long line of supplies from the White House to the Chickahominy, and forced an immediate change of base across the Peninsula.  To that end, from the evening of the 26th, every energy of the army was bent.  Such a change of base in the presence of a powerful enemy is one of the most difficult undertakings in war.  I was confident of the valor and discipline of my brave army, and knew that it could be trusted equally to retreat or advance, and to fight the series of battles now inevitable, whether retreating from victories or marching through defeats ; and, in short, I had no doubt whatever of its ability, even against superior numbers, to fight its way through to the James river, and get a position whence a successful advance upon Richmond would be again possible.  Their superb conduct through the next seven days justified my faith.  On the same day General Van Vliet, chief quartermaster of the Army of the Potomac, by my orders, telegraphed to Colonel Ingalls, quartermaster, at the White House, as follows :

"'Run the cars to the last moment and load them with provisions and ammunition.  Load every wagon you have with subsistence and send them to Savage's station, by way of Bottom's bridge.  If you are obliged to abandon White House, burn every thing that you cannot get off.  You must throw all our supplies up the James river as soon as possible, and accompany them yourself, with all your force.  It will be of vast importance to establish our depots on James river, without delay, if we abandon White House.  I will keep you advised of every movement, so long as the wires work ; after that you must exercise your own judgment.'

"All these commands were obeyed.  So excellent were the

dispositions of the different officers in command of the troops, depots, and gunboats, and so timely the warning of the approach of the enemy, that almost every thing was saved, and but a small amount of stores destroyed to prevent their falling into the hands of the enemy. General Stoneman's communications with the main army being cut off, he fell back upon the White House, and thence to Yorktown, when the White House was evacuated. On the 26th, orders were sent to all the corps commanders on the right bank of the Chickahominy to be prepared to send as many troops as they could spare on the following day to the left bank of the river, as will be seen by the appended telegrams. General Franklin received instructions to hold General Slocum's division in readiness by daybreak on the 27th, and if heavy firing should at that time be heard in the direction of General Porter, to move at once to his assistance, without further orders. At noon on the 26th the approach of the enemy, who had crossed above Meadow bridge, was discovered by the advanced pickets at that point, and at 12.30 P.M. they were attacked and driven in. All the pickets were now called in, and the regiment and battery at Mechanicsville withdrawn."

### The Battle at Mechanicsville.

" Meade's brigade was ordered up as a reserve, in rear of the line, and shortly after Martindale's and Griffin's brigades, of Morrell's division, were moved forward and deployed on the right of McCall's division, toward Shady Grove church, to cover that flank. Neither of these three brigades, however, were warmly engaged, though two of Griffin's regiments relieved a portion of Reynolds' line just at the close of the action. The position of our troops was a strong one, extending along the left bank of Beaver Dam creek, the left resting on the Chickahominy, and the right in thick wood beyond the upper road from Mechanicsville to Coal harbor. The lower or river road crossed the creek at Ellison's mills. Seymour's brigade held the left of the line from the Chickahominy to beyond the mill, partly in woods and partly in cleared ground, and Reynolds's the right, principally in the woods, and covering the upper road. The artillery occupied positions commanding the roads and the open ground across the creek. Timber had been felled, rifle-pits dug, and the position generally prepared with a care that greatly contributed to the success of the day. The passage of the creek was difficult along the whole front and impracticable for artillery, except by the two roads where the main efforts of the enemy were directed. At 3 P.M. he formed his line of battle, rapidly advanced his skirmishers, and soon attacked our whole line, making, at the same time, a determined attempt to force the passage of the upper road, which was successfully resisted by General Reynolds. After a severe struggle he was forced to retire with very heavy loss. A rapid artillery fire, with desultory skirmishing, was maintained along the whole front, while the enemy massed his troops for another effort at the lower road about two hours later, which was likewise repulsed by General Seymour, with heavy slaughter. The firing ceased, and the enemy retired about 9 P.M., the action having lasted six hours, with entire success to our arms. But few, if any, of Jackson's troops were engaged on this day. The portion of the enemy encountered were chiefly from the troops on the right bank of the river, who crossed near Meadow-bridge and at Mechanicsville. The information in my possession soon after the close of this action, convinced me that Jackson was really approaching in large force. The position on Beaver Dam creek, although so successfully defended, had its right flank too much in the rear, and was too far from the main army to make it available to retain it longer. I therefore determined to send the heavy guns at Hogan's and Gaines' houses over the Chickahominy during the night, with as many of the wagons of the Fifth corps as possible, and to withdraw the corps itself to a position stretching around the bridges, where its flanks would be reasonably secure, and it would be within supporting distance of the main army. General Porter carried out my orders to that effect. It was not advisable at that time, even had it been practicable, to withdraw the Fifth corps to the right bank of the Chickahominy. Such a movement would have exposed the rear of the army, placed us between two fires, and enabled Jackson's fresh troops to intercept the movement to James' river, by crossing the Chickahominy in the vicinity of Jones's bridge, before we could reach Malvern hill with our trains. I determined then to resist Jackson with the Fifth corps, reinforced by all our disposable troops in the new position near the bridge heads, in order to cover the withdrawal of the trains and heavy guns, and to give time for the arrangements to secure the adoption of the James river as our line of supplies, in lieu of the Pamunky. The greater part of the heavy guns and wagons having been removed to the right bank of the Chickahominy, the delicate operation of withdrawing the troops from Beaver Dam creek was commenced shortly before daylight, and successfully executed. Meade's and Griffin's brigades were the first to leave the ground; Seymour's brigade covered the rear, with the horse-batteries of Captains Robertson and Tidball; but the withdrawal was so skilful and gradual, and the repulse of the preceding day so complete, that although the enemy followed the retreat slowly and some skirmishing occurred, he did not appear in front of the new line in force till about noon of the 27th, when we were prepared to receive him. About this time General Porter, believing that General Stoneman would be cut off from him, sent him orders to fall back on the White House, and afterwards rejoin the army as best he could."

### The Battle of Gaines' Mill.

"On the morning of the 27th of June, during the withdrawal of his troops from Mechanicsville to the selected position already mentioned, General Porter telegraphed as follows:

"'I hope to do without aid, though I request that Franklin or some other command, be held ready to reinforce me. The enemy are so close that I expect to be hard pressed in front. I hope to have a portion in position to cover the retreat. This is a delicate movement; but relying on the good qualities of the commanders of divisions and brigades, I expect to get back and hold the new line.'

"This shows how closely Porter's retreat was followed. Notwithstanding all the efforts used during the entire night to remove the heavy guns and wagons, some of the siege-guns were still in position at Gaines's house after sunrise, and were finally hauled off by hand. The new position of the Fifth corps was about an arc of a circle, covering the approaches to the bridges which connected our right wing with the troops on the opposite side of the river. Morrill's divison held the left of the line in a strip of woods on the left bank of the Gaines's mill stream, resting its left flank on the descent to the Chickahominy, which was swept by our artillery on both sides of the river, and extending into open ground on the right towards New Coal harbor. In this line, General Butterfield's brigade held the extreme left, General Martindale's joined his right, and General Griffin, still further to the right, joined the left of General Sykes's division, which, partly in woods and partly in open ground, extended in rear of Coal harbor. Each brigade had in reserve two of its own regiments. McCall's division having been engaged on the day before, was formed in a second line in the rear of the first, Meade's brigade on the left, near the Chickahominy, Reynolds's brigade on the right, covering the approaches from Coal harbor and Dispatch station to Sumner's bridge, and Seymour's in reserve to the second line, still further in rear. General P. St. George Cooke, with five companies of the Fifth regular cavalry, two squadrons of the First regulars, and three squadrons of the Sixth Pennsylvania cavalry (Lancers), was posted behind a hill in rear of the position and near the Chickahominy, to aid in watching the left flank and defending the slope to the river. The troops were all in position by noon, with the artillery on the commanding ground, and in the intervals between the divisions and brigades. Besides the division batteries, there were Robertson's and Tidball's horse batteries, from the artillery reserve; the latter posted on the right of Sykes's division, and the former on the extreme left of the line, in the valley of the Chickahominy. Shortly after noon, the enemy was discovered approaching in force, and it soon became evident that the entire position was to be attacked. His skirmishers advanced rapidly, and soon the firing became heavy along our whole front. At 2

P.M. General Porter asked for reinforcements. Slocum's division, of the Sixth corps, was ordered to cross to the left bank of the river, by Alexander's bridge, and proceed to his support. General Porter's first call for reinforcements, through General Barnard, did not reach me, nor his demand for more axes, through the same officer. By 3 P.M. the engagement had become so severe, and the enemy were so greatly superior in numbers, that the entire second line and reserves had been moved forward to sustain the first line against repeated and desperate assaults along our whole front. At 3.30 P.M. Slocum's division reached the field, and was immediately brought into action at the weak points of our line. On the left the contest was for the strip of woods running almost at right angles to the Chickahominy in front of Adams's house, or between that and Gaines's house; the enemy several times charged up to this wood, but were each time driven back with heavy loss. The regulars of Sykes's division on the right also repulsed several strong attacks. But our own loss, under the tremendous fire of such greatly superior numbers, was very severe, and the troops, most of whom had been under arms more than two days, were rapidly becoming exhausted by the masses of fresh men constantly brought against them. When General Slocum's division arrived on the ground it increased General Porter's force to some thirty-five thousand, who were probably contending against about seventy thousand of the enemy. The line was severely pressed in several points, and as its being pierced at any one would have been fatal, it was unavoidable for General Porter, who was required to hold his position until night, to divide Slocum's division, and send parts of it, even single regiments, to the points most threatened. About 5 P.M., General Porter having reported his position as critical, French's and Meagher's brigades, of Richardson's division (Third corps), were ordered to cross to his support. The enemy attacked again, in great force, at 6 P.M., but failed to break our lines, though our loss was very heavy. About 7 P.M., they threw fresh troops against General Porter with still greater fury, and finally gained the woods held by our left. This reverse, aided by the confusion that followed an unsuccessful charge by five companies of the Fifth cavalry, and followed as it was by more determined assaults on the remainder of our lines, now outflanked, caused a general retreat from our position to the hill in rear overlooking the bridge. French's and Meagher's brigades now appeared, driving before them the stragglers who were thronging towards the bridge. These brigades advanced boldly to the front, and by their example as well as by the steadiness of their bearing, reanimated our own troops and warned the enemy that reinforcements had arrived. It was now dusk. The enemy, already repulsed several times with terrible slaughter, and hearing the shouts of the fresh troops, failed to follow up their advantage. This gave an opportunity to rally our men behind the brigades of Generals French and Meagher, and they again advanced up the hill, ready to repulse another attack. During the night our thinned and exhausted regiments were all withdrawn in safety, and by the following morning all had reached the other side of the stream. The regular infantry formed the rear guard, and about 6 o'clock on the morning of the 28th, crossed the river, destroying the bridge behind them. Our loss in this battle, in killed, wounded, and missing, was very heavy, especially in officers, many of whom were killed, wounded, or taken prisoners while gallantly leading on their men, or rallying them to renewed exertions. It is impossible to arrive at the exact numbers lost in this desperate engagement, owing to the series of battles which followed each other in quick succession, and in which the whole army was engaged. No general returns were made until after we had arrived at Harrison's landing, when the losses during the whole seven days were estimated together. Although we were finally forced from our first line after the enemy had been repeatedly driven back, yet the objects sought for had been obtained. The enemy was held at bay, our siege-guns and material were saved, and the right wing had now joined the main body of the army. The number of guns captured by the enemy at this battle was twenty-two, three of which were lost by being run off the bridge during the final withdrawal. Great credit is due for the efficiency and bravery with which this important arm of the service (the artillery) was fought, and it was not until the last successful charge of the enemy that the cannoneers were driven from their pieces or struck down, and the guns captured. Diedrich's, Knierim's, and Grimm's batteries took position during the engagement in the front of General Smith's line, on the right bank of the stream, and with a battery of siege-guns, served by the First Connecticut Artillery, helped to drive back the enemy in front of General Porter."

### The Right Bank of the Chickahominy.

" So threatening were the movements of the enemy on both banks of the Chickahominy, that it was impossible to decide, until the afternoon, where the real attack would be made. Large forces of infantry were seen, during the day, near the old tavern, on Franklin's right, and threatening demonstrations were frequently made along the entire line on this side of the river, which rendered it necessary to hold a considerable force in position to meet them. On the 26th a circular was sent to the corps commanders on the right bank of the river, asking them how many of their troops could be spared to reinforce General Porter, after retaining sufficient to hold their positions for twenty-four hours.

" To this the following replies were received :

5

> " ' HEAD-QUARTERS, THIRD CORPS,
> " *June 26th*—4 P.M.

" '*General R. B. Marcy:*

" I think I can hold the intrenchments with four brigades for twenty-four hours. That would leave two brigades disposable for service on the other side of the river; but the men are so tired and worn out that I fear they would not be in a condition to fight after making a march of any distance.       *       *

> " ' S. P. HEINTZELMAN, *Brigadier-General.*'

" Telegrams from General Heintzelman, on the 25th and 26th, had indicated that the enemy was in large force in front of Generals Hooker and Kearney, and on the Charles City road (Longstreet, Hill, and Huger), and General Heintzelman expressed the opinion, on the night of the 25th, that he could not hold his advanced position without reinforcements.

" General Keys telegraphed : 'As to how many men will be able to hold this position for twenty-four hours, I must answer, all I have, if the enemy is as strong as ever in front, it having at all times appeared to me that our forces on this flank are small enough.'

" On the morning of the 27th, the following despatch was sent to General Sumner :

> " ' HEAD-QUARTERS, ARMY OF THE POTOMAC,
> " *June 27th*—8.45 A.M.

" '*General E. V. Sumner, commanding Second Army Corps:*

" ' General Smith just reports that six or eight regiments have moved down to the woods in front of General Sumner.

> " '(Signed)      " ' R. B. MARCY, *Chief of Staff.*'

" At 11 o'clock, A.M., General Sumner telegraphed as follows : 'The enemy threaten an attack on my right, near Smith.' At 12.30 P.M., he telegraphed : 'Sharp shelling on both sides.' At 2.45 P.M. : 'Sharp musketry firing in front of Burns; we are replying with artillery and infantry. The man on the lookout reports some troops drawn up in line of battle about opposite my right and Smith's left ; the number cannot be made out.'

" In accordance with orders given on the night of the 26th, General Slocum's division commenced crossing the river, to support General Porter, soon after daybreak on the morning of the 27th ; but, as the firing in front of General Porter ceased, the movement was suspended. At 2 P.M., General Porter called for reinforcements. I ordered them at once, and at 3.25 P.M., sent him the following :

" ' Slocum is now crossing Alexander's bridge with his whole command. Enemy has commenced an infantry attack on Smith's left. I have ordered down Sumner's and Heintzelman's reserves, and you can count on the whole of Slocum's. Go on as you have begun.'

" During the day the following despatches were received, which will show the condition of affairs on the right bank of the Chickahominy :

" 'June 27th, 1862.

" ' *To Colonel A. V. Colburn, A. A. G.:*

" 'General Smith thinks the enemy are massing heavy columns in the clearings to the right of James Garnett's house and on the other side of the river, opposite it. Three regiments are reported to be moving from Sumner's to Smith's front. The arrangements are very good—made by Smith.

" '(Signed) " 'W. B. FRANKLIN, *Brigadier-General.*'

"Afterwards he telegraphed : 'The enemy has begun an attack on Smith's left with infantry. I know no details.' Afterwards the following : 'The enemy has opened on Smith from a battery of three pieces to the right of the White House. Our shells are bursting well, and Smith thinks Sumner will soon have a cross-fire upon them that will silence them.' Afterwards (at 5.50 P.M.) the following was sent to General Keyes :

" 'Please send one brigade of Couch's division to these head-quarters without a moment's delay. A staff-officer will be here to direct the brigade where to go.'

" Subsequently the following was sent to Generals Sumner and Franklin :

" 'Is there any sign of the enemy being in force in your front ? Can you spare any more force to be sent to General Porter ? Answer at once.'

"At 5.15, P.M., the following was received from General Franklin :

" 'I do not think it prudent to take any more troops from here at present.'

" General Sumner replied as follows :

" 'If the General desires to trust the defence of my position to my front line alone, I can send French with three regiments and Meagher with his brigade to the right—every thing is so uncertain, that I think it would be hazardous to do it.'

" These two brigades were sent to reinforce General Porter, as has been observed.

"At 5.25 P.M., I sent the following to General Franklin :

" 'Porter is hard pressed. It is not a question of prudence, but of possibilities. Can you possibly maintain your position until dark with two brigades ? I have ordered eight regiments of Sumner's to support Porter, one brigade of Couch's to this place. Heintzelman's reserve to go in rear of Sumner. If possible, send a brigade to support Porter. It should follow the regiments ordered from Sumner.'

"At 7.35, P.M., the following was sent to General Sumner:

"'If it is possible, send another brigade to reinforce General Smith. It is said three heavy columns of infantry are moving on him.'

" From the foregoing despatches it will be seen that all disposable troops were sent from the right bank of the river to reinforce General Porter, and that the corps commanders were left with smaller forces to hold their positions than they deemed adequate. To have done more, even though Porter's reverse had been prevented, would have had the still more disastrous result of imperiling the whole movement across the Peninsula "

### JUNCTION OF FORCES EFFECTED.

"The operations of this day proved the numerical superiority of the enemy, and made it evident that while he had a large army on the left bank of the Chickahominy, which had already turned our right, and was in position to intercept the communications with our depot at the White House, he was also in large force between our army and Richmond. I therefore effected a junction of our forces. This might probably have been executed on either side of the Chickahominy, and if the concentration had been effected on the left bank, it is possible we might, with our entire force, have defeated the enemy there; but at that time they held the roads leading to the White House, so that it would have been impossible to have sent forward supply trains in advance of the army in that direction, and the guarding of those trains would have seriously embarrassed our operations in the battle; we would have been compelled to fight, if concentrated on that bank of the river. Moreover, we would at once have been followed by the enemy's forces upon the Richmond side of the river, operating upon our rear, and if in the chances of war, we had been ourselves defeated in the effort, we would have been forced to fall back to the White House, and, probably, to Fortress Monroe. And as both our flank and rear would then have been entirely exposed, our entire supply train, if not the greater part of the army itself, might have been lost. The movements of the enemy showed that they expected this, and as they themselves acknowledge, they were prepared to cut off our retreat in that direction. I, therefore, concentrated all our forces on the right bank of the river. During the night of the 26th, and morning of the 27th, all our wagons, heavy guns, etc., were gathered there. It may be asked why, after the concentration of our forces on the right bank of the Chickahominy with a large part of the enemy drawn away from Richmond, upon the opposite side, I did not, instead of striking for James river, fifteen miles below that place, at once march directly on Richmond. It will be remembered that at this junction the enemy was on our rear, and there was every reason to believe that he would sever our communications with the supply depot at the White House. We had on hand but a limited amount of rations, and if we had advanced directly on Richmond, it would have required considerable time to carry the strong works around that place, during which our men would have been destitute of food, and even if Richmond had fallen before our arms, the enemy would still have occupied our supply communications between that place and the gunboats and turned the disaster into victory. If, on the other hand, the enemy had concentrated all his forces at Richmond during the progress of our attack and we had been defeated, we must, in all probability, have lost our trains before reaching the flotilla. The battles which continued day after day in the progress of our flank movement to the James river, with the exception of the one at Gaines's mill were successes to our arms, and the closing engagement at Malvern Hill was the most decisive of all."

## THE MOVEMENT TO JAMES RIVER.

"On the evening of the 27th of June I assembled the corps commanders at my head-quarters and informed them of my plan, its reasons, and my choice of route and method of execution. Gen. Keyes was directed to move his corps, with its artillery and baggage, across the White Oak swamp bridge, and to seize strong positions on the opposite side of the swamp, to cover the passage of the other troops and trains. This was executed on the 28th by noon. Before daybreak on the 28th I went to Savage's station, and remained there during the day and night, directing the withdrawal of the trains and supplies of the army. Orders were given to the different commanders to load their wagons with ammunition and provisions and the necessary baggage of the officers and men, and to destroy all property which could not be transported with the army. Orders were also given to leave with those of the sick and wounded who could not be transported, a proper complement of surgeons and attendants, with a bountiful supply of rations and medical stores. The large herd of 2,500 beef-cattle was, by the chief commissary, Colonel Clarke, transferred to the James river without loss. On the morning of the 28th, while General Franklin was withdrawing his command from Golding's farm, the enemy opened upon General Smith's division from Garnett's hill, from the valley above, and from Gaines's hill on the opposite side of the Chickahominy, and shortly afterward two Georgia regiments attempted to carry the works about to be vacated; but this attack was repulsed by the Twenty-third New York and the Forty-ninth Pennsylvania Volunteers, on picket, and a section of Mott's battery. Porter's corps was moved across White Oak swamp during the day and night, and took up positions covering the roads leading from Richmond towards White Oak swamp and Long bridge. McCall's division was ordered on the night of the 28th to move across the swamp and take a proper position to assist in cover-

ing the remaining troops and trains. During the same night
the corps of Sumner and Heintzelman, and the division of Smith,
were ordered to an interior line, the left resting on Keyes' old
intrenchments and curving to the right, so as to cover Savage's
station. General Slocum's division of Franklin's corps was ordered to Savage's station in reserve. They were ordered to hold
this position until dark of the 29th, in order to cover the withdrawal of the trains, and then to fall back across the swamp and
unite with the remainder of the army."

" On the night of the 28th I sent the following to the Secretary of War :

" ' HEAD-QUARTERS, ARMY OF THE POTOMAC,
" ' SAVAGE's STATION, *June 28th*, 1862—12.20 A.M.

" ' I know the full history of the day. On this side of the river—
the right bank—we repulsed several strong attacks. On the
left bank our men did all that men could do, all that soldiers
could accomplish ; but they were overwhelmed by vastly superior
numbers, even after I brought my last reserves into action. The
loss on both sides is terrible. I believe it will prove to be the
most desperate battle of the war. The sad remnants of my men
behave as men ; those battalions who fought most bravely, and
suffered most, are still in the best order. My regulars were
superb, and I count upon what are left to turn another battle in
company with their gallant comrades of the volunteers. Had I
twenty thousand (20,000) or even ten thousand (10,000) fresh
troops to use to-morrow, I could take Richmond ; but I have
not a man in reserve, and shall be glad to cover my retreat and
save the material and *personnel* of the army. If we have lost
the day, we have yet preserved our honor, and no one need blush
for the Army of the Potomac. I have lost this battle because
my force was too small. I again repeat that I am not responsible for this, and I say it with the earnestness of a General who
feels in his heart the loss of every brave man who has been need-
lessly sacrificed to-day. I still hope to retrieve our fortunes ;
but to do this the Government must view the matter in the same
earnest light that I do. You must send me very large reinforcements, and send them at once. I shall draw back to this side
of the Chickahominy, and think I can withdraw all our material. Please understand that in this battle we have lost nothing
but men, and those the best we have. In addition to what I
have already said, I only wish to say to the President that I
think he is wrong in regarding me as ungenerous when I said
that my force was too weak—I merely intimated a truth which
to-day has been too plainly proved. If, at this instant, I could
dispose of (10,000) ten thousand fresh men, I could gain the victory to-morrow. I know that a few thousand more men would
have changed this battle from a defeat to a victory. As it is,

the Government must not, and cannot hold me responsible for the result. I feel too earnestly to-night—I have seen too many dead and wounded comrades to feel otherwise, than that the Government has not sustained this army. If you do not do so now, the game is lost. If I save this army now, I tell you plainly that I owe no thanks to you, or to any other persons in Washington. You have done your best to sacrifice this army.

"'G. B. McCLELLAN.

"'To Hon. E. M. Stanton.'"

"The head-quarters camp at Savage's station was broken up early on the morning of the 29th, and moved across White Oak Swamp. As the essential part of this day's operations was the passage of the trains across the swamp and their protection against attack from the direction of New Market and Richmond, as well as the immediate and secure establishment of our communications with the gunboats, I passed the day in examining the ground, directing the posting of troops, and securing the uninterrupted movement of the trains. In the afternoon I instructed General Keyes to move during the night to James river, and occupy a defensive position near Malvern Hill, to secure our extreme left flank. General F. J. Porter was ordered to follow him and prolong the line towards the right. The trains were to be pushed on toward James river in rear of these corps, and placed under the protection of the gunboats as they arrived. A sharp skirmish with the enemy's cavalry early this day, on the Quaker road, showed that his efforts were about to be directed towards impeding our progress to the river, and rendered my presence in that quarter necessary."

### BATTLE OF ALLEN'S FARM.

"General Sumner vacated his works at Fair Oaks on June 29th, at daylight, and marched his command to Orchard station, halting at Allen's Field, between Orchard and Savage's station. The divisions of Richardson and Sedgwick were formed on the right of the railroad, facing towards Richmond, Richardson holding the right, and Sedgwick joining the right of Heintzelman's corps. The first line of Richardson's division was held by General French, General Caldwell supporting in the second. A log building in front of Richardson's division was held by Colonel Brooks with one regiment (Fifty-third Pennsylvania volunteers), with Hazzard's battery, on an elevated piece of ground, a little in rear of Colonel Brooks' command. At 9 A.M., the enemy commenced a furious attack on the right of General Sedgwick, but were repulsed. The left of General Richardson was next attacked, the enemy attempting in vain to carry the position of Colonel Brooks. Captain Hazzard's battery, and Captain Pettit's battery, which afterwards replaced it,

were served with great effect, while the Fifty-third Pennsylvania
kept up a steady fire on the advancing enemy, compelling them
at last to retire in disorder. The enemy renewed the attack
three times, but were as often repulsed."

## BATTLE OF SAVAGE'S STATION.

" General Slocum arrived at Savage's station at an early hour
on the 29th, and was ordered to cross White Oak swamp, and
relieve General Keyes's corps. As soon as General Keyes was
thus relieved, he moved towards James river, which he reached
in safety with all his artillery and baggage early on the morning
of the 30th, and took up a position below Turkey Creek bridge.
During the morning General Franklin heard that the enemy,
after having repaired the bridges, was crossing the Chickahominy
in large force, and advancing toward Savage's station. He
communicated this information to General Sumner, at Allen's
farm, and moved Smith's division to Savage's station. A little
after noon General Sumner united his forces with those of General Franklin, and assumed command. I had ordered General
Heintzelman, with his corps, to hold the Williamsburg road
until dark, at a point where were several field-works, and a skirt
of timber between these works and the railroad; but he fell back
before night, and crossed White Oak Swamp at Brackett's ford.

General Sumner, in his report of the battle of Savage's
station, says:

" 'When the enemy appeared on the Williamsburg road, I
could not imagine why General Heintzelman did not attack him,
and not till some time afterwards did I learn to my utter amaze-
ment, that General Heintzelman had left the field, and retreated
with his whole corps (about fifteen thousand men) before the
action commenced. This defection might have been attended
with the most disastrous consequences, and, although we beat
the enemy signally, and drove him from the field, we should
certainly have given him a more crushing blow if General
Heintzelman had been there with his corps."

General Heintzelman, in his report of the operations of his
corps, says:

" 'On the night of the 28th of June I received orders to
withdraw the troops of my corps from the advanced position they
had taken on the 25th of June, and to occupy the intrenched
lines about a mile in rear. A map was sent me showing the
positions General Sumner's and General Franklin's corps would
occupy. About sunrise the next day, our troops slowly fell back
to the new position, cautiously followed by the enemy, taking
possession of our camps as soon as we left them. From some
misapprehension, General Sumner held a more advanced position than was indicated on the map furnished me, thus leaving a

space of about three-fourths of a mile between the right of his corps and General Smith's division of General Franklin's corps.    *    *    *    *    *    *    *

"'At 11. A.M., on the 29th, the enemy commenced an attack on General Sumner's troops, a few shells falling within my lines. Late in the forenoon reports reached me that the rebels were in possession of Doctor Trent's house, only a mile and a half from Savage's station. I sent several cavalry reconnoissances, and finally was satisfied of the fact. General Franklin came to my head-quarters when I learned of the interval between his left and General Sumner's right, in which space Dr. Trent's house is. Also, that the rebels had repaired one of the bridges across the Chickahominy, and were advancing.    *    *    *

"'I rode forward to see General Sumner, and met his troops falling back on the Williamsburg road, through my lines. General Sumner informed me that he intended to make a stand at Savage's station, and for me to join him, to determine upon the position.

"'This movement of General Sumner's uncovering my right flank, it became necessary for me to at once withdraw my troops.    *    *    *    *    *    *    *

"'I rode back to find General Sumner. After some delay, from the mass of troops in the field, I found him, and learned that the course of action had been determined on; so I returned to give the necessary orders for the destruction of the railroad cars, ammunition, and provisions still remaining on the ground.

"'The whole open space near Savage's station was crowded with troops, more than I supposed could be brought into action judiciously. An aid from the commanding general had, in the morning, reported to me to point out a road across the White Oak swamp, starting from the left of General Kearney's position, and leading by Brackett's ford.    *    *    *    *    The advance of the column reached the Charles City road at 6½ P.M., and the rear at 10 P.M., without accident.'"

"The orders given by me to Generals Sumner, Heintzelman, and Franklin were to hold the positions assigned them until dark. As stated by General Heintzelman, General Sumner did not occupy the designated position; but as he was the senior officer present on that side of the White Oak swamp, he may have thought that the movements of the enemy justified a deviation from the letter of the orders. It appears from his report that he assumed command of all the troops near Savage's Station, and determined to resist the enemy there, and that he gave General Heintzelman orders to hold the same position as I had assigned him. The aid sent by me to General Heintzelman, to point out the road across the swamp, was to guide him in retiring after dark. On reaching Savage's Station, Sumner's and Franklin's commands were drawn up in line of battle, in the large open field to the left of the railroad, the left resting on the edge of the woods, and the right extending down to the railroad. General Brooks, with his brigade, held the woods to the left of the field, where he did excellent service, receiving a wound, but retaining his command. General Hancock's brigade was thrown into the woods on the right and front. At 4 P.M., the enemy commenced his attack in large force, by the Williamsburg road. It was gallantly met by General Burns's brigade, supported and reinforced by two lines in reserve, and finally by the New York Sixty-ninth, Hazzard's and Pettet's batteries again doing good service. Osborn's and Bramhall's batteries also took part effectively in this action, which was continued with great obstinacy until between 8 and 9 P.M., when the enemy were driven from the field. Immediately after the battle, the orders were repeated for all the troops to fall back and cross White Oak swamp, which we accomplished during the night in good order. By midnight all the troops were on the road to White Oak swamp bridge. General French, with his brigade, acting as rear-guard, and at 5 A.M., on the 30th, all had crossed, and the bridge was destroyed.

## OPERATIONS ON THE 30TH.

"On the afternoon of the 29th, I gave to the corps commanders their instructions for the operations of the following day. As stated before, Porter's corps was to move forward to James river, and with the corps of General Keyes, to occupy a position at or near Turkey Bend, on a line perpendicular to the river, thus covering the Charles City road to Richmond, opening communication with the gunboats, and covering the passage of the supply trains, which were pushed forward as rapidly as possible upon Haxall's plantation. The remaining corps were pressed onward and posted so as to guard the approaches from Richmond, as well as the crossings of the White Oak Swamp, over which the army had passed. General Franklin was ordered to hold the passage of White Oak Swamp bridge, and cover the withdrawal of the trains from that point. His command consisted of his own corps, with General Richardson's division, and General Naglee's brigade, placed under his orders for the occasion. General Slocum's division was on the right of the Charles City road. On the morning of the 30th I again gave to the corps commanders within reach instructions for posting their troops. I found that, notwithstanding all the efforts of my personal staff and other officers, the roads were blocked by wagons, and there was great difficulty in keeping the trains in motion. The engineer officers whom I had sent forward on the 28th to reconnoitre the roads, had neither returned nor sent me any reports or guides. Generals Keyes and Porter had been delayed —one by losing the road, and the other by repairing an old road —and had not been able to send any information. We then knew of but one road for the movement of the troops and our immense trains. It was therefore necessary to post the troops in advance of this road as well as our limited knowledge of the ground permitted, so as to cover the movement of the trains in the rear. I then examined the whole line from the swamp to the left, giving final instructions for the posting of the troops, and the obstructions of the roads toward Richmond; and all corps commanders were directed to hold their positions until the trains had passed, after which a more concentrated position was to be taken up near James river. Our force was too small to occupy and hold the entire line from the White Oak Swamp to the river, exposed as it was, to be taken in reverse by a movement across the lower part of the swamp, or across the Chickahominy below the swamp. Moreover, the troops were then greatly exhausted, and required rest in a more secure position. I extended my examinations of the country as far as Haxall's, looking at all the approaches to Malvern, which position I perceived to be the key to our operations in this quarter, and was thus enabled to expedite very considerably the passage of the trains, and to rectify the positions of the troops.

"Every thing being then quiet, I sent aids to the different corps commanders to inform them what I had done on the left, and to bring me information of the condition of affairs on the right. I returned from Malvern to Haxall's, and having made arrangements for instant communication from Malvern by signals, went on board of Captain Rodgers's gunboat, lying near, to confer with him in reference to the condition of our supply vessels, and the state of things on the river. It was his opinion that it would be necessary for the army to fall back to a position below City Point, as the channel there was so near the southern shore that it would not be possible to bring up the transports, should the enemy occupy it. Harrison's Landing was, in his opinion, the nearest suitable point. Upon the termination of this interview, I returned to Malvern Hill, and remained there till shortly before daylight."

### Battle of Nelson's Farm or Glendale.

"On the morning of the 30th, General Sumner was ordered to march with Sedgwick's division to Glendale (Nelson's farm.) General McCall's division (Pennsylvania reserves) was halted during the morning on the New Market road, just in advance of the point where the road turns off to Quaker Church. This line was formed perpendicularly to the New Market road, with Meade's brigade on the right, Seymour's on the left, and Reynold's brigade, commanded by Colonel S. G. Simmons, of the Fifth Pennsylvania, in reserve; Randall's regular battery on the right, Kern's and Cooper's batteries opposite the centre, and Deitrich's and Kanerhun's batteries, of the artillery reserve, on the left—all in front of the infantry line. The country in General McCall's front was an open field, intersected towards the right by the New Market road, and a small strip of timber parallel to it. The open front was about eight hundred yards; its depth about one thousand yards. On the morning of the 30th, General Heintzelman ordered the bridge at Brackett's Ford to be destroyed, and trees to be felled across that road and the Charles City road. General Slocum's division was to extend to the Charles City road. General Kearney's left to connect with General Slocum's left. General McCall's position was to the left of the Long Bridge road, in connection with General Kearney's left. General Hooker was on the left of General McCall. Between 12 and 1 o'clock the enemy opened a fierce cannonade upon the divisions of Smith and Richardson, and Naglee's brigade, at White Oak Swamp bridge. This artillery fire was continued by the enemy through the day, and he crossed some infantry below our position. Richardson's division suffered severely. Captain Ayres directed our artillery with great effect. Captain Hazzard's battery, after losing many cannoneers, and Captain Hazzard being mortally wounded, was compelled to retire. It was replaced by Pettet's battery, which partially silenced the enemy's guns. General Franklin held his position until after dark, repeatedly driving back the enemy in their attempts to cross the White Oak Swamp. At 2 o'clock in the day the enemy were reported advancing in force by the Charles City road, and at 2½ o'clock the attack was made down the road on General Slocum's left, but was checked by his artillery. After this the enemy, in large force, comprising the divisions of Longstreet and A. P. Hill, attacked General McCall, whose division, after severe fighting, was compelled to retire.

General McCall, in his report of the battle, says:

\* \* \* "'About 2½ o'clock my pickets were driven in by a strong advance, after some skirmishing, without loss on our part.

"'At 3 o'clock the enemy sent forward a regiment on the left centre, and another on the right centre, to feel for a weak point. They were under cover of a shower of shells, and boldly advanced, but were both driven back—on the left by the Twelfth regiment, and on the right by the Seventh regiment. For nearly two hours the battle raged hotly here. \* \* \* At last the enemy was compelled to retire before the well-directed musketry fire of the reserves. The German batteries were driven to the rear, but I rode up and sent them back. It was, however, of little avail, and they were soon after abandoned by the cannoneers. \* \* \* The batteries in front of the centre were boldly charged upon, but the enemy were speedily forced back. \* \* \* Soon after this a most determined charge was made on Randall's battery by a full brigade, advancing in wedge shape, without order, but in perfect recklessness. Somewhat similar charges had, I have stated, been previously made on Cooper's and Kern's batteries by single regiments without success, they having recoiled before the storm of cannister hurled against them. A like result was anticipated by Randall's battery, and the Fourth regiment was requested not to fire until the battery had done with them. Its gallant commander did not doubt his ability to repel the attack, and his guns did indeed mow down the advancing host, but still the gaps were closed, and the enemy came in upon a run to the very muzzle of his guns. It was a perfect torrent of men, and they were in his battery before the guns could be removed. Two guns that were, indeed, successfully limbered had their horses killed and wounded, and were overturned on the spot, and the enemy, dashing past, drove the greater part of the Fourth regiment before them. The left company (B), nevertheless, stood its ground, with its Captain, Fred. A. Conrad, as did likewise certain men of other companies. I had ridden into the regiment and endeavored to check them, but with only partial success.       *       *       *       *       *       *       *

" 'There was no running, but my division, reduced by the previous battles to less than 6,000, had to contend with the divisions of Longstreet and A. P. Hill, considered two of the strongest and best among many of the Confederate Army, numbering that day 18,000 or 20,000 men, and it was reluctantly compelled to give way before heavier force accumulated upon them.' "

" General Heintzelman states that about 5 o'clock, P.M., General McCall's division was attacked in large force, evidently the principal attack; that in less than an hour the division gave way, and adds :

" ' General Hooker being on his left, by moving to his right repulsed the rebels in the handsomest manner, with great slaughter. General Sumner, who was with General Sedgwick in McCall's rear, also greatly aided with his artillery and infantry in driving back the enemy. They now renewed their attack with vigor on General Kearney's left, and were again repulsed with heavy loss.       *       *       *       *       *       *

" 'This attack commenced about 4 P.M., and was pushed by heavy masses with the utmost determination and vigor. Captain Thompson's battery, directed with great precision, firing double charges, swept them back. The whole open space, two hundred paces wide, was filled with the enemy ; each repulse brought fresh troops. The third attack was only repulsed by the rapid volleys and determined charge of the Sixty-third Pennsylvania, Colonel Hayes, and half of the Thirty-seventh New York Volunteers.' "

" General McCall's troops soon began to emerge from the woods into the open field. Several batteries were in position, and began to fire into the woods over the heads of our men in front. Captain DeRussey's battery was placed on the right of

General Sumner's artillery, with orders to shell the woods. General Burns's brigade was then advanced to meet the enemy, and soon drove him back; other troops began to return from the White Oak swamp. Late in the day, at the call of General Kearney, General Taylor's First New Jersey brigade, Slocum's division, was sent to occupy a portion of General McCall's deserted position, a battery accompanying the brigade. They soon drove back the enemy, who shortly after gave up the attack, contenting themselves with keeping up a desultory firing till late at night. Between 12 and 1 o'clock at night, General Heintzelman commenced to withdraw his corps, and soon after daylight both of his divisions, with General Slocum's division, and a portion of General Sumner's command, reached Malvern Hill. On the morning of the 30th, General Sumner, in obedience to orders, had moved promptly to Glendale, and upon a call from General Franklin for reinforcements, sent him two brigades, which returned in time to participate and render good service in the battle near Glendale."

" General Sumner says of this battle :

"'The battle of Glendale was the most severe action since the battle of Fair Oaks. About 3 o'clock, P.M., the action commenced, and after a furious contest, lasting till after dark, the enemy was routed at all points, and driven from the field.'

" The rear of the supply trains and the reserve artillery of the army reached Malvern Hill about 4 P.M. At about this time the enemy began to appear in General Porter's front, and at 5 o'clock advanced in large force against his left flank, posting artillery under cover of a skirt of timber, with a view to engage our force on Malvern Hill, while, with his infantry, and some artillery, he attacked Colonel Warren's brigade. A concentrated fire of about thirty guns was brought to bear on the enemy, which with the infantry fire of Colonel Warren's command, compelled him to retreat, leaving two guns in the hands of Colonel Warren. The gunboats rendered most efficient aid at this time, and helped to drive back the enemy. It was very late at night before my aids returned to give me the results of the day's fighting along the whole line, and the true position of affairs. While waiting to hear from General Franklin before sending orders to Generals Sumner and Heintzelman. I received a message from the latter that General Franklin was falling back, whereupon I sent Colonel Colburn, of my staff, with orders to verify this, and if it were true, to order in Generals Sumner and Heintzelman at once. He had not gone far when he met two officers sent from General Franklin's head-quarters, with the information that he was falling back. Orders were then sent to Generals Sumner and Heintzelman to fall back also, and definite instructions were given as to the movement, which was to commence on the right. The orders met these troops already *en route* to Malvern. Instructions were also sent to General Franklin as to the route he was to follow. General Barnard then received full instructions for posting the troops as they arrived. I then returned to Haxall's, and again left for Malvern soon after daybreak. Accompanied by several general officers, I once more made the entire circuit of the position and then returned to Haxall's, whence I went with Captain Rodgers to select the final location for the army and its depots. I returned to Malvern before the serious fighting commenced, and after riding along the lines, and seeing most cause to feel anxious about the right, remained in that vicinity."

### BATTLE OF MALVERN HILL.

"The position selected for resisting the further advance of the enemy on the first of July, was with the left and centre of our lines resting on Malvern Hill, while the right curved backward through a wooded country towards a point below Haxall's, on James river. Malvern Hill is an elevated plateau, about a mile and a half by three-fourths of a mile in area, well cleared of timber, and with several converging roads running over it. In front are numerous defensible ravines, and the ground slopes gradually toward the north and east to the woodland, giving clear ranges for artillery in those directions. Towards the northwest the plateau falls off more abruptly into a ravine which extends to James river. From the position of the enemy, his most obvious lines of attack would come from the direction of Richmond and White Oak swamp, and would almost of necessity strike us upon our left wing. Here, therefore, the lines were strengthened by massing the troops and collecting the principal part of the artillery. Porter's corps held the left of the line—Sykes' division on the left, Morrell's on the right, with the artillery of his two divisions advantageously posted, and the artillery of the reserve so disposed on the high ground that a concentrated fire of some sixty guns could be brought to bear on any point in his front or left. Colonel Tyler also had, with great exertion, succeeded in getting ten of his siege-guns in position on the highest point of the hill. Conch's division was placed on the right of Porter; next came Kearney and Hooker; next Sedgwick and Richardson; next Smith and Slocum, then the remainder of Keyes' corps, extending by a backwood curve nearly to the river. The Pennsylvania Reserve corps was held in reserve, and stationed behind Porter's and Conch's position. One brigade of Porter's was thrown to the left, on the low ground, to protect that flank from any movement direct from the Richmond road. The line was very strong along the whole front of the open plateau, but from thence to the extreme right, the troops were more deployed. This formation was imperative, as an attack would probably be made upon our left. The right was rendered as secure as possible by slashing the timber, and by barricading the roads. Commodore Rodgers, commanding the flotilla on James river, placed his gunboats so as to protect our flank and to command the approaches from Richmond. Between 9 and 10 A.M., the enemy commenced feeling along our whole left wing with his artillery and skirmishers, as far to the right as Hooker's division. About two o'clock a column of the enemy was observed moving towards our right, within the skirt of woods in front of Heintzelman's corps, but beyond the range of our artillery. Arrangements were at once made to meet the anticipated attack in that quarter; but though the column was long, occupying more than two hours in passing, it disappeared and was not again heard of. The presumption is, that it retired by the rear and participated in the attack afterwards made on our left. About 3 P.M., a heavy fire of artillery opened on Kearney's left and Couch's division, speedily followed up by a brisk attack of infantry on Couch's front. The artillery was replied to with good effect by our own, and the infantry of Couch's division remained lying on the ground until the advancing column was within short musket-range, when they sprang to their feet and poured in a deadly volley, which entirely broke the attacking force, and drove them in disorder back over their own ground. This advantage was followed up until we had advanced the right of our lines some seven or eight hundred yards, and rested upon a thick clump of trees, giving us a stronger position and a better fire. Shortly after 4 o'clock, the firing ceased along the whole front, but no disposition was evinced on the part of the enemy to withdraw from the field. Caldwell's brigade, having been detached from Richardson's division, was stationed upon Couch's right by General Porter, to whom he had been ordered to report. The whole line was surveyed by the General, and every thing held in readiness to meet the coming attack. At 6 o'clock the enemy suddenly opened upon Couch and Porter with the whole strength of his artillery, and at once began pushing forward his columns of attack, to carry the hill. Brigade after brigade formed under cover of the woods, started at a run to cross the open space and charge our batteries, but the heavy fire of our guns, with the cool and steady volleys of our infantry, in every case sent them reeling back to shelter, and covered the ground with their dead and wounded. In several instances our infantry withheld their fire, until the attacking column, which rushed through the storm of cannister and shell from our artillery, had reached within a few yards of our lines. They then poured in a single volley, and dashed forward with the bayonet, capturing prisoners and colors, and driving the routed columns in confusion from the field. About 7 o'clock, as fresh troops were accumulating in front of Porter and Couch, Meagher and Sickels were sent with their brigades as soon as it was considered prudent to withdraw any portion of Sumner's and Heintzelman's troops, to reinforce that part of the line, and hold the position. These brigades relieved such regiments of Porter's corps and Couch's division, as had expended their ammunition, and batteries from the reserve were pushed forward to replace those whose boxes were empty. Until dark the enemy persisted in his efforts to take the position so tenaciously defended, but despite his vastly superior numbers, his repeated and desperate attacks were repulsed with fearful loss, and darkness ended the battle of Malvern Hill, though it was not until after nine o'clock that the artillery ceased its fire. During the whole battle, Commodore Rodgers added greatly to the discomfiture of the enemy, by throwing shell among his reserves and advancing columns. As the army, in its movement from the Chickahominy to Harrison's Landing, was continually occupied in marching by night and fighting by day, its commanders found no time or opportunity for collecting data which would enable them to give exact returns of casualties in each engagement. The aggregate of our entire losses from the 26th of June to the 1st of July, inclusive, was ascertained after arriving at Harrison's Landing, to be as follows:

*List of killed, wounded and missing in the Army of the Potomac, from the 26th of June to the 1st of July, 1862, inclusive.*

| Corps. | Killed. | Wounded. | Missing. | Agg. |
|---|---|---|---|---|
| 1. McCall's division........ | 253 | 1,240 | 1,581 | 3,074 |
| 2. Sumner's................ | 187 | 1,076 | 848 | 2,111 |
| 3. Heintzelman's........... | 189 | 1,051 | 833 | 2,073 |
| 4. Keyes'.................. | 69 | 507 | 201 | 777 |
| 5. Porter's................ | 620 | 2,460 | 1,198 | 4,278 |
| 6. Franklin's.............. | 245 | 1,313 | 1,179 | 2,737 |
| Engineers ................. | | 2 | 21 | 23 |
| Cavalry.................... | 19 | 60 | 97 | 176 |
| Total................ | 1,582 | 7,709 | 5,958 | 15,249 |

## WHY HARRISON'S LANDING WAS SELECTED.

"Although the result of the battle of Malvern was a complete victory, it was nevertheless necessary to fall back still further, in order to reach a point where our supplies could be brought to us with certainty. As before stated, in the opinion of Captain Rodgers, commanding the gunboat flotilla, this could only be done below City Point. Concurring in his opinion. I selected Harrison's bar as the new position of the army. The exhaustion of our supplies of food, forage and ammunition, made it imperative to reach the transports immediately. The greater portion of the transportation of the army having been started for Harrison's Landing during the night of the 30th of June and the 1st of July, the order for the movement of the troops was at once issued upon the final repulse of the enemy at Malvern Hill. The order prescribed a movement by the left and rear,

6

General Keyes's corps to cover the manœuvre. It was not carried out in detail as regards the divisions on the left, the roads
being somewhat blocked by the rear of our trains. Porter and
Couch were not able to move out as early as had been anticipated, and Porter found it necessary to place a rear-guard between his command and the enemy. Colonel Averill, of the
Third Pennsylvania Cavalry, was entrusted with this delicate
duty. He had under his command his own regiment, and Lieutenant-Colonel Buchanan's brigade of regular infantry and one
battery. By a judicious use of the resources at his command,
he deceived the enemy, so as to cover the withdrawal of the left
wing without being attacked, remaining himself on the previous
day's battle-field until about seven o'clock of the 2d of July.
Meantime General Keyes, having received his orders, commenced
vigorous preparations for covering the movement of the entire
army and protecting the trains. It being evident that the immense number of wagons and artillery-carriages pertaining to
the army could not move with celerity along a single road, General Keyes took advantage of every accident of the ground to
open new avenues and to facilitate the movement. He made
preparations for obstructing the roads after the army had passed,
so as to prevent any rapid pursuit, destroying effectually Turkey
Bridge on the main road, and rendering other roads and approaches temporarily impassible by felling trees across them.
He kept the trains well closed-up and directed the march so that
the troops could move on each side of the roads, not obstructing the passage, but being in good position to repel an attack
from any quarter. His dispositions were so successful that, to
use his own words: ' I do not think more vehicles or more public property were abandoned on the march from Turkey Bridge
than would have been left in the same state of the roads, if the
army had been moving toward the enemy instead of away from him.
And when it is understood that the carriages and teams belong-
ing to this army, stretched out in one line, would extend not far
from forty miles, the energy and caution necessary for their safe
withdrawal from the presence of an enemy vastly superior in
numbers will be appreciated.' The last of the wagons did not
reach the site selected at Harrison's bar until after dark on the
3d of July, and the rear-guard did not move into their camp
until every thing was secure. The enemy followed up with a
small force, and on the 3d threw a few shells at the rear-guard,
but were quickly dispersed by our batteries and the fire of the gunboats. Great credit must be awarded to General Keyes for the
skill and energy which characterized his performance of the important and delicate duties entrusted to his charge. High praise
is also due to the officers and men of the First Connecticut Artillery, Colonel Tyler, for the manner in which they withdrew all
the heavy guns during the seven days, and from Malvern Hill.
Owing to the crowded state of the roads, the teams could not be
brought within a couple of miles of the position; but these

energetic soldiers removed the guns by hand for that distance, leaving nothing behind.

" On the 1st of July I received the following from the President :

" ' WASHINGTON, *July 1st*, 1862—3.30 P.M.

" '*Major-General* GEORGE B. McCLELLAN :

" ' It is impossible to reinforce you for your present emergency. If we had a million of men, we could not get them to you in time. We have not the men to send. If you are not strong enough to face the enemy, you must find a place of security ; and wait, rest and repair. Maintain your ground if you can, but save the army at all events, even if you fall back to Fortress Monroe. We still have strength enough in the country, and will bring it out. " 'A. LINCOLN.' "

" In the despatch from the President to me, on the 2d of July, he says :

" ' If you think you are not strong enough to take Richmond just now, I do not ask you to. Try just now to save the army material and *personnel*, and I will strengthen it for the offensive again as fast as I can. The Governors of eighteen (18) States offer me a new levy of three hundred thousand, which I accept.' "

" On the 3d of July, the following kind despatch was received from the President :

" ' WASHINGTON, *July 3d*, 1862—3 P.M.

" '*Major-General* GEORGE B. McCLELLAN :

" ' Yours of 5.30 yesterday is just received. I am satisfied that yourself, officers, and men have done the best you could. All accounts say better fighting was never done. Ten thousand thanks for it. " 'A. LINCOLN.' "

## HIS ADDRESS TO THE ARMY.

On the fourth of July the following address was issued to the troops :

" HEAD-QUARTERS, ARMY OF THE POTOMAC, CAMP NEAR " HARRISON'S LANDING, *July 4th*, 1862.

" SOLDIERS OF THE ARMY OF THE POTOMAC :—Your achievements of the last ten days have illustrated the valor and endurance of the American soldier. Attacked by superior forces, and without hope of reinforcements, you have succeeded in changing your base of operations by a flank movement, always regarded as the most hazardous of military expedients. You have saved all your material, all your trains and all your guns, except a few lost in battle, taking in return guns and colors from the enemy. Upon your march, you have been assailed day after day with desperate fury, by men of the same race and nation, skilfully massed and led. Under every disadvantage of number, and necessarily of position also, you have in every conflict beaten back your foes with enormous slaughter. Your conduct ranks you among the celebrated armies of history. No one will now question that each of you may always with pride say: 'I belong to the Army of the Potomac.' You have reached the new base, complete in organization and unimpaired in spirit. The enemy may at any moment attack you. We are prepared to meet them. I have personally established your lines. Let them come, and we will convert their repulse into a final defeat. Your Government is strengthening you with the resources of a great people. On this, our nation's birthday, we declare to our foes, who are rebels against the best interests of mankind, that this army shall enter the capital of the so-called Confederacy; that our national Constitution shall prevail, and that the Union, which can alone insure internal peace and external security to each State, 'must and shall be preserved,' cost what it may in time, treasure, and blood.

"GEORGE B. McCLELLAN."

## LETTER TO THE PRESIDENT.

On the same day he wrote as follows to the President:

"HEAD-QUARTERS, ARMY OF THE POTOMAC,
"HARRISON BAR, JAMES RIVER, *July 4th*, 1862.

"TO THE PRESIDENT:

"I have the honor to acknowledge the receipt of your despatch of the 2d instant.

"I shall make a stand at this place, and endeavor to give my men the repose they so much require.

"After sending my communication on Tuesday, the enemy attacked the left of our lines, and a fierce battle ensued, lasting until night. They were repulsed with great slaughter.

"Had their attack succeeded, the consequences would have been disastrous in the extreme. This closed the hard fighting which had continued from the afternoon of the 26th ult., in a daily series of engagements wholly unparalleled on this continent for determination and slaughter on both sides. The mutual loss in killed and wounded is enormous—that of the enemy certainly greatest. On Tuesday morning, the 1st, our army commenced its movement from Haxall's to this point, our line of defence there being too extended to be maintained by our weakened forces. Our train was immense, and about 4 P.M. on the 2d a heavy storm of rain began, which continued during the entire day and until the forenoon of yesterday. The roads became horrible. Troops, artillery and wagons moved on steadily, and our whole army, men and material, was finally brought safely into this camp. The last of the wagons reached here at noon yesterday. The exhaustion was very great, but the army preserved its morale, and would have repelled any attack which the enemy was in condition to make. We now occupy a line of heights about two miles from the James, a plain extending from there to the river. Our front is about three miles long. These heights command our whole position, and must be maintained. The gunboats can render valuable support upon both flanks. If the enemy attack us in front, we must hold our ground as we best may, and at whatever cost. Our positions can be carried only by overwhelming numbers. The spirit of the army is excellent; stragglers are finding their regiments, and the soldiers exhibit the best results of discipline. Our position is by no means impregnable, especially as a morass extends on this side of the high ground from our centre to the James on our right. The enemy may attack in vast numbers, and, if so, our front will be the scene of a desperate battle, which, if lost, will be decisive. Our army is fearfully weakened by killed, wounded, and prisoners. I cannot now approximate to any statement of our losses, but we were not beaten in any conflict. The enemy were unable, by their utmost efforts, to drive us from the field. Never did such a change of base, involving a retrograde movement, and under incessant attacks from a most determined and vastly more numerous foe, partake so little of disorder. We have lost no guns, except twenty-five on the field of battle, twenty-one of which were lost by the giving way of McCall's division under the onset of superior numbers. Our communications by the James river are not secure. There are points where the enemy can establish themselves with cannon or musketry and command the river, and where it is not certain that our gunboats can drive them out. In case of this, or in case our front is broken, I will still make every effort to preserve at least the *personnel* of the army, and the events of the last few days leave no question that the troops will do all that their country can ask. Send such reinforcements as you can; I will do what I can. We are shipping our wounded and sick, and landing supplies. The Navy Department should co-operate with us to the extent of its resources. Captain Rodgers is doing all in his power in the kindest and most efficient manner. When all the circumstances of the case are known, it will be acknowledged by all competent judges that the movement just completed by this army is unparalleled in the annals of war. Under the most difficult circumstances, we have preserved our trains, our guns, our material, and, above all, our honor.

"G. B. McClellan,
"*Major-General.*"

LETTERS FROM THE PRESIDENT.

" ' WASHINGTON, *July 5th.* 1862—9 A.M.

" ' MAJOR-GENERAL GEORGE B. McCLELLAN,

" ' *Commanding Army of Potomac:*

" ' A thousand thanks for the relief your two despatches of 12 and 1 P.M., yesterday, gave me. Be assured, the heroism and skill of yourself and officers and men, is and forever will be appreciated.

" ' If you can hold your present position, we shall hive the enemy yet.    " 'A. LINCOLN.' "

" ' WAR DEPARTMENT,

" ' WASHINGTON, D. C., *July 4th,* 1862.

" ' I understand your position, as stated in your letter, and by General Marcy. To reinforce you so as to enable you to resume the offensive within a month, or even six weeks, is impossible. In addition to that arrived and now arriving from the Potomac (about 10,000, I suppose), and about 10,000 I hope you will have from Burnside very soon, and about 5,000 from Hunter a little later, I do not see how I can send you another man within a month. Under these circumstances the defensive for the present must be your only care. Save the army first where you are, if you can, and secondly by removal if you must. You, on the ground, must be the judge as to which you will attempt, and of the means for effecting it. I but give it as my opinion that, with the aid of the gunboats, and the reinforcements mentioned above, you can hold your present position, provided, and so long as you can keep the James river open below you. If you are not tolerably confident you can keep the James river open, you had better remove as soon as possible. I do not remember that you have expressed any apprehension as to the danger of having your communication cut on the river below you; yet I do not suppose it can have escaped your attention.

" ' Yours very truly,    " 'A. LINCOLN.

" ' P.S.—If at any time you feel able to take the offensive, you are not restrained from doing so.    " 'A. L.' "

On July 7th, General McClellan telegraphed as follows to the President:

" HEAD-QUARTERS, ARMY OF THE POTOMAC,

" BERKELEY, *July 7th,* 1862—8.30 A.M.

"As the boat is starting I have only time to acknowledge the receipt of despatch by General Marcy. Enemy have not attacked. My position is very strong, and daily becoming more so. If not attacked to-day I shall laugh at them. I have been anxious about my communications. Had a long consultation about it with Flag-Officer Goldsborough last night. He is confident he can keep the river open. He should have all gunboats possible. Will see him again this morning. My men in splendid spirits, and anxious to try it again. Alarm yourself as little as possible about me, and don't lose confidence in this army. "G. B. McClellan, *Major-General.*"

## GENERAL McCLELLAN GIVES THE PRESIDENT HIS VIEWS ON THE CONDUCT OF THE WAR.

Expecting an attack, however, as a necessity to the enemy, and feeling the critical nature of the position, General McClellan on the same day addressed to the President the following letter :

"Head-quarters, Army of the Potomac, Camp near "Harrison's Landing, Va., *July 7th*, 1862.

"Mr. President: You have been fully informed that the rebel army is in the front, with the purpose of overwhelming us by attacking the positions or reducing us by blocking our river communications. I cannot but regard our condition as critical, and I earnestly desire, in view of possible contingencies, to lay before your Excellency, for your private consideration, my general views concerning the existing state of the rebellion, although they do not strictly relate to the situation of this army or strictly come within the scope of my official duties. These views amount to convictions, and are deeply impressed upon my mind and heart. Our cause must never be abandoned—it is the cause of free institutions and self-government. The Constitution and the Union must be preserved, whatever may be the cost in time, treasure, and blood. If Secession is successful, other dissolutions are clearly to be seen in the future. Let neither military disaster, political faction nor foreign war shake your settled purpose to enforce the equal operation of the laws of the United States upon the people of every State.

"The time has come when the Government must determine upon a civil and military policy covering the whole ground of our national trouble. The responsibility of determining, declaring and supporting such civil and military policy, and of directing the whole course of national affairs in regard to the rebellion, must now be assumed and exercised by you, or our cause will be lost. The Constitution gives you power even for the present terrible exigency.

"This rebellion has assumed the character of a war, as such it should be regarded, and it should be conducted upon the highest principles known to Christian civilization. It should not be a war looking to the subjugation of the people of any State in any event. It should not be at all a war upon population, but against armed forces and political organization. Neither confiscation of property, political executions of persons, territorial organizations of States, or forcible abolition of slavery, should be contemplated for a moment. In prosecuting the war all private property and unarmed persons should be strictly protected, subject only to the necessity of military operations. All private property taken for military use should be paid or receipted for; pillage and waste should be treated as high crimes; all unnecessary trespass sternly prohibited, and offensive demeanor by the military toward citizens promptly rebuked. Military arrests should not be tolerated, except in places where active hostilities exist, and oaths not required by enactments constitutionally made, should be neither demanded nor received. Military government should be confined to the preservation of public order and the protection of political right. Military power should not be allowed to interfere with the relations of servitude, either by supporting or impairing the authority of the master, except for repressing disorder, as in other cases. Slaves contraband under the Act of Congress, seeking military protection, should receive it. The right of the Government to appropriate permanently to its own service claims to slave labor should be asserted, and the right of the owner to compensation therefor should be recognized.

"This principle might be extended upon grounds of military necessity and security to all the slaves of a particular State, thus working manumission in such State; and in Missouri, perhaps in Western Virginia also, and possibly even in Maryland, the expediency of such a measure is only a question of time.

"A system of policy thus constitutional, and pervaded by the influences of Christianity and freedom, would receive the support of almost all truly loyal men, would deeply impress the rebel masses and all foreign nations, and it might be humbly hoped that it would commend itself to the favor of the Almighty.

"Unless the principles governing the future conduct of our struggle shall be made known and approved, the effort to obtain requisite forces will be almost hopeless. A declaration of radical views, especially upon slavery, will rapidly disintegrate our present armies.

"The policy of the Government must be supported by concentrations of military power. The national forces should not be dispersed in expeditions, posts of occupation, and numerous armies; but should be mainly collected into masses and brought to bear upon the armies of the Confederate States. Those armies thoroughly defeated, the political structure which they support would soon cease to exist.

"In carrying out any system of policy which you may form, you will require a commander-in-chief of the army—one who possesses your confidence, understands your views, and who is competent to execute your orders, by directing the military forces of the nation to the accomplishment of the objects by you proposed. I do not ask that place for myself. I am willing to serve you in such position as you may assign me, and I will do so as faithfully as ever subordinate served superior.

"I may be on the brink of eternity, and, as I hope forgiveness from my Maker, I have written this letter with sincerity toward you and from love for my country.

"Very respectfully, your obedient servant,
"GEORGE B. McCLELLAN,
"*Major-General, Commanding.*"

## MORE OFFICIAL DESPATCHES.

During the period that the army was encamped at Harrison's Landing, the following despatches among others passed between the Commanding General and the Washington authorities:

### FROM GENERAL McCLELLAN.

"BERKELEY, *July* 11*th*, 1862.—3 P.M.—We are very strong here now so far as defensive is concerned. Hope you will soon make us strong enough to advance and try it again."

"SAME, *July* 12*th*—Men resting well, but begining to be impatient for another fight. I am more and more convinced that this army ought not to be withdrawn from here, but promptly reinforced and thrown again upon Richmond. If we have a little more than half a chance, we can take it. I dread the effects of any retreat upon the morale of the men."

"SAME, *July* 17*th*.—It appears, manifestly, to be our policy to concentrate here every thing we can possibly spare from less important points, to make sure of crushing the enemy at Richmond, which seems clearly to be the most important point in Rebeldom. Nothing should be left to chance here. I would recommend that General Burnside, with all his troops, be ordered to this army, to enable it to assume the offensive as soon as possible."

"SAME, *July* 18*th*.—Am anxious to have determination of Government that no time may be lost in preparing for it. Hours are very precious now, and perfect unity of action necessary."

"SAME, *July* 28*th*.—Reinforcements reaching Richmond from South. My opinion is more and more firm that here is the defence of Washington, and that I should be at once reinforced by all available troops, to enable me to advance. Retreat would be disastrous to the army and the cause. I am confident of that."

"SAME, *July* 30*th*.—I hope that it may soon be decided what is to be done by this army, and that the decision may be to reinforce it at once. We are losing much valuable time, and that at a moment when energy and decision are sadly needed."

After giving an account of the affair at Coggin's Point, where the enemy planted light batteries and annoyed our right flank by firing across the river, a telegram to General Halleck, dated August 2d, says:

"Sent party across river yesterday to the Coles house, destroyed it and cut down the timber; will complete work to-day, and also send party to Coggin's Point, which I will probably occupy. I will attend to your telegraph about pressing at once; will send Hooker out. Give me Burnside and I will stir these people up. I need more cavalry."

"SAME, *August 3d*.—A few thousand more men would place us in condition at least to annoy and disconcert the enemy very much."

### GENERAL HALLECK TO GENERAL McCLELLAN.

"WASHINGTON, *July 30th*.—A despatch just received from General Pope says that deserters report that the enemy is moving south of James river, and that the force in Richmond is very small. I suggest he be pressed in that direction, so as to ascertain the facts of the case."

"SAME, *July 30th*.—In order to enable you to move in any direction, it is necessary to relieve you of your sick. The Surgeon-General has therefore been directed to make arrangements for them at other places, and the Quartermaster-General to provide transportation. I hope you will send them away as quickly as possible, and advise me of their removal."

To carry out General Halleck's first order, of July 30th, it was necessary first to gain possession of Malvern Hill, which was occupied by the enemy, apparently in some little force, and controlled the direct approach to Richmond. Its temporary occupation, at least, was equally necessary in the event of a movement upon Petersburg, or even the abandonment of the Peninsula. It appears that Hooker failed in the first movement on Malvern Hill, in consequence of the incompetency of guides, but that on August 5th he succeeded.

At an early hour of the morning of August 1st, the rebels opened upon our encampments at Harrison's Landing with batteries in position on the other side of the river, but after a brisk fire from our land batteries and the guns of the fleet, the enemy's cannon were silenced.

On the second, General Halleck telegraphed to General McClellan as follows :

"*August* 2.—You have not answered my telegram of July 30th, about the removal of your sick.   Remove them as rapidly as possible, and telegraph me when they will be out of your way.   The President wishes an answer as early as possible."

### GENERAL McCLELLAN TO GENERAL HALLECK.

"*August* 3.—Answer already sent.   It is impossible for me to decide what cases to send off, unless I know what is to be done with this army.   Were the disastrous measures of retreat adopted, all the sick who cannot march and fight should be despatched by water.   Should the army advance, many of the sick could be of service at the depot.   If it is to remain here any length of time, the question assumes still a different phase.   If I am kept longer in ignorance of what is to be effected, I cannot be expected to accomplish the object in view.   In the meantime I will do all in my power to carry out what I conceive to be your wishes."

### GENERAL HALLECK TO GENERAL McCLELLAN.

"*August* 3.—It is determined to withdraw your army from the Peninsula to Acquia Creek.   You will take immediate measures to effect this, covering the movement the best you can.   Its real object and withdrawal should be concealed even from your own officers.   The entire execution of the movement is left to your discretion and judgment.   You will leave such forces as you may deem proper at Fortress Monroe, Norfolk, and other places, which we must occupy."

## GENERAL McCLELLAN PROTESTS AGAINST LEAVING THE PENINSULA.

Although firmly impressed with the conviction that the withdrawal of the army from Harrison's Landing, where its communications had been made secure by the co-operation of the gunboats, would have at that time the most disastrous effect upon the cause, he proceeded to obey the order.   He however on the fourth addressed the following to General Halleck :

" HEAD-QUARTERS, ARMY OF THE POTOMAC,
" BERKELEY, *August* 4, 1862.—12 M.

"Your telegram of last evening is received.   I must confess that it has caused me the greatest pain I ever experienced, for I am convinced that the order to withdraw this army to Acquia creek will prove disastrous to our cause.   I fear it will be a fatal blow.   Several days are necessary to complete the preparations for so important a movement as this, and while they are in progress, I beg that careful consideration may be given to my statements.

" This army is now in excellent discipline and condition. We hold a debouche on both banks of the James river, so that we are free to act in any direction; and with the assistance of the gunboats, I consider our communications as now secure.

" We are twenty-five (25) miles from Richmond, and are not likely to meet the enemy in force sufficient to fight a battle until we have marched fifteen (15) to eighteen (18) miles, which brings us practically within ten (10) miles of Richmond. Our longest line of land transportation would be from this point twenty-five (25) miles, but with the aid of the gunboats we can supply the army by water during its advance, certainly to within twelve (12) miles of Richmond.

" At Acquia creek we would be seventy-five (75) miles from Richmond, with land transportation all the way.

" From here to Fortress Monroe is a march of about seventy (70) miles, for I regard it as impracticable to withdraw this army and its material, except by land.

" The result of the movement would thus be a march of one hundred and forty-five (145) miles, to reach a point now only twenty-five (25) miles distant, and to deprive ourselves entirely of the powerful aid of the gunboats and water transportation.

" Add to this the certain demoralization of this army which would ensue, the terrible depressing effect upon the people of the north, and the strong probability that it would influence foreign powers to recognize our adversaries; and these appear to me sufficient reasons to make it my imperative duty to urge in the strongest terms afforded by our language, that this order may be rescinded, and that far from recalling this army, it may be promptly reinforced to enable it to resume the offensive.

" It may be said that there are no reinforcements available. I point to Burnside's force; to that of Pope, not necessary to maintain a strict defensive in front of Washington and Harper's Ferry; to those portions of the army of the west not required for a strict defensive there. Here, directly in front of this army, is the heart of the rebellion; it is here that all our resources should be collected to strike the blow which will determine the fate of the nation.

" All points of secondary importance elsewhere should be abandoned, and every available man brought here; a decided victory here, and the military strength of the rebellion is crushed. It matters not what partial reverses we may meet with elsewhere; here is the true defence of Washington; it is here, on the banks of the James, that the fate of the Union should be decided.

" Clear in my convictions of right, strong in the consciousness that I have ever been, and still am, actuated solely by the love of my country, knowing that no ambitious or selfish motives have influenced me from the commencement of this war, I do now, what I never did in my life before, I entreat that this order may be rescinded.

" If my counsel does not prevail, I will with a sad heart obey your orders to the utmost of my power, directing to the movement, which I clearly foresee will be one of the utmost delicacy and difficulty, whatever skill I may possess. Whatever the result may be—and may God grant that I am mistaken in my forebodings—I shall at least have the internal satisfaction that I have written and spoken frankly, and have sought to do the best in my power to avert disaster from my country.

" GEORGE B. MCCLELLAN,
" Major-General Commanding.

"Major-General H. W. HALLECK,
" Commanding United States Army."

This produced the following despatch and letter from General Halleck :

" WASHINGTON, August 5th, 1862—12 M.

" You cannot regret the order of the withdrawal more than I did the necessity of giving it. It will not be rescinded, and you will be expected to execute it with all possible promptness. It is believed that it can be done now without serious danger. This may not be so, if there should be any delay. I will write you my views more fully by mail. " H. W. HALLECK,
" Major General, Commanding United States Army.

"Major-General G. B. MCCLELLAN."

LETTER FROM GENERAL HALLECK.

" HEAD-QUARTERS OF THE ARMY,
" WASHINGTON, August 5th, 1862.

" GENERAL :—Your telegram of yesterday was received this morning, and I immediately telegraphed a brief reply, promising to write you more fully by mail.

" You, General, certainly could not have been more pained at receiving my order than I was at the necessity of issuing it. I was advised by high officers, in whose judgment I had great confidence, to make the order immediately on my arrival here, but I determined not to do so until I could learn your wishes from a personal interview. And even after that interview, I tried every means in my power to avoid withdrawing your army, and delayed my decision as long as I dared to delay it.

" I assure you, General, it was not a hasty and inconsiderate act, but one that caused me more anxious thoughts than any other of my life. But after full and mature consideration of all the pros and cons, I was reluctantly forced to the conclusion that the order must be issued—there was to my mind no alternative.

"Allow me to allude to a few of the facts in the case.

"You and your officers at one interview estimated the enemy's forces in and around Richmond at two hundred thousand men. Since then, you and others report that they have received and are receiving large reinforcements from the South. General Pope's army, covering Washington, is only about forty thousand. Your effective force is only about ninety thousand. You are thirty miles from Richmond, and General Pope eighty or ninety, with the enemy directly between you, ready to fall with his superior numbers upon one or the other as he may elect; neither can reinforce the other in case of such an attack.

"If General Pope's army be diminished to reinforce you, Washington, Maryland, and Pennsylvania would be left uncovered and exposed. If your force be reduced to strengthen Pope, you would be too weak to even hold the position you now occupy, should the enemy turn round and attack you in full force. In other words, the old Army of the Potomac is split into two parts, with the entire force of the enemy directly between them. They cannot be united by land without exposing both to destruction, and yet they must be united. To send Pope's forces by water to the Peninsula, is, under present circumstances, a military impossibility. The only alternative is to send the forces on the Peninsula to some point by water, say Fredericksburg, where the two armies can be united.

"Let me now allude to some of the objections which you have urged; you say that the withdrawal from the present position will cause the certain demoralization of the army, 'which is now in excellent discipline and condition.'

"I cannot understand why a simple change of position to a new and by no means distant base will demoralize an army in excellent discipline, unless the officers themselves assist in that demoralization, which I am satisfied they will not.

"Your change of front from your extreme right at Hanover Court-House to your present condition, was over thirty miles, but I have not heard that it demoralized your troops, notwithstanding the severe losses they sustained in effecting it.

"A new base on the Rappahannock at Fredericksburg brings you within about sixty miles of Richmond, and secures a reinforcement of forty or fifty thousand fresh and disciplined troops.

"The change with such advantages will, I think, if properly represented to your army, encourage rather than demoralize your troops. Moreover, you yourself suggested that a junction might be effected at Yorktown, but that a flank march across the isthmus would be more hazardous than to retire to Fortress Monroe.

"You will remember that Yorktown is two or three miles further than Fredericksburg is. Besides, the latter is between

Richmond and Washington, and covers Washington from any attack of the enemy.

" The political effect of the withdrawal may at first be unfavorable; but I think the public are beginning to understand its necessity, and that they will have much more confidence in a united army than in its separated fragments.

" But you will reply, why not reinforce me here, so that I can strike Richmond from my present position? To do this, you said, at our interview, that you required thirty thousand additional troops. I told you that it was impossible to give you so many. You finally thought that you would have some chance of success with twenty thousand. But you afterwards telegraphed me that you would require thirty-five thousand, as the enemy was being largely reinforced.

" If your estimate of the enemy's strength was correct, your requisition was perfectly reasonable; but it was utterly impossible to fill it until new troops could be enlisted and organized, which would require several weeks.

" To keep your army in its present position until it could be so reinforced, would almost destroy it in that climate.

" The months of August and September are almost fatal to whites who live on that part of James river; and even after you received the reinforcements asked for, you admitted that you must reduce Fort Darling and the river batteries before you could advance on Richmond.

" It is by no means certain that the reduction of these fortifications would not require considerable time—perhaps as much as those at Yorktown.

" This delay might not only be fatal to the health of your army, but in the meantime General Pope's forces would be exposed to the heavy blows of the enemy, without the slightest hope of assistance from you.

" In regard to the demoralizing effect of a withdrawal from the Peninsula to the Rappahannock, I must remark that a large number of your highest officers, indeed a majority of those whose opinions have been reported to me, are decidedly in favor of the movement. Even several of those who originally advocated the line of the Peninsula, now advise its abandonment.

" I have not inquired and do not wish to know, by whose advice or for what reasons the army of the Potomac was separated into two parts with the enemy between them. I must take things as I find them.

" I find the forces divided, and I wish to unite them. Only one feasible plan has been presented for doing this. If you, or any one else, had presented a better plan, I certainly should have adopted it. But all of your plans require reinforcements, which it is impossible to give you.

" It is very easy to *ask* for reinforcements, but it is not so easy to give them when you have no disposable troops at your command.

" I have written very plainly as I understand the case, and I hope you will give me credit for having fully considered the matter, although I may have arrived at very different conclusions from your own.

" Very respectfully, your obedient servant,

" H. W. HALLECK, *General-in-Chief.*

"*Major-General* GEORGE B. McCLELLAN,

" *Commanding, etc., Berkeley, Virginia.*"

### GENERAL McCLELLAN TO GENERAL HALLECK.

" MALVERN HILL, *August 5th.*—This is a very advantageous position to cover an advance on Richmond, and only fourteen and three-quarter miles distant, and I feel confident that with reinforcements I would march this army there in five days."

" SAME, *August 5th.*—I am sending off sick as rapidly as our transports will take them. I am also doing every thing in my power to carry out your orders, to push reconnoissances towards the rebel capital, and hope soon to find out whether the reports regarding the abandonment of that place are true."

### GENERAL HALLECK TO GENERAL McCLELLAN.

" WASHINGTON, *August 6th,* 3 A.M.—I have no reinforcements to send you."

Further telegrams followed from General McClellan to General Halleck, and *vice versa*, General Halleck urging General McClellan to ship his sick first, and then batteries and troops more rapidly, and General McClellan insisting that he is doing so as fast as the means of transportation at his disposal permitted, and strengthening his statement by the reports of his subordinates that there has not been an hour of unnecessary delay.

### GENERAL McCLELLAN TO GENERAL HALLECK.

"*August 12th,* 11 P.M.—It is positively the fact that no more men could have been embarked hence than have gone, and that no unnecessary delay has occurred. I am sure you have been misinformed as to the availability of the vessels on hand. There shall be no unnecessary delay; but I cannot manufacture vessels. I state these difficulties from experience, and because it appears to me that we have been lately working at cross-purposes, because you have not been properly informed by those around you, who ought to know the inherent difficulties of such an undertaking. It is not possible for any one to place this army where you wish it, ready to move, in less than a month.

If Washington is in danger now this army can scarcely arrive in time to save it. It is in much better position to do so from here than from Acquia. Our material can only be saved by using the whole army to cover it, if we are pressed. If sensibly weakened by detachments, the results might be the loss of much material and many men. I will be at the telegraph office to-morrow morning."

GENERAL HALLECK TO GENERAL McCLELLAN.

"*August 14th*, 1.40 A.M.—I have read your despatch. There is no change of plans. You will send up your troops as rapidly as possible. There is no difficulty in landing them. According to your own accounts, there is now no difficulty in withdrawing your forces. Do so with all possible rapidity."

General McClellan says that before he had time to decipher and reply to this despatch, the telegraph-operator in Washington informed him that General Halleck had gone out of the office immediately after writing this despatch, without leaving any intimation of the fact to me, or waiting for any further information as to the object of my journey across the Bay. As there was no possibility of other communication with him at that time, I sent the following despatch and returned to Harrison's Landing:

"CHERRY STONE INLET, *August 14th*, 1.40 A.M.—Your orders will be obeyed. I return at once."

## EVACUATION OF HARRISON'S LANDING.

By the morning of the sixteenth all the troops and material were *en route* both by land and water, and late in the afternoon of the same day, when the last man had disappeared from the deserted camps, General McClellan himself bade farewell to Harrison's Landing. On the night of the seventeenth the troops were all safely across the Chickahominy, except the rear-guard, and that crossed early on the following morning. General Porter's corps proceeded directly to Newport News and on the twentieth sailed for Acquia Creek, and on the twenty-first Heintzelman's corps sailed from Yorktown, and on the twenty-third, Franklin's corps. Immediately on reaching

7

Fortress Monroe, General McClellan gave directions for strengthening the defences of Yorktown, and leaving General Keyes with his corps to attend to the work. On the evening of the twenty-third he sailed for Acquia Creek, where he arrived at daylight on the following morning.

## THE SERVICES OF THE ARMY OF THE PO-TOMAC.

On the eighteenth, General McClellan sent the following appeal to General Halleck:

"Please say a kind word to my Army, that I can repeat to them in General Orders, in regard to their conduct at Yorktown, Williamsburgh, West Point, Hanover Court-House, and on the Chickahominy, as well as in regard to the Seven Days and the recent retreat. No one has ever said any thing to cheer them but myself. Say nothing about me; merely give my men and officers credit for what they have done. It will do you much good, and will strengthen you much with them, if you issue a handsome order to them in regard to what they have accomplished. They deserve it."

As no reply was received to this communication, and no order was issued by the General-in-Chief, he concluded the suggestion did not meet with his approbation.

On closing his Peninsular campaign, he thus expressed his opinion of his gallant army:

"From the commencement to the termination of this most arduous campaign, the Army of the Potomac always evinced the most perfect subordination, zeal, and alacrity in the performance of all the duties required of it.

"The amount of severe labor accomplished by this army in the construction of intrenchments, roads, bridges, etc., was enormous; yet all the work was performed with the most gratifying cheerfulness and devotion to the interests of the service.

"During the campaign, ten severely-contested and sanguinary battles had been fought, besides numerous smaller engagements, in which the troops exhibited the most determined enthusiasm and bravery. They submitted to exposure, sickness, and even death, without a murmur. Indeed, they had become veterans in their country's cause, and richly deserved the warm commendation of the Government."

## GENERAL McCLELLAN AT ALEXANDRIA.

Upon arriving at Acquia Creek, General McClellan telegraphed to Washington for further orders, and on the twenty-sixth proceeded to Alexandria and immediately adopting measures to ascertain the state of affairs at the front, was enabled to transmit much information as to the movements of Pope's army, which the authorities were unable to receive direct from the commander of the Army of Virginia. Among other telegrams that passed were the following:

### GENERAL McCLELLAN TO GENERAL HALLECK.

"ALEXANDRIA *August* 27*th*—10 A M.—I have sent orders to Franklin to prepare to march with his corps at once, and to repair here in person, to inform me, as to his means of transportation."

### GENERAL HALLECK TO GENERAL McCLELLAN.

"*August* 27*th*—I can get no satisfactory information from the front, either of the enemy or of our troops. There seems to have been great neglect and carelessness about Manassas. Franklin's corps should march in that direction as soon as possible."

### GENERAL McCLELLAN TO GENERAL HALLECK.

"*August* 27*th*—1.35 P.M.—I learn that Taylor's brigade, sent this morning to Bull Run Bridge, is either captured or cut to pieces. That the force against them had many guns and about 5,000 infantry, receiving reinforcements every minute. Also, that Gainesville is in possession of the enemy. Please send some cavalry out towards Drainsville via Chain Bridge to watch Lewinsville and Drainsville, and go as far as they can. If you will give me even one squadron of good cavalry here, I will ascertain the state of the case. I think our policy now is to make these works perfectly safe, and mobilize a couple of corps as soon as possible, but not to advance them until they can have their artillery and cavalry. I have sent for Colonel Tyler, to place his artillerymen in the works. Is Fort Marcy securely held?"

"*August* 27*th*—2.30 P.M.—If there is any cavalry in Washington it should be ordered to report to me at once. I still think that we should first provide for the immediate defence of Washington on both sides of the Potomac. I am not responsible for the past and cannot be for the future unless I receive authority to dispose of the available troops according to my judgment. Please inform me at once what my position is. I do not wish to act in the dark."

"*August 27th*—6 P.M.—I now have at my disposal here about 10,000 men of Franklin's corps, about 2,800 of General Tyler's brigade, and Colonel Tyler's 1st Connecticut Artillery, which I recommend should be held in hand for the defence of Washington. If you wish me to order any part of this force to the front, it is in readiness to march at a moment's notice to any point you may indicate."

"*August 28th*—4.10 P.M.—Pope must cut through to-day, or adopt the plan I suggested. I have ordered troops to garrison the works at Upton's Hill. They must be held at any cost. As soon as I can see the way to spare them, I will send a corps of good troops there. It is the key to Washington, which cannot be seriously menaced as long as it is held."

### GENERAL HALLECK TO GENERAL McCLELLAN.

"*August 28th*—The principal thing to be feared now is a cavalry raid into this city, especially in the night time. Please send some of your officers to-day to see that every precaution is taken at the forts against a raid, also at the bridge."

### GENERAL McCLELLAN TO GENERAL HALLECK.

"*August 29th*—10.30 A.M.—Franklin's corps is in motion. Started about 6 A.M. I can give him but two squadrons of cavalry. Franklin has but forty rounds of ammunition, and no wagons to move more. I do not think he is in a condition to accomplish much, if he meets with serious resistance. I should not have moved him but for your pressing order of last night."

"*August 29th*—1 P.M.—Shall I do as seems best to me with all the troops in this vicinity, including Franklin, who I really think ought not under present circumstances, to advance beyond Anandale?"

"*August 29th*—10.30 P.M.—By referring to my telegrams you will see why Franklin's corps halted at Anandale. His small cavalry force, all I had to give him, was ordered to push on as far as possible toward Manassas. It was not safe for him to move beyond Anandale, under the circumstances, until we knew what was at Vienna.

"I am responsible for both these circumstances, and do not see that either was in disobedience to your orders. Please give distinct orders with reference to Franklin's movements to-morrow. I desire definite instructions, as it is not agreeable to me to be accused of disobeying orders, when I have simply exercised the discretion you committed to me."

"*August 29th*--11 P.M.—Not hearing from you, I have sent orders to General Franklin to place himself in communication with General Pope as soon as possible, and at the same time cover the transit of Pope's supplies; and I am having inspections made of all the forts around Washington."

On the same day the President telegraphed:

"What news from direction of Manassas Junction? What generally?"

To which the following reply was sent:

"CAMP NEAR ALEXANDRIA,
"*August 29th*, 1862—2.45 P.M.

"The last news I received from the direction of Manassas was from stragglers to the effect that the enemy were evacuating Centreville and retiring towards Thoroughfare Gap. This by no means reliable.

"I am clear that one of two courses should be adopted: 1st. To concentrate all our available forces to open communications with Pope; 2d. To leave Pope to get out of his scrape, and at once use all our means to make the Capital perfectly safe.

"No middle ground will now answer. Tell me what you wish me to do, and I will do all in my power to accomplish it. I wish to know what my orders and authority are. I ask for nothing, but will obey whatever orders you give. I only ask a prompt decision, that I may at once give the necessary orders. It will not do to delay longer.

"G. B. McCLELLAN, *Major-General*."

To this the President replied, that he considered the first of the two courses suggested by the General the proper one, but he did not wish to control, and would leave all to General Halleck, aided "by your counsels."

On the thirtieth of August an order was issued by the War Department to the effect that General McClellan would command that portion of the Army of the Potomac that had not been sent forward to General Pope's command, the Army of Virginia.

The following despatches were sent on the following day and the day after:

"*August 30th*—11.30 A.M.—Ever since General Franklin received notice that he was to march from Alexandria, he has been endeavoring to get transportation from the Quartermaster at

Alexandria, but he has uniformly been told there was none disposable, and his command marched without wagons.

"General Sumner endeavored by application to the Quartermaster's Department to get wagons to carry his reserve ammunition, but without success, and was obliged to march with what he could carry in his cartridge boxes."

### General Halleck to General McClellan.

"*August* 30*th*—1.45 p.m.—Ammunition, and particularly for artillery, must be immediately sent forward to Centreville for General Pope. It must be done with all possible despatch."

### General McClellan's Reply.

"*August* 30*th*—2.10 p.m.—I know nothing of the calibres of Pope's artillery. All I can do is to direct my ordnance officer to load up all the wagons sent to him.

"I can do nothing more than give the order that every available wagon in Alexandria shall be loaded at once.

"I have no sharpshooters except the guard around my camp. I have sent off every man but those, and will now send them as you direct. I will also send my only remaining squadron of cavalry with General Sumner. I can do no more; you now have every man of the Army of the Potomac who is within my reach."

### General McClellan to General Halleck.

"*August* 30*th*—10.30 p.m.—I have sent to the front all my troops, with the exception of Couch's division, and have given the orders necessary to insure its being disposed of as you directed.

"I cannot express to you the pain and mortification I have experienced to-day, in listening to the distant sound of the firing of my men. As I can be of no further use here, I respectfully ask that, if there is a probability of the conflict being renewed to-morrow, I may be permitted to go to the scene of battle with my staff, merely to be with my own men, if nothing more. They will fight none the worse for my being with them. If it is not deemed best to entrust me with the command even of my own army, I simply ask to be permitted to share their fate on the field of battle.

"Please reply to this to-night. I have been engaged for the last few hours in doing what I can to make arrangements for the wounded. I have started out all the ambulances now landed. As I have sent my escort to the front, I would be glad to take some of Gregg's cavalry with me, if allowed to go."

### General Halleck's Reply.

"*August* 31*st*, 9.18 a.m.—I have just seen your telegram of last night. The substance was stated to me when received, but I did not know that you asked for a reply immediately. I cannot answer without seeing the President, as General Pope is in command, by his orders, of the Department.

"I think Couch's division should go forward as rapidly as possible, and find the battle-field."

### GENERAL McCLELLAN TO GENERAL HALLECK.

"*August 31st.*—Under the War Department order of yesterday, I have no control over any thing except my staff, some one hundred men in my camp here, and the few remaining near Fortress Monroe. I have no control over the new regiments; do not know where they are, or any thing about them, except those near here. Their commanding officers and those of the works are not under me. Where I have seen evils existing under my eye, I have corrected them."

### GENERAL HALLECK'S REJOINDER.

"*August 31st*—10.7 P.M.—Since receiving your despatch relating to command, I have not been able to answer any not of absolute necessity. I have not seen the order as published, but will write to you in the morning. You will retain the command of every thing in this vicinity.

"I beg of you to assist me in this crisis with your ability and experience. I am entirely tired out."

### GENERAL McCLELLAN TO GENERAL HALLECK.

"CAMP NEAR ALEXANDRIA, *August 31st*—11.30 P.M.—I recommend that no more of Couch's division be sent to the front, that Burnside be brought here as soon as practicable, and that every thing available this side of Fairfax be drawn in at once—including the mass of the troops on the railroad. I apprehend that the enemy will, or have by this time, occupied Fairfax Court-House, and cut off Pope entirely, unless he falls back tonight via Sangster's and Fairfax Station.

"I think these orders should be sent at once. I have no confidence in the dispositions made as I gather them. To speak frankly, and the occasion requires it, there appears to be a total absence of brains, and I fear the total destruction of the army. I have some cavalry here that can carry out any orders you may have to send. The occasion is grave, and demands grave measures. The question is the salvation of the country. I learn that our loss yesterday amounted to (15,000) fifteen thousand. We cannot afford such losses without an object.

"It is my deliberate opinion that the interests of the nation demand that Pope should fall back to-night, if possible, and not one moment is to be lost. I will use all the cavalry I have to watch our right. Please answer at once. I feel confident that you can rely upon the information I give you. I shall be up all night, and ready to obey any orders you give me."

GENERAL HALLECK TO GENERAL McCLELLAN.

"*September 1st*—1.30 A.M.—Retain remainder of Couch's forces and make arrangements to stop all retreating troops in line of works, or where you can best establish an entire line of defence. I must wait for more definite information before I can order a retreat, as the falling back on the line of works must necessarily be directed, in case of a serious disaster."

## "LITTLE MAC" REQUESTED TO USE HIS IN-FLUENCE WITH THE ARMY.

On the first of September the young commander, who really, after the hardships and experiences of protracted warfare, without the brilliant successes, which upon his first arrival at Fortress Monroe he had pictured as future rewards for the bravery of his troops, now found himself without a command, went to Washington and had an interview with the President and the General-in-Chief, the former of whom requested him to use his influence to ensure a cordial co-operation between the Army of the Potomac and General Pope, as he could accomplish such an object and no one else could. In obedience to the request the following despatch was sent to General Porter :

" WASHINGTON, *September* 1, 1862.

" I ask of you, for my sake, that of the country, and the old Army of the Potomac, that you and all my friends will lend the fullest and most cordial co-operation to General Pope, in all the operations now going on. The destinies of our country, the honor of our arms, are at stake, and all depends now upon the cheerful co-operation of all in the field. This week is the crisis of our fate. Say the same thing to my friends in the Army of the Potomac, and that the last request I have to make of them is, that, for their country's sake, they will extend to General Pope the same support they ever have to me.

" I am in charge of the defences of Washington, and am doing all I can to render your retreat safe, should that become necessary.    " GEORGE B. McCLELLAN."

General Porter replied that all the friends of McClellan would cordially co-operate with General Pope, and would ever give their constant support in the execution of his plans.

## THE END OF THE POPE CAMPAIGN—"LITTLE MAC" AGAIN IN COMMAND.

On the morning of the second of September, the President and General Halleck informed General McClellan that our army was in full retreat for Washington, and instructed him to prepare for their reception and to go out and meet the returning troops, take command of them and place them in the best position. An order was then issued by the War Department, announcing that "by direction of the President, Major-General McClellan will have command of the fortifications at Washington and of all the troops for the defence of the capital.

This order actually placed him again in command of the Army of the Potomac. No time was lost by the gallant chieftain in acceding to the instructions, and in a few hours he had not only informed General Pope what disposition he wished made of troops as they arrived within our lines of defence, but had himself crossed the river and advanced to meet the retreating soldiers, and by his cheering voice encouraged them, and at the same time assured them that they were approaching a haven of safety of which he was the master pilot. The enemy soon became aware that they had their old foe to confront them, and two days later they relinquished the pursuit and moved towards the Upper Potomac, with the evident intention of crossing the stream and carrying out their long-cherished plan of invading the North, and devastating the fertile and highly cultivated valleys of Maryland and Pennsylvania. General McClellan immediately ordered his troops, fatigued as they were by the hardships and sufferings which they recently endured during the memorable Pope campaign, to intercept the enemy. The fact that their old commander was again at his post reinvigorated their wearied frames and revived their spirits, which had naturally drooped under the repeated defeats, and although the ranks had been sadly depleted in the numerous battles and skirmishes which were fought during the retreat, without a moment's unnecessary delay the army was in motion.

## THE MARYLAND CAMPAIGN.

General McClellan left Washington on the seventh, having temporarily transferred the command of the defences of the capital to General Banks, and after cautious marching, made so by the inability to ascertain whether the enemy actually intended to invade Pennsylvania or to march on Washington from the North, on the fourteenth, four of the corps on the right wing and centre, arrived at South Mountain, and the balance of the army was within supporting distance. During the entire march the army was moved in such order, that it might be concentrated at any time. On the thirteenth the right wing and the centre passed through Frederick, from which place the enemy had just retired towards Harper's Ferry, thus making it necessary for General McClellan to force the passes through the mountain ranges and gain possession of Boonsboro' and Rohrersville, before he could extend relief to Colonel Miles, commanding at Harper's Ferry. On the thirteenth he came into possession of an order issued four days previous by General Lee, prescribing the manner in which the different Divisions of his army should move.

Before leaving Washington, General McClellan suggested that the troops at Harper's Ferry should be withdrawn to the North side of the Potomac, but as the recommendation was not observed, it was too late when the matter was left to his discretion to do any thing but attempt to relieve them. Immediate arrangements were made for that purpose, and the left was ordered to move through Crampton's Pass, while the centre and right marched upon Turner's Pass in front of Middletown. On the thirteenth Colonel Miles sent word that he could hold out with certainty two days longer, in answer to which three copies of the following were sent by three different couriers on three different routes.

"MIDDLETOWN, *September 14th*, 1862.

"COLONEL:—The army is being rapidly concentrated here. We are now attacking the pass on the Hagerstown road over the Blue Ridge. A column is about attacking the Burkettsville and Boonsboro' pass. You may count on our making every effort to relieve you. You may rely upon my speedily accomplishing that object. Hold out to the last extremity. If it is possible, reoccupy the Maryland Heights with your whole force. If you can do that, I will certainly be able to relieve you. As the Catoctin Valley is in our possession, you can safely cross the river at Berlin or its vicinity, so far as opposition on this side of the river is concerned. Hold out to the last.

"GEORGE B. McCLELLAN,

"*Major-General Commanding.*"

"*Colonel* D. S. MILES."

On the previous day he had sent a despatch to General Franklin, advising him of the enemy's movements, and instructing him to relieve Colonel Miles as soon as possible. "If you effect this," he wrote, "you will order him to join you at once with all his disposable troops, first destroying the bridges over the Potomac, if not already done, and leaving a sufficient garrison to prevent the enemy from passing the ford. You will then return by Rohrersville on the direct road to Boonsboro', if the main column has not succeeded in its attack. If it has succeeded, take the road to Rohrersville, to Sharpsburg and Williamsport, in order either to cut off the retreat of Hill and Longstreet towards the Potomac, or prevent the repassage of Jackson. My general idea is to cut the enemy in two and beat him in detail."

Again, on the 14th, he sent the following:

" HEAD-QUARTERS, ARMY OF THE POTOMAC,
" FREDERICK, *September* 14*th*, 1862—2 P.M.

" MAJOR-GENERAL FRANKLIN:

" Your despatch of 12.30 just received. Send back to hurry up Couch. Mass your troops and carry Burkettsville at any cost. We shall have strong opposition at both passes. As fast as the troops come up, I will hold a reserve in readiness to support you. If you find the enemy in very great force at any of these passes, let me know at once, and amuse them as best you can, so as to retain them there. In that event, I will probably throw the mass of the army on the pass in front of here. If I carry that, it will clear the way for you, and you must follow the enemy as rapidly as possible.

" GEORGE B. McCLELLAN,
"*Major-General Commanding.*"

## THE BATTLES OF CRAMPTON'S GAP AND SOUTH MOUNTAIN—GENERAL McCLELLAN'S OFFICIAL REPORT.

Here follows General McClellan's official reports of the battles of Crampton's Gap and South Mountain:

" General Franklin pushed his corps rapidly forward towards Crampton's Pass, and, at about 12 o'clock on the 14th, arrived at Burkettsville, immediately in rear of which he found the enemy's infantry posted in force on both sides of the road, with artillery in strong positions to defend the approaches to the pass. Slocum's division was formed upon the right of the road leading through the gap, and Smith's upon the left. A line formed of Bartlett's and Torbett's brigades, supported by Newton, whose activity was conspicuous, advanced steadily upon the enemy, at a charge, on the right. The enemy were driven from their position at the base of the mountain, where they were protected by a stone wall, steadily forced back up the slope, until they reached the position of their battery on the road, well up the mountain. There they made a stand. They were, however, driven back, retiring their artillery in *echelon*, until, after an action of three hours, the crest was gained, and the enemy hastily fled down the mountain on the other side.

" On the left of the road Brooks's and Irwin's brigades, of Smith's division, formed for the protection of Slocum's flank, charged up the mountain in the same steady manner, driving the enemy before them until the crest was carried. Four hundred prisoners, from seventeen different organizations; seven hundred stand of arms, one piece of artillery, and three colors, were captured by our troops in this brilliant action. It was conducted by General Franklin in all its details.

" The loss in General Franklin's corps was one hundred and

fifteen killed, four hundred and sixteen wounded, and two missing. The enemy's loss was about the same. The enemy's position was such that our artillery could not be used with any effect. The close of the action found General Franklin's advance in Pleasant Valley, on the night of the 14th, within three and one-half miles of the point on Maryland Heights, where he might on the same night, or on the morning of the 15th, have formed a junction with the garrison of Harper's Ferry, had it not been previously withdrawn from Maryland Heights."

At midnight the following despatch was sent to General Franklin :

"BOLIVAR, *September 15th*—1 A.M.

"*General Franklin* :—GENERAL :—

"The Commanding General directs that you occupy with your command the road from Rohrersville to Harper's Ferry, placing a sufficient force at Rohrersville to hold that position in case it should be attacked by the enemy from Boonsboro'. Endeavor to open communication with Colonel Miles at Harper's Ferry, attacking and destroying such of the enemy as you may find in Pleasant Valley. Should you succeed in opening communication with Colonel Miles, direct him to join you with his whole command, with all the guns and public property that he can carry with him. The remainder of the guns will be spiked or destroyed; the rest of the public property will also be destroyed. You will then proceed to Boonsboro', which place the Commanding General intends to attack to-morrow, and join the main body of the army at that place. Should you find, however, that the enemy have retreated from Boonsboro' towards Sharpsburg, you will endeavor to fall upon him and cut off his retreat.

"By command of      " MAJOR-GENERAL McCLELLAN.

"*Geo. D. Ruggles, Colonel, and Aide-de-Camp.*"

On the 15th the following were received from General Franklin :

"AT THE FOOT OF MOUNT PLEASANT,

"IN PLEASANT VALLEY, THREE MILES FROM ROHRERSVILLE,

"*September 15th*—8.50 A.M.

"GENERAL :—My command started at daylight this morning, and I am waiting to have it closed up here. General Couch arrived about ten o'clock last night. I have ordered one of his brigades and one battery to Rohrersville or to the strongest point in its vicinity. The enemy is drawn up in line of battle about two miles to our front, one brigade in sight. As soon as I am sure that Rohrersville is occupied I shall move forward to attack the enemy. This may be two hours from now. If

Harper's Ferry has fallen, and the cessation of firing makes me fear that it has, it is my opinion that I should be strongly rein- forced.

"W. B. FRANKLIN,

"*Major-General Commanding Corps.*

"GENERAL G. B. McCLELLAN."

"*September 15th—11 A.M.*

"GENERAL:—I have received your despatch by Captain O'Keefe. The enemy is in large force in my front, in two lines of battle, stretching across the valley, and a large column of artillery and infantry on the right of the valley, looking towards Harper's Ferry. They outnumber me two to one. It will of course not answer to pursue the enemy under these circumstances. I shall communicate with Burnside as soon as possible. In the meantime I shall wait here until I learn what is the prospect of reinforcement. I have not the force to justify an attack on the force I see in front. I have had a very close view of it, and its position is very strong.    "Respectfully,

"W. B. FRANKLIN, *Major-General.*

"GENERAL G. B. McCLELLAN, *Commanding.*"

"Col. Miles surrendered Harper's Ferry at 8 A.M. on the 15th, as the cessation of the firing indicated, and Gen. Franklin was ordered to remain where he was to watch the large force in front of him, and protect our left and rear until the night of the 16th, when he was ordered to join the main body of the army at Keedysville, after sending Couch's division to Maryland Heights. While the events which have just been described were taking place at Crampton's Gap, the troops of the centre and right wing, which had united at Frederick on the 13th, were engaged in the contest for the possession of Turner's Gap.

"On the morning of the 13th, General Pleasanton was or- dered to send McReynolds's brigade and a section of artillery in the direction of Gettysburg, and Rush's regiment towards Jefferson, to communicate with Franklin, to whom the Sixth United States cavalry and a section of artillery had previously been sent, and to proceed with the remainder of his force in the direction of Middletown, in pursuit of the enemy. After skir- mishing with the enemy all the morning and driving them from several strong positions, he reached Turner's Gap of the South Mountain, in the afternoon, and found the enemy in force, and apparently determined to defend the pass. He sent back for infantry to General Burnside, who had been directed to support him, and proceeded to make a reconnoissance of the position.

"The South Mountain is at this point about one thousand feet in height, and its general direction is from northeast to southwest. The National Road from Frederick to Hagerstown crosses it nearly at right angles, through Turner's Gap, a de- pression which is some four hundred feet in depth. The mountain on the north side of the turnpike is divided into two crests or ridges, by a narrow valley, which, though deep at the pass, becomes a slight depression at about a mile to the north. There are two country-roads, one to the right of the turnpike and the other to the left, which give access to the crests overlooking the main road. The one on the left, called the 'Old Sharpsburg Road,' is nearly parallel to and about half a mile distant from the turnpike, until it reaches the crest of the mountain, when it bends off to the left. The other road, called the 'Old Hagerstown Road,' passes up a ravine in the mountains, about a mile from the turnpike, and bending to the left over and along the first crest, enters the turnpike at the Mountain House, near the summit of the pass. On the night of the 13th, the positions of the different corps were as follows :

"Reno's corps at Middletown, except Redman's division at Frederick.

"Hooker's corps on the Monocacy, two miles from Frederick.
"Sumner's corps near Frederick.
"Banks's corps near Frederick.
"Sykes's division near Frederick.
"Franklin's corps at Buckeyestown.
"Couch's division at Licksville."

The orders from head-quarters for the march on the 14th were as follows :

"13th, 11.30 P.M.—Hooker to march at daylight to Middletown.

"13th, 11.30 P.M.—Sykes to move at 6 A.M. after Hooker, on the Middletown and Hagerstown road.

"14th, 1 A.M.—Artillery reserve to follow Sykes closely.

"13th, 8.45 P.M.—Turner to move at 7 A.M.

"14th, 9 A.M.—Sumner ordered to take the Shookstown road to Middletown.

"13th, 6.45 P.M.—Couch ordered to move to Jefferson with his whole division.

"On the 14th, General Pleasanton continued his reconnoissance. Gibson's battery, and afterward Benjamin's battery (of Reno's corps) were placed on high ground to the left of the turnpike, and obtained a direct fire on the enemy's position in the gap."

General Cox's division, which had been ordered up to support General Pleasanton, left its bivouac near Middletown at 6 A.M. The first brigade reached the scene of action about 9 A.M., and was sent up the Old Sharpsburg road by General Pleasanton to feel the enemy, and ascertain if he held the crest on that side in strong force.

"This was soon found to be the case, and General Cox having arrived with the other brigade, and information having been re ceived from General Reno, that the column would be supported by the whole corps, the division was ordered to assault the position. Two 20-pounder Parrots of Simmons's battery, and two sections of McMullan's battery were left in the rear, in position near the turnpike, where they did good service during the day against the enemy's batteries in the gap. Colonel Scammon's brigade was deployed, and, well covered by skirmishers, moved up the slope to the left of the road, with the object of turning the enemy's right, if possible. It succeeded in gaining the crest and establishing itself there, in spite of the vigorous efforts of the enemy, who was posted behind stone walls and in the edges of timber, and the fire of a battery which poured in canister and case shot on the regiment on the right of the brigade. Colonel Crook's brigade marched in columns at supporting distance. A section of McMullan's battery, under Lieutenant Croome (killed while serving one of his guns), was moved up with great difficulty, and opened with canister at very short range, on the enemy's infantry, by whom, after having done considerable execution, it was soon silenced and forced to withdraw.

"One regiment of Crook's brigade was now deployed on Scammon's left, and the other two in his rear, and they several times entered the first line and relieved the regiments in front of them when hard pressed. A section of Sumner's battery was brought up and placed in the open space in the woods, where it did good service during the rest of the day. The enemy several times attempted to retake the crest, advancing with boldness, but were each time repulsed. They then withdrew their battery to a point more to the right and formed columns on both our flanks. It was now about noon, and a lull occurred in the contest which lasted about two hours, during which the rest of the corps was coming up. General Wilcox's division was the first to arrive. When he reached the base of the mountain, General Cox advised him to consult General Pleasanton as to a position. The latter indicated that on the right, afterwards taken up by General Hooker. General Wilcox was in the act of moving to occupy this ground, when he received an order from General Reno to move up the Old Sharpsburg road and take a position to its right, overlooking the turnpike. Two regiments were detached to support General Cox, at his request. One section of Cook's battery was placed in position near the turn of the road (on the crest), and opened fire on the enemy's batteries across the gap; the division was proceeding to deploy to the right of the road, when the enemy suddenly opened at 150 yards with a battery which enfiladed the road at this point, drove off Cook's cannoneers with their limbers, and caused a temporary panic in which the guns were nearly lost.

But the Seventy-ninth New York and Seventeenth Michigan
promptly rallied, changed front under a heavy fire, and moved
out to protect the guns with which Captain Cook had remained.
Order was soon restored and the division formed in line on the
right of Cox, and was kept concealed as much as possible,
under the hill-side, until the whole line advanced. It was exposed not only to the fire of the battery in front, but also to
that of the batteries on the other side of the turnpike, and lost
heavily.

"Shortly before this time, Generals Burnside and Reno arrived at the base of the mountain, and the former directed the
latter to move up the divisions of Generals Sturgis and Rodman
to the crest held by Cox and Wilcox, and to move upon the
enemy's position with his whole force as soon as he was informed
that General Hooker (who had just been directed to attack on
the right) was well advanced up the mountain. General Reno
then went to the front and assumed the direction of affairs, the
positions having been explained to him by General Pleasanton.
Shortly before this time, I arrived at the point occupied by
General Burnside, and my head-quarters were located there
until the conclusion of the action. General Sturgis had left his
camp at 1 P.M., and reached the scene of action about 3½ P.M.
Clark's battery of his division was sent to assist Cox's left, by
order of General Reno, and two regiments (Second Maryland
and Sixth New Hampshire) were detached by General Reno and
sent forward a short distance on the left of the turnpike. His
division was formed in rear of Wilcox's, and Rodman's division
was divided, Colonel Fairchilds's brigade being placed on the extreme left, and Colonel Harland's, under General Rodman's
personal supervision, on the right.

"My order to move the whole line forward and take or silence
the enemy's batteries in front, was executed with enthusiasm.
The enemy made a desperate resistance, charging our advancing
lines with fierceness, but they were everywhere routed, and fled.
Our chief loss was in Wilcox's division. The enemy's battery
was found to be across a gorge, and beyond the reach of our
infantry, but its position was made untenable, and it was hastily
removed, and not again put in position near us. But the batteries across the gap still kept up a fire of shot and shell.

"General Wilcox praises very highly the conduct of the
Seventeenth Michigan in this advance, a regiment which had
been organized scarcely a month, but which charged the advancing enemy in flank in a manner worthy of veteran troops,
and also that of the Forty-fifth Pennsylvania, which bravely
met them in front. Cook's battery now re-opened fire ; Sturgis's division was moved to the front of Wilcox's, occupying the
new ground gained on the further side of the slope, and his
artillery opened on the batteries across the gap. The enemy
made an effort to turn our left about dark, but were repulsed by

8

Fairchilds's brigade and Clark's battery. At about seven o'clock the enemy made another effort to regain the lost ground, attacking along Sturgis's front, and part of Cox's; a lively fire was kept up until nearly nine o'clock, several charges being made by the enemy and repulsed with slaughter, and we finally occupied the highest part of the mountain. General Reno was killed just before sunset, while making a reconnoissance to the front, and the command of the corps devolved upon General Cox. In General Reno the nation lost one of its best General officers. He was a skilful soldier, a brave and honest man.

"There was no firing after ten o'clock, and the troops slept on their arms, ready to renew the fight at daylight, but the enemy quietly retired from our front during the night, abandoning their wounded, and leaving their dead in large numbers scattered over the field. While these operations were progressing on the left of the main column, the right, under General Hooker, was actively engaged. His corps left the Monocacy early in the morning, and its advance reached the Catoctin Creek about 1 P.M. General Hooker then went forward to examine the ground.

"At about one o'clock General Meade's division was ordered to make a diversion in favor of Reno.

"The division left Catoctin Creek about 2 o'clock, and turned off to the right from the main road, on the Old Hagerstown road, to Mount Tabor Church, where General Hooker was, and deployed a short distance in advance, its right resting about one and one-half miles from the turnpike. The enemy fired a few shots from the battery on the mountain-side, but did no considerable damage. Cooper's battery B, First Pennsylvania artillery, was placed in position on high ground, at about $3\frac{1}{2}$ o'clock, and fired at the enemy on the slope, but soon ceased by order of General Hooker; and the position of our lines prevented any further use of artillery by us on this part of the field. The First Massachusetts cavalry was sent up the valley to the right, to observe the movement, if any, of the enemy, in that direction, and one regiment of Meade's division was posted to watch a road coming in the same direction. The other divisions were deployed as they came up, General Hatch's on the left, and General Ricketts's, which arrived at 5 P.M., in the rear. General Gibbon's brigade was detached from General Hatch's division by General Burnside, for the purpose of making a demonstration on the enemy's centre, up the main road, as soon as the movements on the right and left had sufficiently progressed. The First Pennsylvania rifles, of General Seymour's brigade, were sent forward as skirmishers to feel the enemy, and it was found that he was in force. Meade was then directed to advance his division to the right of the road so as to outflank them, if possible, and then to move forward and attack, while Hatch was directed to take with his division the crest on the left of the Old Hagerstown road, Ricketts's division being held in reserve, Seymour's

brigade was sent up to the top of the slope on the right of the
ravine through which the road runs, and then moved along the
summit parallel to the road, while Colonel Gallagher's and
Colonel McGilton's brigades moved in the same direction along
the slope and in the ravine. The ground was of the most difficult character for the movement of troops, the hill-side being
very steep and rocky, and obstructed by stone walls and timber.
The enemy was very soon encountered, and in a short time the
action became general along the whole front of the division.
The line advanced steadily up the mountain side, where the
enemy was posted behind trees and rocks, from which he was
gradually dislodged. During this advance Colonel Gallagher,
commanding the Third brigade, was severely wounded, and the
command devolved upon Lieutenant-Colonel Robert Anderson.

"General Meade, having reason to believe that the enemy
were attempting to outflank him on his right, applied to General
Hooker for reinforcements. General Duryea's brigade, of Ricketts's division, was ordered up; but it did not arrive until the
close of the action. It was advanced on Seymour's left, but
only one regiment could open fire before the enemy retired and
darkness intervened. General Meade speaks highly of General
Seymour's skill in handling his brigade on the extreme right,
securing, by his manœuvres, the great object of the movement,
the outflanking of the enemy. While General Meade was gallantly driving the enemy on the right, General Hatch's division
was engaged in a severe contest for the possession of the crest
on the left of the ravine. It moved up the mountain in the
following order: Two regiments of General Patrick's brigade,
deployed as skirmishers, with the other two regiments of the
same brigade supporting them, Colonel Phelps's brigade in
line of battalions in mass at deploying distance, General Doubleday's brigade, in the same order, bringing up the rear. The
Twenty-first New York having gone straight up the slope, instead of around to the right, as directed, the Second United
States sharpshooters was sent out in its place.

"Phelps's and Doubleday's brigades were deployed in turn
as they reached the woods, which began about half up the
mountain. General Patrick, with his skirmishers, soon drew the
fire of the enemy, and found him strongly posted behind a fence
which bounded the cleared space on the top of the ridge, having
on his front the woods through which our line was advancing,
and in his rear a corn-field full of rocky ledges, which afforded
good cover to fall back to, if dislodged. Phelps's brigade gallantly advanced, under a hot fire, to close quarters, and, after ten
or fifteen minutes of heavy firing on both sides (in which General Hatch was wounded while urging on his men) the fence was
carried by a charge, and our line advanced a few yards beyond
it, somewhat sheltered by the slope of the hill. Doubleday's
brigade, now under the command of Lieutenant-Colonel Hoffman

(Colonel Wainwright having been wounded,) relieved Phelps, and continued firing for an hour and a half; the enemy, behind ledges of rocks some thirty or forty paces in our front, making a stubborn resistance, and attempting to charge, on the least cessation of our fire. About dusk, Colonel Christian's brigade, of Ricketts's division, came up and relieved Doubleday's brigade, which fell back into line behind Phelps's. Christian's brigade continued the action for thirty or forty minutes, when the enemy retired, after having made an attempt to flank us on the left, which was repulsed by the Seventy-fifth New York and Seventh Indiana.

" The remaining brigade of General Ricketts's division (General Hartsuff's) was moved up in the centre, and connected Meade's left with Doubleday's right. We now had possession of the summit of the first ridge, which commanded the turnpike on both sides of the mountain, and the troops were ordered to hold their positions until further orders, and slept on their arms. Late in the afternoon General Gibbon, with his brigade and one section of Gibbon's battery (B, Fourth artillery), was ordered to move up the main road on the enemy's centre. He advanced a regiment on each side of the road, preceded by skirmishers, and followed by the other two regiments in double column—the artillery moving on the road until within range of the enemy's guns, which were firing on the column from the gorge.

" The brigade advanced steadily, driving the enemy from his positions in the woods and behind stone walls, until they reached a point well up towards the top of the pass, when the enemy, having been reinforced by three regiments, opened a heavy fire on the front and on both flanks. The fight continued until nine o'clock, the enemy being entirely repulsed, and the brigade, after having suffered severely and having expended all its ammunition, including even the cartridges of the dead and wounded, continued to hold the ground it had so gallantly won, until twelve o'clock, when it was relieved by General Gorman's brigade, of Sedgwick's division, Sumner's corps (except the Sixth Wisconsin, which remained on the field all night). General Gibbon, in this delicate movement, handled his brigade with as much precision and coolness as if upon parade, and the bravery of his troops could not be excelled. The Second corps (Sumner's) and the Twelfth corps (Williams's) reached their final positions shortly after dark. General Richardson's division was placed near Mount Tabor Church, in a position to support our right, if necessary; the Twelfth corps and Sedgwick's division bivouacked around Bolivar, in a position to support our centre and left.

" General Sykes's division of regulars, and the artillery reserve halted for the night at Middletown. Thus, on the night of the 14th, the whole army was massed in the vicinity of the field of battle, in readiness to renew the action the next day, or to move in pursuit of the enemy. At daylight our skirmishers were advanced, and it was found that he had retreated during the night, leaving his dead on the field, and his wounded uncared for.

"About fifteen hundred prisoners were taken by us during the battle, and the loss to the enemy in killed was much greater than our own, and probably also in wounded. It is believed that the force opposed to us at Turner's Gap consisted of D. H. Hill's corps (15,000), and a part, if not the whole, of Longstreet's and perhaps a portion of Jackson's, probably some thirty thousand in all.

"We went into action with about 30,000 men, and our losses amounted to 1,568 aggregate,—312 killed, 1,234 wounded, and 22 missing.            "GEORGE B. McCLELLAN,

*"Major-General Commanding U. S. A."*

On the next day General McClellan received the following despatch from the President.

"WAR DEPARTMENT, 2.45 P.M.

"WASHINGTON, *September 15th*, 1862.

"Your despatch of to-day received. God bless you and all with you. Destroy the rebel army, if possible.

"A. LINCOLN.

*"To Major-General* McCLELLAN."

## THE BATTLE OF ANTIETAM.

On the night of the battle of South Mountain the corps commanders were ordered to advance their pickets at daylight, which order was obeyed, and it being discovered that the enemy had retired, pursuit was commenced; the cavalry under Pleasanton, and the corps of Sumner, Hooker and Mansfield (the latter having arrived that morning and assumed command of the Twelfth), by the National turnpike and Boonsboro'; the corps of Burnside and Porter, by the old Sharpsburg road; and Franklin, to move into Pleasant Valley, occupy Rohrersville, and endeavor to relieve Harper's Ferry. Generals Burnside and Porter were ordered upon reaching the Boonsboro' and Rhorersville road, to reinforce Franklin or to move on Sharpsburg, according to circumstances.

Franklin moved towards Brownsville, but finding the enemy in force, and that firing had ceased at Harper's

Ferry, waited for reinforcements, as stated in his despatch heretofore published.

Our cavalry overtook the rebel cavalry at Boonsboro', made a brilliant charge, killing and wounding a number, and capturing 250 prisoners and two guns.

General McClellan thus describes the battle of Antietam in his official report, with the movements previous thereto :

" General Richardson's division of the Second corps, pressing the rear-guard of the enemy with vigor, passed Boonsboro' and Keedysville, and came upon the main body of the enemy, occupying in large force a strong position a few miles beyond the latter place.

" It had been hoped to engage the enemy during the 15th. Accordingly, instructions were given that if the enemy were overtaken on the march they should be attacked at once ; if found in heavy force and in position, the corps in advance should be placed in position for attack, and await my arrival. On reaching the advanced position of our troops, I found but two divisions, Richardson's and Sykes's, in position ; the other troops were halted in the road ; the head of the column some distance in rear of Richardson.

" The enemy occupied a strong position on the heights, on the west side of Antietam creek, displaying a large force of infantry and cavalry, with numerous batteries of artillery, which opened on our columns as they appeared in sight on the Keedysville road and Sharpsburg turnpike, which fire was returned by Captain Tidball's light battery, Second United States artillery, and Pettet's battery, First New York artillery.

" The division of General Richardson, following close on the heels of the retreating foe, halted and deployed near Antietam river, on the right of the Sharpsburg road. General Sykes, leading on the division of regulars on the old Sharpsburg road, came up and deployed to the left of General Richardson, on the left of the road.

"Antietam creek, in this vicinity, is crossed by four stone bridges—the upper one on the Keedysville and Williamsport road ; the second on the Keedysville and Sharpsburg turnpike, some two and a half miles below ; the third about a mile below the second, on the Rohrersville and Sharpsburg road ; and the fourth near the mouth of Antietam creek, on the road leading from Harper's Ferry to Sharpsburg. some three miles below the third. The stream is sluggish, with few and difficult fords. After a rapid examination of the position, I found that it was too late to attack that day, and at once directed the placing of the batteries in position in the centre, and indicated the bivouacs for the different corps, massing them near and on both sides of the Sharpsburg turnpike. The corps were not all in their positions until the next morning after sunrise.

"On the morning of the 16th, it was discovered that the enemy had changed the position of his batteries. The masses of his troops, however, were still concealed behind the opposite heights. Their left and centre were upon and in front of the Sharpsburg and Hagerstown turnpike, hidden by woods and irregularities of the ground; their extreme left resting upon a wooded eminence near the cross-roads to the north of J. Miller's farm; their left resting upon the Potomac. Their line extended south, the right resting upon the hills to the south of Sharpsburg, near Shaveley's farm.

"The bridge over the Antietam, described as No. 3, near this point, was strongly covered by riflemen protected by rifle-pits, stone fences, etc., and enfiladed by artillery. The ground in front of this line consisted of undulating hills, their crests in turn commanded by others in their rear. On all favorable points the enemy's artillery was posted, and their reserves, hidden from view by the hills, on which their line of battle was formed, could manœuvre unobserved by our army, and from the shortness of their line could rapidly reinforce any point threatened by our attack. Their position, stretching across the angle formed by the Potomac and Antietam, their flanks and rear protected by these streams, was one of the strongest to be found in this region of country, which is well adapted to defensive warfare.

"On the right, near Keedysville, on both sides of the Sharpsburg turnpike, were Sumner's and Hooker's corps. In advance, on the right of the turnpike and near the Antietam river, General Richardson's division of General Sumner's corps were posted. General Sykes's division of General Porter's corps was on the left of the turnpike and in line with General Richardson, protecting the bridge No. 2, over the Antietam. The left of the line, opposite to and some distance from bridge No. 3, was occupied by General Burnside's corps.

"Before giving General Hooker his orders to make the movement which will presently be described, I rode to the left of the line to satisfy myself that the troops were properly posted there to secure our left flank from any attack made along the left bank of the Antietam, as well as to enable us to carry bridge No. 3.

"I found it necessary to make considerable changes in the position of General Burnside's corps, and directed him to advance to a strong position in the immediate vicinity of the bridge, and to reconnoitre the approaches to the bridge carefully. In front of General Sumner's and Hooker's corps, near Keedysville, and on the ridge of the first line of hills overlooking the Antietam, and between the turnpike and Fry's house on the right of the road, were placed Captain Taft's, Langner's, Von Kleizer's and Lieutenant Weaver's batteries of twenty-pounder

Parrott guns.  On the crest of the hill in the rear and right of bridge No. 3, Captain Weed's three-inch and Lieutenant Benjamin's twenty-pounder batteries.  General Franklin's corps and General Couch's division held a position in Pleasant valley in front of Brownsville, with a strong force of the enemy in their front.  General Morell's division of Porter's corps was *en route* from Boonsboro', and General Humphrey's division of new troops *en route* from Frederick, Maryland.  About daylight on the 16th the enemy opened a heavy fire of artillery on our guns in position, which was promptly returned; their fire was silenced for the time, but was frequently renewed during the day.  In the heavy fire of the morning, Major Arndt, commanding first battalion first New York artillery, was mortally wounded while directing the operations of his batteries.

"It was afternoon before I could move the troops to their positions for attack, being compelled to spend the morning in reconnoitring the new position taken up by the enemy, examining the ground, finding fords, clearing the approaches, and hurrying up the ammunition and supply trains, which had been delayed by the rapid march of the troops over the few practicable approaches from Frederick.  These had been crowded by the masses of infantry, cavalry, and artillery pressing on with the hope of overtaking the enemy before he could form to resist an attack.  Many of the troops were out of rations on the previous day, and a good deal of their ammunition had been expended in the severe action of the 14th.

"My plan for the impending general engagement was to attack the enemy's left with the corps of Hooker and Mansfield, supported by Sumner's, and if necessary by Franklin's; and, as soon as matters looked favorably there, to move the corps of Burnside against the enemy's extreme right, upon the ridge running to the south and rear of Sharpsburg, and having carried their position, to press along the crest towards our right; and whenever either of these flank movements should be successful, to advance our centre with all the forces then disposable.

"About 2 P.M. General Hooker, with his corps, consisting of General Ricketts's, Meade's and Doubleday's divisions, was ordered to cross the Antietam at a ford, and at bridge No 1, a short distance above, to attack and, if possible, turn the enemy's left.  General Sumner was ordered to cross the corps of General Mansfield (the 12th) during the night, and hold his own (the 2d) corps ready to cross early the next morning.  On reaching the vicinity of the enemy's left a sharp contest commenced with the Pennsylvania reserves, the advance of General Hooker's corps, near the house of D. Miller.  The enemy were driven from the strip of woods where he was first met.  The firing lasted until after dark, when General Hooker's corps rested on their arms on ground won from the enemy.

"During the night General Mansfield's corps, consisting of Generals Williams's and Green's divisions, crossed the Antietam at the same ford and bridge that General Hooker's troops had passed, and bivouacked on the farm of J. Poffenberger, about a mile in rear of General Hooker's position. At daylight on the 17th the action was commenced by the skirmishers of the Pennsylvania reserves. The whole of General Hooker's corps was soon engaged, and drove the enemy from the open field in front of the first line of woods into a second line of woods beyond, which runs to the eastward of and nearly parallel to the Sharpsburg and Hagerstown turnpike.

" This contest was obstinate, and as the troops advanced the opposition became more determined and the number of the enemy greater. General Hooker then ordered up the corps of General Mansfield, which moved promptly toward the scene of action.

" The first division, General Williams's, was deployed to the right on approaching the enemy; General Crawford's brigade on the right, its right resting on the Hagerstown turnpike; on his left General Gordon's brigade. The second division, General Green's, joining the left of Gordon's, extended as far as the burnt buildings to the north and east of the white church on the turnpike. During the deployment, that gallant veteran General Mansfield fell mortally wounded, while examining the ground in front of his troops. General Hartsuff, of Hooker's corps, was severely wounded, while bravely pressing forward his troops, and was taken from the field.

" The command of the Twelfth corps fell upon General Williams. Five regiments of first division of this corps were new troops. One brigade of the second division was sent to support General Doubleday.

" The One-hundred-and-twenty-fourth Pennsylvania volunteers were pushed across the turnpike into the woods beyond J. Miller's house, with orders to hold the position as long as possible.

" The line of battle of this corps was formed, and it became engaged about 7 A.M., the attack being opened by Knapp's (Pennsylvania,) Cothran's (New York,) and Hampton's (Pittsburg) batteries. To meet this attack the enemy had pushed a strong column of troops into the open fields in front of the turnpike, while he occupied the woods on the west of the turnpike in strong force. The woods (as was found by subsequent observation) were traversed by outcropping ledges of rock. Several hundred yards to the right and rear was a hill which commanded the debouche of the woods, and in the fields between was a long line of stone fences, continued by breastworks of rails, which covered the enemy's infantry from our musketry. The same woods formed a screen behind which his movements were concealed, and his batteries on the hill and the rifle works covered from the fire of our artillery in front.

" For about two hours the battle raged with varied success, the enemy endeavoring to drive our troops into the second line of wood, and ours in turn to get possession of the line in front

"Our troops ultimately succeeded in forcing the enemy back into the woods near the turnpike, General Green with his two brigades crossing into the woods to the left of the Dunbar church. During this conflict General Crawford, commanding first division after General Williams took command of the corps, was wounded and left the field.

"General Green being much exposed and applying for reinforcements, the Thirteenth New Jersey, Twenty-seventh Indiana, and the Third Maryland, were sent to his support with a section of Knapp's battery.

"At about nine o'clock A.M. General Sedgwick's division of General Sumner's corps arrived. Crossing the ford previously mentioned, this division marched in three columns to the support of the attack on the enemy's left. On nearing the scene of action the columns were halted, faced to the front, and established by General Sumner in three parallel lines by brigade, facing toward the south and west; General Gorman's brigade in front, General Dana's second, and General Howard's third, with a distance between the lines of some seventy paces. The division was then put in motion and moved upon the field of battle, under fire from the enemy's concealed batteries on the hill beyond the roads. Passing diagonally to the front across the open space and to the front of the first division of General Williams's corps, this latter division withdrew.

"Entering the woods on the west of the turnpike, and driving the enemy before them, the first line was met by a heavy fire of musketry and shell from the enemy's breastworks and the batteries on the hill commanding the exit from the woods; meantime a heavy column of the enemy had succeeded in crowding back the troops of General Green's division, and appeared in rear of the left of Sedgwick's division. By command of General Sumner, General Howard faced the third line to the rear preparatory to a change of front to meet the column advancing on the left; but this line, now suffering from a destructive fire both in front and on its left, which it was unable to return, gave way towards the right and rear in considerable confusion, and was soon followed by the first and second lines.

"General Gorman's brigade, and one regiment of General Dana's, soon rallied and checked the advance of the enemy on the right. The second and third lines now formed on the left of General Gorman's brigade, and poured a destructive fire upon the enemy.

"During General Sumner's attack, he ordered General Williams to support him. Brigadier-General Gordon, with a portion of his brigade, moved forward, but when he reached the woods, the left of General Sedgwick's division had given way; and finding himself, as the smoke cleared up, opposed to the enemy in force with his small command, he withdrew to the rear of the batteries at the second line of woods. As General

Gordon's troops unmasked our batteries on the left, they opened with canister; the batteries of Captain Cothran, First New York, and I, First artillery, commanded by Lieutenant Woodruff, doing good service. Unable to withstand this deadly fire in front and the musketry fire from the right, the enemy again sought shelter in the woods and rocks beyond the turnpike.

"During this assault Generals Sedgwick and Dana were seriously wounded, and taken from the field. General Sedgwick, though twice wounded, and faint from loss of blood, retained command of his division for more than an hour after his first wound, animating his command by his presence.

"About the time of General Sedgwick's advance, General Hooker, while urging on his command, was severely wounded in the foot and taken from the field, and General Meade was placed in command of his corps. General Howard assumed command after General Sedgwick retired.

"The repulse of the enemy offered opportunity to re-arrange the lines and re-organize the commands on the right, now more or less in confusion. The batteries of the Pennsylvania Reserve, on high ground, near I. Poffenburger's house, opened fire, and checked several attempts of the enemy to establish batteries in front of our right, to turn that flank and enfilade the lines.

"While the conflict was so obstinately raging on the right, General French was pushing his division against the enemy still further to the left. This division crossed the Antietam at the same ford as General Sedgwick, and immediately in his rear. Passing over the stream in three columns, the division marched about a mile from the ford, then facing to the left, moved in three lines towards the enemy: General Max Weber's brigade in front; Colonel Dwight Morris's brigade of raw troops, undrilled, and moving for the first time under fire, in the second, and General Kimball's brigade in the third. The division was first assailed by a fire of artillery, but steadily advanced, driving in the enemy's skirmishers, and encountered the infantry in some force at the group of houses on Roulette's farm. General Weber's brigade gallantly advanced with an unwavering front and drove the enemy from their position about the houses

"While General Weber was hotly engaged with the first line of the enemy, General French received orders from General Sumner, his corps commander, to push on with renewed vigor to make a diversion in favor of the attack on the right. Leaving the new troops, who had been thrown into some confusion from their march through corn-fields, over fences, etc., to form as a reserve, he ordered the brigade of General Kimball to the front, passing to the left of General Weber. The enemy was pressed back to near the crest of the hill, where he was encountered in greater strength posted in a sunken road, forming a natural rifle-pit running in a northwesterly direction. In a

cornfield in rear of this road were also strong bodies of the
enemy. As the line reached the crest of the hill a galling fire
was opened on it from the sunken road and cornfield. Here a
terrific fire of musketry burst from both lines, and the battle
raged along the whole line with great slaughter.

"The enemy attempted to turn the left of the line, but were
met by the Seventh Virginia and One-hundred-and-thirty-sec-
ond Pennsylvania volunteers and repulsed. Foiled in this, the
enemy made a determined assault on the front, but were met
by a charge from our lines, which drove them back with severe
loss, leaving in our hands some three hundred prisoners and
several stand of colors. The enemy having been repulsed by
the terrible execution of the batteries and the musketry fire on
the extreme right, now attempted to assist the attack on General French's division by assailing him on his right and endeavoring to turn this flank, but this attack was met and
checked by the Fourteenth Indiana and Eighth Ohio volunteers, and by canister from Captain Tompkins's battery, First
Rhode Island artillery. Having been under an almost continuous fire for nearly four hours, and the ammunition nearly
expended, this division now took position immediately below
the crest of the heights on which they had so gallantly fought,
the enemy making no attempt to regain their lost ground.

"On the left of General French, General Richardson's division was hotly engaged. Having crossed the Antietam about
9.30 A.M. at the ford crossed by the other divisions of Sumner's
corps, it moved on a line nearly parallel to the Antietam, and
formed in a ravine behind the high grounds overlooking Roulette's house; the Second (Irish) brigade, commanded by General Meagher, on the right; the Third brigade, commanded by
General Caldwell, on his left, and the brigade commanded by
Colonel Brooks, Fifty-third Pennsylvania volunteers, in support.
As the division moved forward to take its position on the field,
the enemy directed a fire of artillery against it, but, owing to
the irregularities of the ground, did but little damage.

"Meagher's brigade advancing steadily soon became engaged
with the enemy posted to the left and in front of Roulette's
house. It continued to advance under a heavy fire nearly to
the crest of the hill overlooking Piper's house, the enemy being
posted in a continuation of the sunken road and cornfield before referred to. Here the brave Irish brigade opened upon the
enemy a terrific musketry fire.

"All of General Sumner's corps was now engaged: General
Sedgwick on the right; General French in the centre, and General Richardson on the left. The Irish brigade sustained its
well-earned reputation. After suffering terribly in officers and
men, and strewing the ground with their enemies as they drove
them back, their ammunition nearly expended, and their commander, General Meagher, disabled by the fall of his horse shot

under him, this brigade was ordered to give place to General
Caldwell's brigade, which advanced to a short distance in its
rear. The lines were passed by the Irish brigade breaking by
company to the rear, and General Caldwell's by company to the
front as steadily as on drill. Colonel Brooks's brigade now
became the second line.

"The ground over which General Richardson's and French's
divisions were fighting was very irregular, intersected by numerous ravines, hills covered with growing corn, enclosed by stone
walls, behind which the enemy could advance unobserved upon
any exposed point of our lines. Taking advantage of this, the
enemy attempted to gain the right of Richardson's position in a
cornfield near Roulette's house, where the division had become
separated from that of General French's. A change of front
by the Fifty-second New York and Second Delaware volunteers, of Colonel Brooks's brigade, under Colonel Frank, and
the attack made by the Fifty-third Pennsylvania volunteers,
sent further to the right by Colonel Brooks to close this gap in
the line, and the movement of the One-hundred-and-thirty-
second Pennsylvania and Seventh Virginia volunteers of General French's division, before referred to, drove the enemy from
the cornfield and restored the line.

"The brigade of General Caldwell, with determined gallantry,
pushed the enemy back opposite the left and centre of this
division, but sheltered in the sunken road, they still held our
forces on the right of Caldwell in check. Colonel Barlow, commanding the Sixty-first and Sixty-fourth New York regiments
of Caldwell's brigade, seeing a favorable opportunity, advanced
the regiments on the left, taking the line in the sunken road in
flank, and compelled them to surrender, capturing over three
hundred prisoners and three stands of colors.

"The whole of the brigade, with the Fifty-seventh and Sixty-
sixth New York regiments of Colonel Brooks's brigade, who
had moved these regiments into the first line, now advanced
with gallantry, driving the enemy before them in confusion into
the cornfield beyond the sunken road. The left of the division
was now well advanced, when the enemy, concealed by an inter-
vening ridge, endeavored to turn its left and rear.

"Colonel Cross, Fifth New Hampshire, by a change of front
to the left and rear, brought his regiment facing the advancing
line. Here a spirited contest arose to gain a commanding
height, the two opposing forces moving parallel to each other,
giving and receiving fire. The Fifth gaining the advantage,
faced to the right and delivered its volley. The enemy stag-
gered, but rallied and advanced desperately at a charge. Being
reinforced by the Eighty-first Pennsylvania, these regiments
met the advance by a counter charge. The enemy fled, leaving
many killed, wounded, and prisoners, and the colors of the
Fourth North Carolina, in our hands.

"Another column of the enemy, advancing under shelter of a stone wall and cornfield, pressed down on the right of the division; but Colonel Barlow again advanced the Sixty-first and Sixty-fourth New York against these troops, and with the attack of Kimball's brigade on the right drove them from this position.

" Our troops on the left of this part of the line having driven the enemy far back, they, with reinforced numbers, made a determined attack directly in front. To meet this, Colonel Barlow brought his two regiments to their position in line, and drove the enemy through the cornfield into the orchard beyond, under a heavy fire of musketry, and a fire of canister from two pieces of artillery in the orchard, and a battery further to the right, throwing shell and case shot. This advance gave us possession of Piper's house, the strong point contended for by the enemy at this part of the line, it being a defensible building several hundred yards in advance of the sunken road. The musketry fire at this point of the line now ceased. Holding Piper's house, General Richardson withdrew the line a little way to the crest of a hill, a more advantageous position. Up to this time the division was without artillery, and in the new position suffered severely from artillery fire which could not be replied to. A section of Robertson's horse battery, commanded by Lieutenant Vincent, Second artillery, now arrived on the ground and did excellent service. Subsequently a battery of brass guns, commanded by Captain Graham, First artillery, arrived, and was posted on the crest of the hill, and soon silenced the two guns in the orchard. A heavy fire soon ensued between the battery further to the right and our own. Captain Graham's battery was bravely and skilfully served, but unable to reach the enemy, who had rifled guns of greater range than our smooth-bores, retired by order of General Richardson, to save it from useless sacrifice of men and horses. The brave general was himself mortally wounded while personally directing its fire.

" General Hancock was placed in command of the division after the fall of General Richardson. General Meagher's brigade, now commanded by Colonel Burke, of the Sixty-third New York, having refilled their cartridge-boxes, was again ordered forward, and took position in the centre of the line. The division now occupied one line in close proximity to the enemy, who had taken up a position in the rear of Piper's house. Colonel Dwight Morris, with the Fourteenth Connecticut and a detachment of the One-hundred-and-eighth New York, of General French's division, was sent by General French to the support of General Richardson's division. This command was now placed in an interval in the line between General Caldwell's and the Irish brigades.

" The requirements of the extended line of battle had so

engaged the artillery that the application of General Hancock for artillery for the division could not be complied with immediately by the chief of artillery or the corps commanders in his vicinity. Knowing the tried courage of the troops, General Hancock felt confident that he could hold his position, although suffering from the enemy's artillery, but was too weak to attack, as the great length of the line he was obliged to hold prevented him from forming more than one line of battle, and, from his advanced position, this line was already partly enfiladed by the batteries of the enemy on the right, which were protected from our batteries opposite them by the wood at the Dunker church.

"Seeing a body of the enemy advancing on some of our troops to the left of his position, General Hancock obtained Hexamer's battery from General Franklin's corps, which assisted materially in frustrating this attack. It also assisted the attack of the Seventh Maine, of Franklin's corps, which, without other aid, made an attack against the enemy's line, and drove in skirmishers who were annoying our artillery and troops on the right. Lieutenant Woodruff, with battery I, Second artillery, relieved Captain Hexamer, whose ammunition was expended. The enemy at one time seemed to be about making an attack in force upon this part of the line, and advanced a long column of infantry towards this division; but on nearing the position, General Pleasanton opening on them with sixteen guns, they halted, gave a desultory fire, and retreated, closing the operations on this portion of the field. I return to the incidents occurring still farther to the right.

"Between 12 and 1 P.M., General Franklin's corps arrived on the field of battle, having left their camp near Crampton's pass, at 6 A.M., leaving General Couch with orders to move with his division to occupy Maryland heights. General Smith's division led the column, followed by General Slocum's.

"It was first intended to keep this corps in reserve on the east side of the Antietam, to operate on either flank or on the centre, as circumstances might require; but on nearing Keedysville, the strong opposition on the right, developed by the attacks of Hooker and Sumner, rendered it necessary at once to send this corps to the assistance of the right wing.

"On nearing the field, hearing that one of our batteries, (A,) Fourth United States artillery, commanded by Lieutenant Thomas, who occupied the same position as Lieutenant Woodruff's battery in the morning, was hotly engaged without supports. General Smith sent two regiments to its relief from General Hancock's brigade. On inspecting the ground, General Smith ordered the other regiments of Hancock's brigade, with Frank's and Cowen's batteries, First New York artillery, to the threatened position. Lieutenant Thomas and Captain Cothran, commanding batteries, bravely held their positions against the advancing enemy, handling their batteries with skill.

"Finding the enemy still advancing, the Third brigade, of Smith's division, commanded by Colonel Irwin, Forty-ninth Pennsylvania volunteers, was ordered up, and passed through Lieutenant Thomas's battery, charged upon the enemy, and drove back the advance until abreast of the Dunker church. As the right of the brigade came opposite the woods it received a destructive fire, which checked the advance and threw the brigade somewhat into confusion. It formed again behind a rise of ground in the open space in advance of the batteries.

"General French having reported to General Franklin that his ammunition was nearly expended, that officer ordered General Brooks, with his brigade, to reinforce him. General Brooks formed his brigade on the right of General French, where they remained during the remainder of the day and night, frequently under the fire of the enemy's artillery.

"It was soon after the brigade of Colonel Irwin had fallen back behind the rise of ground that the Seventh Maine, by order of Colonel Irwin, made the gallant attack already referred to.

"The advance of General Franklin's corps was opportune. The attack of the enemy on this position, but for the timely arrival of his corps, must have been disastrous, had it succeeded in piercing the line between Generals Sedgwick's and French's divisions.

"General Franklin ordered two brigades of General Slocum's division, General Newton's and Colonel Torbert's, to form in column to assault the woods that had been so hotly contested before by Generals Sumner and Hooker. General Bartlett's brigade was ordered to form as a reserve. At this time General Sumner, having command on the right, directed further offensive operations to be postponed, as the repulse of this, the only remaining corps available for attack, would peril the safety of the whole army.

"General Porter's corps, consisting of General Sykes's division of regulars and volunteers, and General Morell's division of volunteers, occupied a position on the east side of Antietam creek, upon the main turnpike leading to Sharpsburg, and directly opposite the centre of the enemy's line. This corps filled the interval between the right wing and General Burnside's command, and guarded the main approach from the enemy's position to our trains of supply. It was necessary to watch this part of our line with the utmost vigilance, lest the enemy should take advantage of the first exhibition of weakness here to push upon us a vigorous assault, for the purpose of piercing our centre and turning our rear, as well as to capture or destroy our supply trains. Once having penetrated this line, the enemy's passage to our rear could have met with but feeble resistance, as there were no reserves to reinforce or close up the gap.

"Towards the middle of the afternoon, proceeding to the right, I found that Sumner's, Hooker's, and Mansfield's corps had met with serious losses. Several general officers had been carried from the field severely wounded, and the aspect of affairs was any thing but promising. At the risk of greatly exposing our centre, I ordered two brigades from Porter's corps, the only available troops, to reinforce the right. Six battalions of Sykes's regulars had been thrown forward across the Antietam bridge on the main road to attack and drive back the enemy's sharpshooters, who were annoying Pleasanton's horse batteries in advance of the bridge; Warren's brigade, of Porter's corps, was detached to hold a position on Burnside's right and rear; so that Porter was left at one time with only a portion of Sykes's division and one small brigade of Morell's division (but little over three thousand men) to hold his important position.

"General Sumner expressed the most decided opinion against another attempt during that day to assault the enemy's position in front, as portions of our troops were so much scattered and demoralized. In view of these circumstances, after making changes in the position of some of the troops, I directed the different commanders to hold their positions, and being satisfied that this could be done without the assistance of the two brigades from the centre, I countermanded the order, which was in course of execution.

"General Slocum's division replaced a portion of General Sumner's troops, and positions were selected for batteries in front of the woods. The enemy opened several heavy fires of artillery on the position of our troops after this, but our batteries soon silenced them.

"On the morning of the 17th General Pleasanton, with his cavalry division and the horse batteries, under Captains Robertson, Tidball, and Lieutenant Haines, of the Second artillery, and Captain Gibson, Third artillery, was ordered to advance on the turnpike towards Sharpsburg, across bridge No. 2, and support the left of General Sumner's line. The bridge being covered by a fire of artillery and sharpshooters, cavalry skirmishers were thrown out, and Captain Tidball's battery advanced by piece and drove off the sharpshooters with canister sufficiently to establish the batteries above mentioned, which opened on the enemy with effect. The firing was kept up for about two hours, when, the enemy's fire slackening, the batteries were relieved by Randall's and Van Reed's batteries, United States artillery. About three o'clock Tidball, Robertson, and Haines returned to their positions on the west of Antietam, Captain Gibson having been placed in position on the east side to guard the approaches to the bridge. These batteries did good service, concentrating their fire on the column of the enemy about to attack General Hancock's position, and compelling it to find shelter behind the hills in rear.

"General Sykes's division had been in position since the 15th, exposed to the enemy's artillery and sharpshooters. General Morell had come up on the 16th, and relieved General Richardson on the right of General Sykes. Continually, under the vigilant watch of the enemy, this corps guarded a vital point.

9

"The position of the batteries under General Pleasanton being one of great exposure, the battalion of the Second and Tenth United States infantry, under Captain Pollard, Second infantry, was sent to his support.  Subsequently four battalions of regular infantry, under Captain Dryer, Fourth infantry, were sent across to assist in driving off the sharpshooters of the enemy.

"The battalion of the Second and Tenth infantry, advancing far beyond the batteries, compelled the cannoneers of a battery of the enemy to abandon their guns.  Few in numbers, and unsupported, they were unable to bring them off.  The heavy loss of this small body of men attests their gallantry.

"The troops of General Burnside held the left of the line opposite bridge No. 3.  The attack on the right was to have been supported by an attack on the left.  Preparatory to this attack, on the evening of the 16th, General Burnside's corps was moved forward and to the left, and took up a position nearer the bridge.

"I visited General Burnside's position on the 16th, and after pointing out to him the proper dispositions to be made of his troops during the day and night, informed him that he would probably be required to attack the enemy's right on the following morning, and directed him to make careful reconnoissances.

"General Burnside's corps, consisting of the divisions of Generals Cox, Wilcox, Rodman, and Sturgis, was posted as follows: Colonel Brooks's brigade, Cox's division, on the right, General Sturgis's division immediately in rear.  On the left was General Rodman's division, with General Scammon's brigade, Cox's division, in support.

"General Wilcox's division was held in reserve.

"The corps bivouacked in position on the night of the 16th.

"Early on the morning of the 17th I ordered General Burnside to form his troops, and hold them in readiness to assault the bridge in his front, and to await further orders.

"At 8 o'clock an order was sent to him by Lieutenant Wilson, topographical engineers, to carry the bridge, then to gain possession of the heights beyond, and to advance along their crest upon Sharpsburg and its rear.

"After some time had elapsed, not hearing from him, I despatched an aid to ascertain what had been done.  The aid returned with the information that but little progress had been made.  I then sent him back with an order to General Burnside to assault the bridge at once, and carry it at all hazards.  The aid returned to me a second time with the report that the bridge was still in the possession of the enemy.  Whereupon I directed Colonel Sackett, Inspector-General, to deliver to General Burnside my positive order to push forward his troops without a moment's delay, and, if necessary, to carry the bridge at the point of the bayonet; and I ordered Colonel Sackett to remain with General Burnside and see that the order was executed promptly.

"After these three hours' delay, the bridge was carried at one o'clock by a brilliant charge of the Fifty-first New York and Fifty-first Pennsylvania volunteers. Other troops were then thrown over, and the opposite bank occupied, the enemy retreating to the heights beyond.

"A halt was then made by General Burnside's advance until 3 P.M., upon hearing which I directed one of my aids, Colonel Key, to inform General Burnside that I desired him to push forward his troops with the utmost vigor, and carry the enemy's position on the heights; that the movement was vital to our success; that this was a time when we must not stop for loss of life, if a great object could thereby be accomplished. That if, in his judgment, his attack would fail, to inform me so at once, that his troops might be withdrawn and used elsewhere on the field. He replied that he would soon advance, and would go up the hill as far as a battery of the enemy on the left would permit. Upon this report, I again immediately sent Colonel Key to General Burnside with orders to advance at once, if possible, to flank the battery, or storm it and carry the heights; repeating, that if he considered the movement impracticable, to inform me so, that his troops might be recalled. The advance was then gallantly resumed, the enemy driven from the guns, the heights handsomely carried, and a portion of the troops even reached the outskirts of Sharpsburg. By this time it was nearly dark, and strong reinforcements just then reaching the enemy from Harper's Ferry, attacked General Burnside's troops on their left flank, and forced them to retire to a lower line of hills nearer the bridge.

"If this important movement had been consummated two hours earlier, a position would have been secured upon the heights, from which our batteries might have enfiladed the greater part of the enemy's line, and turned their right and rear; our victory might thus have been much more decisive.

"The following is the substance of General Burnside's operations, as given in his report:

"Colonel Crook's brigade was ordered to storm the bridge. This bridge, No. 3, is a stone structure of three arches with stone parapets. The banks of the stream on the opposite side are precipitous, and command the eastern approaches to the bridge. On the hill-side, immediately by the bridge, was a stone fence running parallel to the stream; the turns of the roadway, as it wound up the hill, were covered by rifle-pits and breastworks of rails, etc. These works, and the woods that covered the slopes, were filled with the enemy's riflemen, and batteries were in position to enfilade the bridge and its approaches.

"General Rodman was ordered to cross the ford below the bridge. From Colonel Crook's position it was found impossible to carry the bridge.

"General Sturgis was ordered to make a detail from his division for that purpose. He sent forward the Second Maryland and the Sixth New Hampshire. These regiments made several successive attacks in the most gallant style, but were driven back.

"The artillery on the left were ordered to concentrate their fire on the woods above the bridge. Colonel Crook brought a section of Captain Simmons's battery to a position to command the bridge. The Fifty-first New York and Fifty-first Pennsylvania were then ordered to assault the bridge. Taking advantage of a small spur of the hills which ran parallel to the river, they moved towards the bridge. From the crest of this spur they rushed with bayonets fixed and cleared the bridge.

"The division followed the storming party, also the brigade of Colonel Crook's as a support. The enemy withdrew to still higher ground, some five or six hundred yards beyond, and opened a fire of artillery on the troops in the new position on the crest of the hill above the bridge.

"General Rodman's division succeeded in crossing the ford after a sharp fire of musketry and artillery, and joined on the left of Sturgis. Scammon's brigade crossing as support. General Wilcox's division was ordered across to take position on General Sturgis's right.

"These dispositions being completed about 3 o'clock, the command moved forward, except Sturgis's division, left in reserve. Clark's and Durell's batteries accompanied Rodman's division; Cook's battery with Wilcox's division, and a section of Simmons's battery with Colonel Crook's brigade. A section of Simmons's battery and Mullenburgh's and McMullan's batteries were in position. The order for the advance was obeyed by the troops with alacrity. General Wilcox's division, with Crook in support, moved up on both sides of the turnpike leading from the bridge to Sharpsburg, General Rodman's division, supported by Scammon's brigade, on the left of General Wilcox. The enemy retreated before the advance of the troops. The Ninth New York, of General Rodman's division, captured one of the enemy's batteries and held it for some time. As the command was driving the enemy to the main heights on the left of the town, the light division of General A. P. Hill arrived upon the field of battle from Harper's Ferry, and with a heavy artillery fire made a strong attack on the extreme left. To meet this attack the left division diverged from the line of march intended, and opened a gap between it and the right. To fill up this it was necessary to order the troops from the second line. During these movements General Rodman was mortally wounded. Colonel Harland's brigade, of General Rodman's division, was driven back. Colonel Scammon's brigade, by a change of front to rear on his right flank, saved the left from being driven completely in. The fresh troops of the enemy pouring in, and the accumulation of artillery against this command, destroyed all hope of its being able to accomplish any thing more.

" It was now nearly dark. General Sturgis was ordered forward to support the left. Notwithstanding the hard work in the early part of the day, his division moved forward with spirit. With its assistance the enemy were checked and held at bay.

" The command was ordered to fall back by General Cox, who commanded on the field the troops engaged in this affair beyond the Antietam. The artillery had been well served during the day. Night closed the long and desperately contested battle of the 17th. Nearly two hundred thousand men and five hundred pieces of artillery were for fourteen hours engaged in this memorable battle. We had attacked the enemy in a position selected by the experienced engineer then in person directing their operations. We had driven them from their line on one flank, and secured a footing within it on the other. The Army of the Potomac, notwithstanding the moral effect incident to previous reverses, had achieved a victory over an adversary invested with the prestige of recent success. Our soldiers slept that night conquerors on a field won by their valor and covered with the dead and wounded of the enemy.

" The night, however, brought with it grave responsibilities. Whether to renew the attack on the 18th, or to defer it, even with the risk of the enemy's retirement, was the question before me.

" After a night of anxious deliberation and a full and careful survey of the situation and condition of our army, the strength and position of the enemy, I concluded that the success of an attack on the 18th was not certain. I am aware of the fact that, under ordinary circumstances, a general is expected to risk a battle if he has a reasonable prospect of success; but at this critical juncture I should have had a narrow view of the condition of the country had I been willing to hazard another battle with less than an absolute assurance of success. At that moment—Virginia lost, Washington menaced, Maryland invaded—the national cause could afford no risks of defeat. One battle lost, and almost all would have been lost. Lee's army might then have marched as it pleased on Washington, Baltimore, Philadelphia, or New York. It could have levied its supplies from a fertile and undevastated country; extorted tribute from wealthy and populous cities; and nowhere east of the Alleghanies was there another organized force able to arrest its march.

" The following are among the considerations which led me to doubt the certainty of success in attacking before the 19th :

" The troops were greatly overcome by the fatigue and exhaustion attendant upon the long continued and severely contested battle of the 17th, together with the long day and night marches to which they had been subjected during the previous three days.

" The supply trains were in the rear, and many of the troops had suffered from hunger. They required rest and refreshment.

"One division of Sumner's and all of Hooker's corps, on the right, had, after fighting most valiantly for several hours, been overpowered by numbers, driven back in great disorder, and much scattered, so that they were for the time somewhat demoralized.

"In Hooker's corps, according to the return made by General Meade, commanding, there were but 6,729 men present on the 18th; whereas, on the morning of the 22d, there were 13,-093 men present for duty in the same corps, showing that previous to and during the battle 6,364 men were separated from their command.

"General Meade, in an official communication upon this subject, dated September 18, 1862, says:

"'I enclose a field return of the corps made this afternoon, which I desire you will lay before the commanding general. I am satisfied the great reduction in the corps since the recent engagements is not due solely to the casualties of battle, and that a considerable number of men are still in the rear, some having dropped out on the march, and many dispersing and leaving yesterday during the fight. I think the efficiency of the corps, so far as it goes, good. To resist an attack in our present strong position I think they may be depended on, and I hope they will perform duty in case we make an attack, though I do not think their morale is as good for an offensive as a defensive movement.'

"One division of Sumner's corps had also been overpowered, and was a good deal scattered and demoralized. It was not deemed by its corps commander in proper condition to attack the enemy vigorously next day.

"Some of the new troops on the left, although many of them fought well during the battle, and are entitled to great credit, were, at the close of the action, driven back, and their morale impaired.

"On the morning of the 18th General Burnside requested me to send him another division to assist in holding his position on the other side of the Antietam, and to enable him to withdraw his corps if he should be attacked by a superior force. He gave me the impression that if he were attacked again that morning he would not be able to make a very vigorous resistance. I visited his position early, determined to send General Morell's division to his aid, and directed that it should be placed on this side of the Antietam, in order that it might cover the retreat of his own corps from the other side of the Antietam, should that become necessary, at the same time it was in position to reinforce our centre or right, if that were needed.

"Late in the afternoon I found that, although he had not been attacked, General Burnside had withdrawn his own corps to this side of the Antietam, and sent over Morell's division alone to hold the opposite side.

"A large number of our heaviest and most efficient batteries had consumed all their ammunition on the 16th and 17th, and it was impossible to supply them until late on the following day.

"Supplies of provisions and forage had to be brought up and issued, and infantry ammunition distributed.

"Finally, reinforcements to the number of 14,000 men—to say nothing of troops expected from Pennsylvania—had not arrived, but were expected during the day.

"The 18th was, therefore, spent in collecting the dispersed, giving rest to the fatigued, removing the wounded, burying the dead, and the necessary preparations for a renewal of the battle.

"Of the reinforcements, Couch's division, marching with commendable rapidity, came up into position at a late hour in the morning. Humphrey's division of new troops, in their anxiety to participate in the battle, which was raging when they received the order to march from Frederick at about half-past three P.M., on the 17th, pressed forward during the entire night, and the mass of the division reached the army during the following morning. Having marched more than twenty-three miles after half-past four o'clock on the preceding afternoon, they were of course, greatly exhausted, and needed rest and refreshment. Large reinforcements expected from Pennsylvania never arrived. During the 18th orders were given for a renewal of the attack at daylight on the 19th.

"On the night of the 18th the enemy, after passing troops in the latter part of the day from the Virginia shore to their position behind Sharpsburg, as seen by our officers, suddenly formed the design of abandoning their position, and retreating across the river. As their line was but a short distance from the river, the evacuation presented but little difficulty, and was effected before daylight.

"About 2,700 of the enemy's dead were, under the direction of Major Davis, assistant inspector general, counted and buried upon the battle-field of Antietam. A portion of their dead had been previously buried by the enemy. This is conclusive evidence that the enemy sustained much greater loss than we.

"Thirteen guns, thirty-nine colors, upwards of fifteen thousand stand of small arms, and more than six thousand prisoners, were the trophies which attest the success of our army in the battles of South Mountain, Crampton's Gap, and Antietam.

"Not a single gun or color was lost by our army during these battles. "GEORGE B. McCLELLAN,
*Major-General Commanding.*"

The Maryland victories renewed the enthusiasm and veneration for General McClellan, who had thus with an army shattered and dispirited by repeated defeats and retreats, during its brief campaign in the Valley of Virginia under General Pope, conquered the flower of the rebel army. That success would attend the invasion was the confident belief of every Southern officer and soldier. The crossing of the Potomac had been long held out to them as an inducement to persevere in their treasonable cause, and the people and press of the South had for months urged and insisted upon the promise being fulfilled. What their plans were in the event of a successful occupation, may be gleaned from the following editorial, published in the Richmond *Despatch*, of the seventeenth of September, 1862.

"Let not a blade of grass." says the editor, "or a stalk of corn, or a barrel of flour, or a bushel of meal, or a sack of salt, or a horse, or a cow, or a hog, or a sheep, be left wherever they move along. Let vengeance be taken for all that has been done until retribution itself shall stand aghast. This is the country of the smooth-spoken, would-be gentleman, McClellan. He has caused a loss to us, in Virginia, of at least thirty thousand negroes, the most valuable property that a Virginian can own They have no negroes in Pennsylvania. Retaliation must therefore fall upon something else. A Dutch farmer has no negroes, but he has horses that can be seized, grain that can be confiscated, cattle that can be killed, and houses that can be burned. By advancing into Pennsylvania with rapidity, our army can easily get possession of the Pennsylvania Central Railroad, and break it down so thoroughly that it cannot be repaired in six months. They have already possession of the Baltimore and Ohio railroad and the York River railroad. By breaking down these and the railroad from Philadelphia to Baltimore, they will completely isolate both Washington and Baltimore. No reinforcements can reach them from either North or West, except by the Potomac and the bay."

When these prophecies of victory and confident boastings were made, it was not supposed that General McClellan would be the leader of the hosts against which they would be called upon to contend ; and when the fact was announced to the half-clad soldiers of the rebel army, the confidence in success with which they had started upon their march Northward, was changed to apprehensions of defeat, which were realized to the utmost.

The protracted sojourn which General Lee had promised to his followers, was unexpectedly terminated by the fatal check he received at South Mountain and Antietam, and when our cavalry on the morning of the nineteenth reached the bank of the Potomac, they discovered that nearly all the enemy's forces had crossed into Virginia during the night, their rear escaping under cover of eight batteries, placed in strong positions upon the elevated bluffs on the opposite bank. General Porter, commanding the Fifth Corps, ordered a detachment under General Griffin to cross the river at dark and carry the enemy's batteries. This was gallantly done under the fire of the enemy; several guns, caissons, etc., were taken, and their supports driven back half a mile.

The information obtained indicated that the mass of the enemy had retreated towards Winchester. To verify this, and to ascertain how far the enemy had retired, General Porter was authorized to detach from his corps, on the morning of the twentieth, a reconnoitering party in greater force. This detachment crossed the river at Shepherdstown, and advanced about a mile, when it was attacked by a large body of the enemy lying in ambush, and driven back across the river with considerable loss. This reconnoissance showed that the enemy was still in force on the Virginia bank of the Potomac, prepared to resist our further advance.

On the nineteenth, General Stuart made his appearance at Williamsport with some four thousand cavalry and six pieces of artillery. General Couch marched at once with his division, and a part of Pleasanton's cavalry, with Franklin's corps, within supporting distance, to Williamsport, and attacked the enemy, but they made their escape across the river.

General McClellan then despatched the following report to the General-in-Chief:

"HEAD-QUARTERS, ARMY OF THE POTOMAC,
"SHARPSBURG, *September* 19*th*, 1862.

"I have the honor to report that Maryland is entirely freed from the presence of the enemy, who has been driven across the Potomac. No fears need now be entertained for the safety of Pennsylvania. I shall at once occupy Harper's Ferry.

"GEORGE B. McCLELLAN,
"*Major-General Commanding.*

"*Major-General* H. W. HALLECK,
"*Commanding United States Army.*"

On the following day he received this answer :

"WASHINGTON, *September* 20*th*, 1862.—2 P.M.

"We are still left entirely in the dark in regard to your own movements and those of the enemy. This should not be so. You should keep me advised of both, so far as you know them.

"H. W. HALLECK,
"*General-in-Chief.*

"*Major-General* G. B. McCLELLAN."

To which General McClellan replied :

"HEAD-QUARTERS, ARMY OF THE POTOMAC,
"*Near Sharpsburg, September* 20*th*, 1862—8 P.M.

"Your telegram of to-day is received. I telegraphed you yesterday all I knew, and had nothing more to inform you of until this evening. Williams's corps (Banks's) occupied Maryland Heights at 1 P.M. to-day. The rest of the army is near here, except Couch's division, which is at this moment engaged with the enemy in front of Williamsport ; the enemy is retiring, *via* Charlestown and Martinsburg, on Winchester. He last night re-occupied Williamsport by a small force, but will be out of it by morning. I think he has a force of infantry near Shepherdstown.

"I regret that you find it necessary to couch every despatch I have the honor to receive from you in a spirit of fault-finding, and that you have not yet found leisure to say one word in commendation of the recent achievements of this army, or even to allude to them.

"I have abstained from giving the number of guns, colors, small arms, prisoners, etc., captured, until I could do so with some accuracy. I hope by to-morrow evening to be able to give at least an approximate statement.

"GEORGE B. McCLELLAN,
"*Major-General Commanding.*

"*Major-General* HALLECK,
"*General-in-Chief, Washington.*"

General McClellan also suggested, that as Lee must procure his supplies from Richmond, General Banks should send out a cavalry force from Washington to cut off his communications.

Maryland Heights were occupied by General Williams's corps on the same day, and on the twenty-second, General Sumner took possession of Harper's Ferry, and fortified it and the adjacent heights.

## WHY THE REBEL ARMY WAS NOT PURSUED.

To have followed the enemy would have been madness. Our losses in the two Maryland battles had sadly reduced the numbers of the rank and file; the brave fellows, who were left, although ready to obey whatever order their beloved commander might give them, were exhausted by the fatigues they had been compelled to endure since leaving Washington; a renewal of clothing was necessary, and the means of transportation were inadequate to furnish even a single day's subsistence in advance.

On the twenty-second, General McClellan telegraphed to General Halleck, informing him that as soon as possible the army should be re-organized, as it was necessary for its efficiency that the skeleton regiments should be filled up at once, and officers appointed to supply the existing vacancies.

On the twenty-third he telegraphed that Lee's army was still opposite to his position, and that there were indications that heavy reinforcements were moving towards them on the Winchester road. He also reported the disposition he had made of his troops to guard against a recrossing. General McClellan then continues:

"HEAD-QUARTERS, ARMY OF THE POTOMAC,
"NEAR SHEPHERDSTOWN, *September* 23rd, 1862—9.30 A.M.
"As I mentioned to you before, our army has been very much reduced by casualties in the recent battles, and in my judgment all the reinforcements of old troops that can possibly be dispensed with around Washington and other places should be

instantly pushed forward by rail to this army. A defeat at this juncture would be ruinous to our cause. I cannot think it possible that the enemy will bring any forces to bear upon Washington till after the question is decided here; but if he should, troops can soon be sent back from this army by rail to reinforce the garrison there."

"G. B. McCLELLAN,

"Major-General Commanding.

" MAJOR-GENERAL HALLECK:

" General-in-Chief, Washington."

On the 27th he made the following report:

" HEAD-QUARTERS, ARMY OF THE POTOMAC,

"September 27th, 1862—10 A.M.

"All the information in my possession goes to prove that the main body of the enemy is concentrated not far from Martinsburg, with some troops at Charlestown; not many in Winchester. Their movements of late have been an extension towards our right and beyond it. They are receiving reinforcements in Winchester. mainly, I think, of conscripts—perhaps entirely so.

" This army is not now in condition to undertake another campaign, nor to bring on another battle, unless great advantages are offered by some mistake of the enemy, or pressing military exigencies render it necessary. We are greatly deficient in officers. Many of the old regiments are reduced to mere skeletons. The new regiments need instruction. Not a day should be lost in filling the old regiments—our main dependence —and in supplying vacancies among the officers by promotion.

" My present purpose is to hold the army about as it is now, rendering Harper's Ferry secure and watching the river closely, intending to attack the enemy should he attempt to cross to this side.

" Our possession of Harper's Ferry gives us the great advantage of a secure debouche, but we cannot avail ourselves of it until the railroad bridge is finished, because we cannot otherwise supply a greater number of troops than we now have on the Virginia side at that point. When the river rises so that the enemy cannot cross in force, I purpose concentrating the army somewhere near Harper's Ferry, and then acting according to circumstances, viz: moving on Winchester, if from the position and attitude of the enemy we are likely to gain a great advantage by doing so, or else devoting a reasonable time to the organization of the army and instruction of the new troops, preparatory to an advance on whatever line may be determined. In any event, I regard it as absolutely necessary to send new regiments at once to the old corps, for purposes of instruction, and that the old regiments be filled at once. I have no fears as to an attack on Washington by the line of Manassas. Holding Harper's Ferry as I do, they will not run the risk of an attack on their flank and rear while they have the garrison of Washington in their front.

"I rather apprehend a renewal of the attempt in Maryland should the river remain low for a great length of time, and should they receive considerable addition to their force. I would be glad to have Peck's division as soon as possible. I am surprised that Sigel's men should have been sent to Western Virginia without my knowledge. The last I heard from you on the subject was that they were at my disposition. In the last battles the enemy was undoubtedly greatly superior to us in number, and it was only by very hard fighting that we gained the advantage we did. As it was, the result was at one period very doubtful, and we had all we could do to win the day. If the enemy receives considerable reinforcements and we none, it is possible that I may have too much on my hands in the next battle. My own view of the proper policy to be pursued is to retain in Washington merely the force necessary to garrison it, and to send every thing else available to reinforce this army. The railways give us the means of promptly reinforcing Washington should it become necessary. If I am reinforced, as I ask, and am allowed to take my own course, I will hold myself responsible for the safety of Washington. Several persons recently from Richmond say that there are no troops there except conscripts, and they few in number. I hope to give you details as to late battles by this evening. I am about starting again for Harper's Ferry.            "G. B. McCLELLAN,
                         "*Major-General Commanding.*

" MAJOR-GENERAL HALLECK,
    "*General-in-Chief, Washington.*"

The work of reorganizing the army and placing it in a condition for active service was begun by its commander at the earliest practicable moment, the different fords along an extent of one hundred and fifty miles at the same time being guarded, and reconnoissances being made by our cavalry, which, although sadly reduced in strength, and in the number of horses, performed much important service. When Stuart made his celebrated raid around our lines and into Pennsylvania, not more than eight hundred Union cavalrymen could be mounted for pursuit.

## GENERAL McCLELLAN ORDERED TO CROSS THE POTOMAC.

On the 5th of October, the division of General Cox (about 5,000 men) was ordered from his command to

Western Virginia, and two days later he received the following telegram :

"WASHINGTON, D. C., *October 6th*, 1862.

"I am instructed to telegraph you as follows : The President directs that you cross the Potomac and give battle to the enemy, or drive him south. Your army must move now, while the roads are good. If you cross the river between the enemy and Washington, and cover the latter by your operation, you can be reinforced with 30,000 men. If you move up the valley of the Shenandoah, not more than 12,000 or 15,000 can be sent to you. The President advises the interior line between Washington and the enemy, but does not order it. He is very desirous that your army move as soon as possible. You will immediately report what line you adopt, and when you intend to cross the river ; also to what point the reinforcements are to be sent. It is necessary that the plan of your operations be positively determined on, before orders are given for building bridges and repairing railroads. I am directed to add, that the Secretary of War and the general-in-chief fully concur with the President in these instructions.      "H. W. HALLECK,
                                                        "*General-in-Chief.*

"*Major-General* McCLELLAN."

## STUART'S REBEL RAID.

On the 10th of October, Stuart crossed the Potomac with two thousand cavalry and a battery of horse artillery, on a raid into Maryland and Pennsylvania. General McClellan, upon hearing of the daring feat, immediately made such dispositions of his troops—Cavalry, Artillery, and Infantry—as he thought would ensure the capture or destruction of the rebel cavalry, but, unfortunately, all the orders he had given were not carried out, and Stuart escaped.

## SCARCITY OF ARMY SUPPLIES AND HORSES

At the time General McClellan received the order of October 6th, to cross the river and attack the enemy, the army was wholly deficient in cavalry, and a large part of his troops were in want of shoes, blankets, and other indispensable articles of clothing, notwithstanding all the forts that had been made since the battle of Antietam, and even prior to that date, to refit the army with clothing, as well as horses. In referring to this scarcity and its causes, the General remarks as follows :

"I at once consulted with Colonel Ingalls, the chief quarter-master, who believed that the necessary articles could be supplied in about three days. Orders were immediately issued to the different commanders who had not already sent in their requisitions, to do so at once, and all the necessary steps were forthwith taken by me to insure a prompt delivery of the supplies. The requisitions were forwarded to the proper department at Washington, and I expected that the articles would reach our depots during the three days specified ; but day after day elapsed, and only a small portion of the clothing arrived. Corps commanders, upon receiving notice from the quartermasters that they might expect to receive their supplies at certain dates, sent the trains for them, which, after waiting, were compelled to return empty. Several instances occurred where these trains went back and forth from the camps to the depots, as often as four or five different times, without receiving their supplies, and I was informed by one corps commander that his wagon train had travelled over 150 miles, to and from the depots, before he succeeded in obtaining his clothing.

"The corps of General Franklin did not get its clothing until after it had crossed the Potomac, and was moving into Virginia. General Reynolds's corps was delayed a day at Berlin, to complete its supplies, and General Porter only completed his on reaching the vicinity of Harper's Ferry.

"I made every exertion in my power, and my quartermasters did the same, to have these supplies hurried forward rapidly; and I was repeatedly told that they had filled the requisitions at Washington, and that the supplies had been forwarded. But they did not come to us, and of course were inaccessible to the army. I did not fail to make frequent representation of this condition of things to the general-in-chief, and it appears that he referred the matter to the Quartermaster General, who constantly replied that the supplies had been promptly ordered. Notwithstanding this, they did not reach our depots."

Colonel Ingalls, Chief Quartermaster, in his report upon this subject, says :

"There was great delay in receiving our clothing. The orders were promptly given by me and approved by General Meigs, but the roads were slow to transport, particularly the Cumberland Valley road.

"For instance, clothing ordered to Hagerstown on the 7th of

October for the corps of Franklin, Porter, and Reynolds, did not arrive there until about the 18th, and by that time, of course, there were increased wants and changes in position of troops. The clothing of Sumner arrived in great quantities near the last of October, almost too late for issue, as the army was crossing into Virginia. We finally left 50,000 suits at Harper's Ferry, *partly on the cars just arrived*, and partly in store."

The condition of the cavalry was another cause of great annoyance and delay; and, to show how sadly they were in need of horses, we give the following extract from the official report on the subject, of Colonel Ingalls, Chief Quartermaster. He says:

"Immediately after the battle of Antietam, efforts were made to supply deficiencies in clothing and horses. Large requisitions were prepared and sent in. The artillery and cavalry required large numbers to cover losses sustained in battle, on the march, and by diseases. Both of these arms were deficient when they left Washington. A most violent and destructive disease made its appearance at this time, which put nearly 4,000 animals out of service. Horses reported perfectly well one day would be dead-lame the next, and it was difficult to foresee where it would end, or what number would cover the loss. They were attacked in the hoof and tongue. No one seemed able to account for the appearance of this disease. Animals kept at *rest* would recover in time, but *could not be worked*. I made application to send West and purchase horses at once, but it was refused, on the ground that the outstanding contracts provided for enough, *but they were not delivered sufficiently fast*, nor in sufficient numbers, until late in October and early in November. I was authorized to buy 2,500 late in October, but the delivery was not completed until in November, after we had reached Warrenton."

## CORRESPONDENCE WITH GENERAL HALLECK.

Knowing the solicitude of the President for an early movement, and sharing with him fully his anxiety for prompt action, on the 21st of October, General McClellan telegraphed to the General-in-Chief as follows:

"HEAD-QUARTERS, ARMY OF THE POTOMAC,
"*October* 21st, 1862.

"Since the receipt of the President's order to move on the enemy, I have been making every exertion to get this army supplied with clothing absolutely necessary for marching.

"This, I am happy to say, is now nearly accomplished.   I have also, during the same time, repeatedly urged upon you the importance of supplying cavalry and artillery horses to replace those broken down by hard service, and steps have been taken to insure a prompt delivery.

"Our cavalry, even when well supplied with horses, is much inferior in numbers to that of the enemy, but in efficiency has proved itself superior.   So forcibly has this been impressed upon our old regiments by repeated successes, that the men are fully persuaded that they are equal to twice their number of rebel cavalry.

"Exclusive of the cavalry force now engaged in picketing the river, I have not at present over about one thousand (1000) horses for service.   Officers have been sent in various directions to purchase horses, and I expect them soon.   Without more cavalry horses our communications, from the moment we march, would be at the mercy of the large cavalry force of the enemy, and it would not be possible for us to cover our flanks properly, or to obtain the necessary information of the position and movements of the enemy, in such a way as to insure success.   My experience has shown the necessity of a large and efficient cavalry force.

"Under the foregoing circumstances, I beg leave to ask whether the President desires me to march on the enemy at once, or to await the reception of the new horses, every possible step having been taken to insure their prompt arrival.

"GEORGE B. McCLELLAN,"<br>"Major-General Commanding.

" <i>Major-General</i> H. W. HALLECK,
    "<i>General-in-Chief, Washington.</i>"

On the same day General Halleck replied as follows :

" WASHINGTON, October 21st, 1862—3 P.M.

" Your telegram of 12 M. has been submitted to the President. He directs me to say that he has no change to make in his order of the 6th instant.

" If you have not been, and are not now, in condition to obey it, you will be able to show such want of ability.   The President does not expect impossibilities ; but he is very anxious that all this good weather should not be wasted in inactivity.   Telegraph when you will move, and on what lines you propose to march.

" H. W. HALLECK, General-in-Chief."

From the tenor of this despatch, General McClellan conceived that it was left to him to decide whether or not it was possible to advance with safety at that time, a responsibility which he says " I exercised with the more

10

confidence, in view of the strong assurances of his trust in me as commander of that army, with which the President had seen fit to honor me." Horses were still wanting, and he designated the 1st of November as the earliest date upon which he could commence the forward movement. To advance before that date he considered would be attended with the highest degree of peril, with great suffering and sickness among the men, and with imminent danger of being cut off from supplies by the superior cavalry force of the enemy, and with no reasonable prospect of gaining any advantage over him.

## A CONVINCING RESPONSE.

General Halleck having expressed his opinion that there had been no such want of supplies in the army as to prevent an advance, General McClellan responded in the following convincing language :

"I have found it impossible to resist the force of my own convictions, that the commander of an army who, from the time of its organization, has for eighteen months been in constant communication with its officers and men, the greater part of the time engaged in active service in the field, and who has exercised this command in many battles, must certainly be considered competent to determine whether his army is in proper condition to advance on the enemy or not; and he must necessarily possess greater facilities for forming a correct judgment in regard to the wants of his men, and the condition of his supplies, than the general-in-chief in his office at Washington city. The movement from Washington into Maryland, which culminated in the battles of South Mountain and Antietam, was not a part of an offensive campaign, with the object of the invasion of the enemy's territory and an attack upon his capital, but was defensive in its purposes, although offensive in its character, and would be technically called a 'defensive-offensive campaign.'

"It was undertaken at a time when our army had experienced severe defeats, and its object was to preserve the national capital and Baltimore, to protect Pennsylvania from invasion, and to drive the enemy out of Maryland. These purposes were fully and finally accomplished by the battle of Antietam, which brought the army of the Potomac into what might be termed an accidental position on the upper Potomac. Having gained the immediate object of the campaign, the first thing to be done was to insure Maryland from a return of the enemy; the second, to prepare our own army, exhausted by a series of severe battles, destitute to a great extent of supplies, and very deficient in artillery and cavalry horses, for a definite offensive movement, and to determine upon the line of operations for a further advance. At the time of the battle of Antietam the Potomac was very low, and presented a comparatively weak line of defence unless watched by large masses of troops. The re-occupation of Harper's Ferry, and the disposition of troops above that point, rendered the line of the Potomac secure against every thing except cavalry raids. No time was lost in placing the army in proper condition for an advance, and the circumstances which caused the delay after the battle of Antietam have been fully enumerated elsewhere. I never regarded Harper's Ferry or its vicinity as a proper base of operations for a movement upon Richmond. I still considered the line of the Peninsula as the true approach, but, for obvious reasons, did not make any proposal to return to it.

"On the 6th of October, as stated above, I was ordered by the President, through his general-in-chief, to cross the Potomac and give battle to the enemy, or drive him south. Two lines were presented for my choice:

"1st. Up the valley of the Shenandoah, in which case I was to have 12,000 to 15,000 additional troops.

"2d. To cross between the enemy and Washington—that is, east of the Blue Ridge—in which event I was to be reinforced with 30,000 men.

"At first I determined to adopt the line of the Shenandoah, for these reasons: The Harper's Ferry and Winchester railroad and the various turnpikes converging upon Winchester afforded superior facilities for supplies. Our cavalry being weak, this line of communication could be more easily protected. There was no advantage in interposing at that time the Blue Ridge and the Shenandoah between the enemy and myself. At the period in question the Potomac was still very low, and I apprehended that, if I crossed the river below Harper's Ferry, the enemy would promptly check the movement by re-crossing into Maryland, at the same time covering his rear by occupying in strong force the passes leading through the Blue Ridge from the southeast into Shenandoah valley. I anticipated, as the result of the first course, that Lee would fight me near Winchester, if he could do so under favorable circumstances; or else that he would abandon the lower Shenandoah, and leave the army of the Potomac free to act upon some other line of operations. If he abandoned the Shenandoah, he would naturally fall back upon his railway communications. I have since been confirmed in the belief that, if I had crossed the Potomac below Harper's Ferry in the early part of October, General Lee would have re-crossed into Maryland.

" As above explained, the army was not in condition to move until late in October, and in the meantime circumstances had changed. The period had arrived when a sudden and great rise of the Potomac might be looked for at any moment; the season of bad roads and difficult movements was approaching, which would naturally deter the enemy from exposing himself very far from his base, and his movements all appeared to indicate a falling back from the river towards his supplies. Under these circumstances, I felt at liberty to disregard the possibility of the enemy's re-crossing the Potomac, and determined to select the line east of the Blue Ridge, feeling convinced that it would secure me the largest accession of force, and the most cordial support of the President, whose views, from the beginning, were in favor of that line.

" The subject of the defence of the line of the upper Potomac, after the advance of the main army, had long occupied my attention. I desired to place Harper's Ferry and its dependencies in a strong state of defence, and frequently addressed the general-in-chief upon the subject of the erection of field-works and permanent bridges there, asking for the funds necessary to accomplish the purpose. Although I did my best to explain, as clearly as I was able, that I did not wish to erect permanent works of masonry, and that neither the works nor the permanent bridges had any reference to the advance of the army, but solely to the permanent occupation of Harper's Ferry, I could never make the general-in-chief understand my wishes, but was refused the funds necessary to erect the field-works, on the ground that there was no appropriation for the erection of permanent fortifications; and was not allowed to build the permanent bridge, on the ground that the main army could not be delayed in its movements until its completion. Of course I never thought of delaying the advance of the army for that purpose, and so stated repeatedly."

## ASKS HOW THE UPPER POTOMAC IS TO BE GUARDED.

On the 25th of October General McClellan sent to the General-in-Chief the following telegram :

" HEAD-QUARTERS, ARMY OF THE POTOMAC,
" October 25th, 1862—10.45 P.M.

" As the moment is at hand for the advance of this army, a question arises for the decision of the general-in-chief, which, although perhaps impliedly decided by the President in his letter of the 13th, should be clearly presented by me, as I do not regard it as in my province to determine it.

" This question is the extent to which the line of the Potomac should be guarded, after the army leaves, in order to cover Maryland and Pennsylvania from invasion by large or small parties of the enemy.

"It will always be somewhat difficult to guard the immediate line of the river, owing to its great extent and the numerous passages which exist.

"It has long appeared to me that the best way of covering this line would be by occupying Front Royal, Strasburg, Wardensville and Moorefield, or the debouches of the several valleys in which they are situated.

"These points, or suitable places in their vicinity, should be strongly intrenched and permanently held. One great advantage of this arrangement would be the covering the Baltimore and Ohio railroad, and an essential part of the system would be the construction of the link of railway from Winchester to Strasburg, and the rebuilding of the Manassas Gap railway bridge over the Shenandoah.

"The intrenchment of Manassas Junction would complete the system for the defence of the approaches to Washington and the upper Potomac. Many months ago I recommended this arrangement; in fact, gave orders for it to be carried into effect. I still regard it as essential under all circumstances.

"The views of the chief engineer of this army, in regard to the defences and garrison of Harper's Ferry and its defences, are in your possession.

"The only troops under my command, outside of the organization of the army of the Potomac, are the Maryland brigade, under General Kenley; the Fifty-fourth Pennsylvania, Colonel Voss; Twelfth Illinois cavalry, and Colonel Davis's Eighth New York cavalry; total 2,894 infantry, one battery, and about 900 cavalry men.

"There are also two of my regiments of cavalry (about 750 men), guarding the Baltimore and Ohio railroad between Hancock and Cumberland.

"As I have no department, and command simply an active army in the field, my responsibility for the safety of the line of the Potomac and the States north of it must terminate the moment I advance so far beyond that line as to adopt another for my base of operations. The question for the general-in-chief to decide, and which I regard as beyond my province, is this:

"1st. Shall the safety of Harper's Ferry and the line of the Potomac be regarded as assured by the advance of the army south of the Blue Ridge, and the line left to take care of itself?

"2d. If it is deemed necessary to hold the line, or that hereinbefore indicated in advance of it, how many troops shall be placed there, at what points (and in what numbers and of what composition at each), and where shall they be supplied—*i. e.*, from the army, or from other sources?

"Omitting the detached troops mentioned above, and the

arison, may be reduced so much as to be inadequate to the purposes contemplated. If it is preserved intact, Maryland, Pennsylvania, and the Baltimore and Ohio railroad may be unduly exposed.

"An important element in the solution of this problem is the fact that a great portion of Bragg's army is probably now at liberty to unite itself with Lee's command.

"I commence crossing the river at Berlin in the morning, and must ask a prompt decision of the questions proposed herein.   "GEORGE B. McCLELLAN,
*"Major-General Commanding."*

To which he received the following reply from General Halleck:

"Since you left Washington I have advised and suggested in relation to your movements, but I have given you no orders; I do not give you any now. The Government has entrusted you with defeating and driving back the rebel army in your front. I shall not attempt to control you in the measures you may adopt for that purpose. You are informed of my views, but the President has left you at liberty to adopt them or not, as you may deem best.

"You will also exercise your own discretion in regard to what points on the Potomac and the Baltimore and Ohio railroad are to be occupied or fortified. I will only add that there is no appropriation for *permanent* intrenchments on that line. Moreover, I think it will be time enough to decide upon fortifying Front Royal, Strasburg, Wardensville, and Moorefield, when the enemy is driven south of them, and they come into our possession."

On the 29th, General McClellan sent the following:

"HEAD-QUARTERS, ARMY OF THE POTOMAC,
*"October 29th, 1862—1.15 P.M.*

to decide what steps should be taken to guard the line of the

Potomac when this army leaves here. To this I received your reply that I had been entrusted by the President with defeating and driving away the rebel army; that you had given me no orders heretofore—did not give me any then, etc. Under these circumstances I have only to make such arrangements for guarding this extended line as the means at my disposal will permit, at the same time keeping in view the supreme necessity of maintaining the moving army in adequate force to meet the rebel army before us.

"The dispositions I have ordered are as follows, viz: Ten thousand men to be left at Harper's Ferry; one brigade of infantry in front of Sharpsburg; Kenley's brigade of infantry at Williamsport; Kelley's brigade, including Colonel Campbell's Fifty-fourth Pennsylvania infantry, at Cumberland; and between that point and Hancock. I have also left four small cavalry regiments to patrol and watch the river and the Baltimore and Ohio railroad from Cumberland down to Harper's Ferry.

"I do not regard this force as sufficient to cover securely this great extent of line, but I do not feel justified in detaching any more troops from my moving columns; I would, therefore, recommend that some new regiments of infantry and cavalry be sent to strengthen the forces left by me.

"There should be a brigade of infantry and section of artillery in the vicinity of Cherry run, another brigade at Hancock, an additional brigade at Williamsport, one regiment at Hagerstown, and one at Chambersburg, with a section of artillery at each place, if possible. This is on the supposition that the enemy retain a considerable cavalry force west of the Blue Ridge; if they go east of it, the occupation of the points named in my despatch of the 25th instant will obviate the necessity of keeping many of these troops on the river.

"There are now several hundred of our wounded, including General Richardson, in the vicinity of Sharpsburg, that cannot possibly be moved at present.

"I repeat, that I do not look upon the forces I have been able to leave from this army as sufficient to prevent cavalry raids into Maryland and Pennsylvania, as cavalry is the only description of troops adequate to this service, and I am, as you are aware, deficient in this arm. "GEORGE B. McCLELLAN,

"*Major-General Commanding.*

"MAJOR-GENERAL HALLECK,
"*General-in-Chief, Washington.*"

To which he received on the 30th this reply:

"WASHINGTON, *October 30th,* 1862—11.30 A.M.
"Your telegram of yesterday was received late last evening. The troops proposed for Thoroughfare Gap will be sent to that place whenever you are in position for their co-operation, as

previously stated, but no new regiments can be sent from here to the upper Potomac. The guarding of that line is left to your own discretion with the troops now under your command.

"H. W. HALLECK, *General-in-Chief.*

"*Major-General* GEORGE B. McCLELLAN."

General McClellan accordingly left the Twelfth-corps at Harper's Ferry, detaching one brigade to the vicinity of Sharpsburg. General Morell was placed in command of the line from the mouth of the Antietam to Cumberland, and General Slocum in command of Harper's Ferry and the line east of the mouth of the Antietam.

## THE ADVANCE INTO VIRGINIA.

On the 25th of October the pontoon bridge at Berlin was constructed, there being already one across the Potomac, and another across the Shenandoah, at Harper's Ferry. On the 26th two divisions of the Ninth corps, and Pleasanton's brigade of cavalry, crossed at Berlin and occupied Lovettsville. The First, Sixth, and Ninth corps, the cavalry, and the reserve artillery, crossed at Berlin between the 26th of October and the 2d of November. The Second and Fifth corps crossed at Harper's Ferry between the 29th of October and the 1st of November.

The plan of campaign during this advance was to move the army parallel to the Blue Ridge, taking Warrenton as the point of direction for the main army; seizing each pass on the Blue Ridge by detachments, as we approached it, and guarding them after we had passed as long as they would enable the enemy to trouble our communications with the Potomac. He expected to unite with the Eleventh corps and Sickles's division near Thoroughfare Gap. Harper's Ferry and Berlin were depended upon for supplies until the Manassas Gap railway was reached; when that occurred the passes in our rear were to be abandoned, and the army massed ready for action or movement in any direction.

It was the intention of the commander of the Army of the Potomac, if, upon reaching either of the passes, he found that the enemy were in force between it and the Potomac in the valley of the Shenandoah, to move into the valley and endeavor to gain their rear.

He says he hardly hoped to accomplish this, but did expect that by striking in between Culpeper Court-House and Little Washington, he could either separate their army and beat them in detail, or else force them to concentrate as far back as Gordonsville, and thus place the Army of the Potomac in position either to adopt the Fredericksburg line of advance upon Richmond, or to be removed to the Peninsula.

Having safely crossed the Potomac, the various corps moved gradually along the route prescribed, occupying village after village, and repulsing the enemy wherever they were daring enough to attempt to impede the march of the army.

On the seventh of November, the following was the position of the troops:

The First, Second and Fifth corps, reserve artillery, and general head-quarters, at Warrenton; the Ninth corps on the line of the Rappahannock, in the vicinity of Waterloo; the Sixth corps at New Baltimore; the Eleventh corps at New Baltimore, Gainesville, and Thoroughfare Gap; Sickles's division of the Third corps, on the Orange and Alexandria railroad, from Manassas Junction to Warrenton Junction; Pleasanton across the Rappahannock at Amissville, Jefferson, etc., with his pickets at Hazel river, facing Longstreet, six miles from Culpeper Court-House; Bayard near Rappahannock Station.

The army was thus massed near Warrenton, ready to act in any required direction, and in admirable condition and spirits. Indeed, General McClellan says he doubts whether during the entire period he had the honor to com-

mand the Army of the Potomac, it was in such excellent
condition to fight a great battle.   The best information indicated that Longstreet was immediately in front near
Culpeper; Jackson, with one, perhaps both, of the Hills,
near Chester and Thornton's gaps, with the mass of their
force west of the Blue Ridge; and the reports from General Pleasanton on the advance indicated the possibility of
separating the two wings of the enemy's forces, and either
beating Longstreet separately, or forcing him to fall back
at least upon Gordonsville, to effect his junction with the
rest of the army.

## "LITTLE MAC" RELIEVED FROM COMMAND.

The well-concerted plans of the able strategist were,
however, to meet with an unexpected impediment, and
the expectations of his officers and men that the hour of
victory was again at hand, were to be suddenly disappointed.   Orders had been issued for the movements on
the two subsequent days, which were believed would lead
to a brilliant success, or series of successes, when an officer
arrived from Washington with an order dated on the fifth,
relieving the idol of the Army of the Potomac from his
command, and directing him to report at Trenton, New
Jersey, and designating General Burnside as his successor.
It was late on the night of the seventh, when he received
the unexpected order, but he immediately obeyed its provisions.   Before leaving his head-quarters, he penned the
following modest and patriotic address to his Army :

## HIS FAREWELL ADDRESS TO THE ARMY OF THE POTOMAC.

" HEAD-QUARTERS, ARMY OF THE POTOMAC,
" CAMP NEAR RECTORTOWN. *Nov. 7th*, 1862.
"*Officers and Soldiers of the Army of the Potomac:*
"An order of the President devolves upon Major-General
Burnside the command of this army.   In parting from you, I
cannot express the love and gratitude I bear you.   As an army

you have grown up under my care.  In you I have never found doubt or coldness.  The battles you have fought under my command will proudly live in our nation's history.  The glory you have achieved, our mutual perils and fatigues, the graves of our comrades fallen in battle and by disease, the broken forms of those whom wounds and sickness have disabled—the strongest associations which can exist among men—unite us still by an indissoluble tie.  We shall ever be comrades in supporting the Constitution of our country and the nationality of its people.

" GEORGE B. McCLELLAN,<br>
" <i>Major-General, U. S. A.</i>"

## HE BIDS ADIEU TO HIS OFFICERS AND SOLDIERS, AND LEAVES FOR TRENTON.

On the Sunday evening previous to his departure, the officers assembled at his tent for the purpose of bidding adieu to their gallant leader, and from the eyes of many of their number dropped scalding tears of sorrow and regret. The following day he reviewed the army of heroes who had followed him through many months and many scenes, and as he rode along their lines, pronouncing the last farewell, wild and unrestrained huzzas rent the air ; and they rushed from the ranks and in every conceivable manner gave evidence of their devotion and confidence, and of their annoyance and regret at the separation.  On the tenth he took the railroad cars at Warrenton, and upon reaching Warrenton Junction was again received with the most gratifying manifestations.  In answer to the unanimous request for a parting speech, General McClellan said : "I wish you to stand by General Burnside as you have stood by me, and all will be well.  Good-bye."

At other stations on the road he was also greeted with enthusiastic cheering.  Reaching Washington, he quietly went to the Philadelphia depot, and then passing through the city of his nativity without tarrying, much to the disappointment of hosts of admirers, he proceeded to Trenton.

## OFFICIAL REPORT OF THE ARMY OF THE POTOMAC.

We cannot conclude the sketch of General McClellan's

active service with the Army of the Potomac better than by publishing the following from his Report to the War Department:

"This Report is, in fact, the history of the Army of the Potomac.

"During the period occupied in the organization of that army, it served as a barrier against the advance of a lately victorious enemy, while the fortifications of the capital were in progress; and under the discipline which it then received it acquired strength, education, and some of that experience which is necessary to success in active operations, and which enabled it afterwards to sustain itself under circumstances trying to the most heroic men. Frequent skirmishes occurred along the lines, conducted with great gallantry, which inured our troops to the realities of war.

"The army grew into shape but slowly; and the delays which attended on the obtaining of arms, continuing late into the winter of 1861-'62, were no less trying to the soldiers than to the people of the country. Even at the time of the organization of the Peninsula campaign, some of the finest regiments were without rifles; nor were the utmost exertions on the part of the military authorities adequate to overcome the obstacles to active service.

"When, at length, the army was in condition to take the field, the Peninsula campaign was planned, and entered upon with enthusiasm by officers and men. Had this campaign been followed up as it was designed, I cannot doubt that it would have resulted in a glorious triumph to our arms, and the permanent restoration of the power of the government in Virginia and North Carolina, if not throughout the revolting States. It was, however, otherwise ordered, and instead of reporting a victorious campaign, it has been my duty to relate the heroism of a reduced army, sent upon an expedition into an enemy's country, there to abandon one and originate another and new plan of campaign, which might and would have been successful if supported with appreciation of its necessities, but which failed because of the repeated failure of promised support, at the most critical, and, as it proved, the most fatal moments. That heroism surpasses ordinary description. Its illustration must be left for the pen of the historian in times of calm reflection, when the nation shall be looking back to the past from the midst of peaceful days.

"For me, now, it is sufficient to say that my comrades were victors on every field save one, and there the endurance of but little more than a single corps accomplished the object of the fighting, and by securing to the army its transit to the James, left to the enemy a ruinous and barren victory.

"The Army of the Potomac was first reduced by the withdrawal from my command of the division of General Blenker, which was ordered to the Mountain department, under General Fremont. We had scarcely landed on the Peninsula when it was further reduced by a despatch revoking a previous order giving me command at Fortress Monroe, and under which I had expected to take ten thousand men from that point to aid in our operations. Then, when under fire before the defences of Yorktown, we received the news of the withdrawal of General McDowell's corps of about 35,000 men. This completed the overthrow of the original plan of the campaign. About one-third of my entire army (five divisions out of fourteen, one of the nine remaining being but little larger than a brigade) was thus taken from me. Instead of a rapid advance which I had planned, aided by a flank movement up the York river, it was only left to besiege Yorktown. That siege was successfully conducted by the army, and when these strong works at length yielded to our approaches, the troops rushed forward to the sanguinary but successful battle of Williamsburg, and thus opened an almost unresisted advance to the banks of the Chickahominy. Richmond lay before them surrounded with fortifications, and guarded by an army larger than our own; but the prospect did not shake the courage of the brave men who composed my command. Relying still on the support which the vastness of our undertaking and the grand results depending on our success seemed to insure us, we pressed forward. The weather was stormy beyond precedent; the deep soil of the Peninsula was at times one vast morass; the Chickahominy rose to a higher stage than had been known for years before. Pursuing the advance, the crossings were seized, and the right wing extended to effect a junction with reinforcements now promised and earnestly desired, and upon the arrival of which the complete success of the campaign seemed clear. The brilliant battle of Hanover Court-House was fought, which opened the way for the first corps, with the aid of which, had it come, we should then have gone into the enemy's capital. It never came. The bravest army could not do more, under such overwhelming disappointment, than the Army of the Potomac then did. Fair Oaks attests their courage and endurance when they hurled back, again and again, the vastly superior masses of the enemy. But mortal men could not accomplish the miracle that seemed to have been expected of them. But one course was left—a flank march in the face of a powerful enemy to another and better base—one of the most hazardous movements in war. The Army of the Potomac, holding its own safety and almost the safety of our cause, in its hands, was equal to the occasion. The seven days are classical in American history; those days in which the noble soldiers of the Union and Constitution fought an outnumbering enemy by day, and retreated from successive victories by night, through a week of battle, closing the terrible series of conflicts with the ever-memorable victory of Malvern, where they drove back, beaten and shattered, the entire eastern army of the confederacy, and thus secured for themselves a place of rest and a point for a new advance upon the capital from the banks of the James. Richmond was still within our grasp, had the Army of the Potomac been reinforced and permitted to advance. But counsels, which I cannot but think subsequent events proved unwise, prevailed in Washington, and we were ordered to abandon the campaign. Never did soldiers better deserve the thanks of a nation than the Army of the Potomac for the deeds of the Peninsula campaign, and although that meed was withheld from them by the authorities, I am persuaded they have received the applause of the American people.

" The army of the Potomac was recalled from within sight of Richmond, and incorporated with the army of Virginia. The disappointments of the campaign on the Peninsula had not damped their ardor or diminished their patriotism. They fought well, faithfully, gallantly, under General Pope ; yet were compelled to fall back on Washington, defeated and almost demoralized.

" The enemy, no longer occupied in guarding his own capital, poured his troops northward, entered Maryland, threatened Pennsylvania, and even Washington itself. Elated by his recent victories, and assured that our troops were disorganized and dispirited, he was confident that the seat of war was now permanently transferred to the loyal States, and that his own exhausted soil was to be relieved from the burden of supporting two hostile armies. But he did not understand the spirit which animated the soldiers of the Union. I shall not, nor can I living, forget that when I was ordered to the command of the troops for the defence of the capital, the soldiers, with whom I had shared so much of the anxiety, and pain, and suffering of the war, had not lost their confidence in me as their commander. They sprang to my call with all their ancient vigor, discipline, and courage. I led them into Maryland. Fifteen days after they had fallen back defeated before Washington, they vanquished the enemy on the rugged height of South Mountain, pursued him to the hard-fought field of Antietam, and drove him, broken and disappointed, across the Potomac into Virginia.

" The army had need of rest. After the terrible experiences of battles and marches, with scarcely an interval of repose, which they had gone through from the time of leaving for the Peninsula ; the return to Washington ; the defeat in Virginia ; the victory at South Mountain, and again at Antietam, it was not surprising that they were in a large degree destitute of the absolute necessaries to effective duty. Shoes were worn out ; blankets were lost ; clothing was in rags : in short, the army was unfit for active service, and an interval for rest and equipment was necessary. When the slowly forwarded supplies came to us I led the army across the river, renovated, refreshed, in good order and discipline, and followed the retreating foe to a position where I was confident of decisive victory, when, in the midst of the movement, while my advance guard was actually in contact with the enemy, I was removed from the command.

"I am devoutly grateful to God that my last campaign with this brave army was crowned with a victory which saved the nation from the greatest peril it had then undergone. I have not accomplished my purpose if, by this report, the army of the Potomac is not placed high on the roll of the historic armies of the world. Its deeds ennoble the nation to which it belongs. Always ready for battle, always firm, steadfast, and trustworthy, I never called on it in vain; nor will the nation ever have cause to attribute its want of success, under myself, or under other commanders, to any failure of patriotism or bravery in that noble body of American soldiers.

"No man can justly charge upon any portion of that army, from the commanding general to the private, any lack of devotion to the service of the United States government, and to the cause of the Constitution and the Union. They have proved their fealty in much sorrow, suffering, danger, and through the very shadow of death. Their comrades dead on all the fields where we fought have scarcely more claim to the honor of a nation's reverence than their survivors to the justice of a nation's gratitude.

"GEORGE B. McCLELLAN,
"*Major-General, United States Army.*"

## OVATIONS TENDERED AT THE NORTH.

Upon his arrival at Trenton, he was received with all the enthusiasm which the people of that city could give to such a distinguished General, and from all parts of the North came letters and verbal messages requesting his presence in different cities, towns, and hamlets, and beseeching that he would afford the friends and relatives of the brave soldiers, who fought so long under his banner, an opportunity to shake him by the hand.

However, these complimentary invitations were refused; but subsequently, upon visiting New York and some of the points from whence invitations and deputations had come, he was tendered ovations of the most gratifying character.

Up to the present time (February, 1864) General Mc-
Clellan has not been assigned to another command, but
has been living in rural retirement, in New Jersey.

## RUMORS OF RETURN TO COMMAND—THE EFFECT AT GETTYSBURG.

From time to time rumor has asserted that he was again
to be ordered to the field, but, to the disappointment of
his friends and admirers in civil and military life, the reports have been without foundation.   Especially was this
disappointment experienced at and before the battle of
Gettysburg.   When our troops, after long and forced
marches, had arrived within attacking distance of the
rebel army, and every arrangement had been perfected
for an early conflict, with the speed of an electric current,
passed from regiment to regiment, the report that " Little
Mac" had been sent for in that hour of the country's peril,
to lead the army against the invaders.   Another, and apparently no less authentic rumor, had it, that he was advancing from Harrisburg at the head of a large body of
Pennsylvania militia, to reinforce the Army of the Potomac;
and, consequently, between the two, the men confidently
believed that their favorite leader was really near at hand,
and, incited by the belief, fought with redoubled determination and valor, and achieved a brilliant victory.   It is
said that even distinguished generals, remarking the
beneficial effects resulting from the rumors, aided in circulating the deceptive stories.

## THE SOLDIERS' LOVE FOR "LITTLE MAC."

It is useless to deny that, although the soldiers have
implicit confidence in his gallant successor, they still look
forward to the day when they believe their old commander will return ; and this feeling has pervaded their
ranks since the day he bade them farewell in the valley of Virginia.   A correspondent of a Western journal,

writing some months since from Falmouth, thus confirms the statement: " I asked Colonel ——," he writes, " whether the stories of the attachment of the Army of the Potomac to McClellan were true, and he said they certainly were true—that the Army loved General McClellan, and longed to have him again for their Commander, and that there was a positive faith among the soldiers that it would be his destiny yet to come back and lead them.   The feeling for him was especially strong in the old regiments that had served long under him, and the new regiments were infected with it."

Like all prominent men, in whatever sphere they display unusual ability or talent, General McClellan has his personal and political enemies, but even many of the latter bear testimony to his sagacity, industry, energy and perseverance.   When General Scott designated him as the proper person to succeed him in the command of the armies of the Union, he did so because he had been convinced by constant observation of the superior capacity of the young officer for the responsible position.

To use the language of a military writer, " The simple and unostentatious habits, the industrious, diligent, strict but just manner, in which he attends to the regular business of his army, the precision of his orders, the indefatigable energy, the cool, deliberate courage and self-possession with which he moves and directs operations under the hottest fire ; the never-failing word of encouragement and cheer in the battle, and of consolation in the hospital ; the swiftness with which he moves ; the eagle-eye that, always calm, surveys the situation at a glance, and devises the means to become its master ; show the characteristic qualities of General McClellan, and prove that they are the same which upon the heights of " Cerro-Gordo," elicited the official commendation of General Scott ; which at the battle of Contreras, August 29th, 1847, made him

11

spring forward to take the post of the killed commander
of a howitzer battery and fight it with so much spirit and
ability, that General Twiggs recommended him for
efficiency and gallantry, and for which he was immediately
brevetted first Lieutenant of Engineers; which at the
assault upon the Castle of Chapultepec made General
Worth recommend him for gallantry of conduct and
signal service as an engineer; which, at Mexico, made
him push the first officer into the city, entering at three
o'clock in the morning at the head of his sappers and
miners under the most dreadful of all attacks, the firing
from the windows and house-tops, kept up by two
thousand released convicts; when he was for gallant and
meritorious conduct at Chapultepec and Mexico brevetted
Captain, an honor he had declined when conferred upon
him on the 12th of September; '*en-fin*' the same rare
qualities of conspicuous gallantry, daring and professional
excellence by which George B. McClellan had won his
captaincy upon bloody fields before he was twenty-two
years old."

## AN IMPARTIAL OPINION OF McCLELLAN.

In conclusion, we quote the following summary of General McClellan's services. It is from "The Round Table,"
a weekly journal of the highest character, free from all
partisan bias, and sustained by a corps of the ablest liter-
ary, political, and military writers. It condenses into
comparatively few words the *gist* of the reports we have
given, and will unquestionably be the verdict of history.

"It was charged against that officer (General McClellan) that when he held the position of General-in-Chief,
he really had no plans adequate to the occasion, and this
belief, more than any thing else, led to the acquiescence
of the country in his removal from the supreme control of
military affairs. Subsequent revelations have proved that

he had a continental scheme equal to the occasion, and which would in all probability have ended the rebellion, or, at the worst, the close of the year 1862 would have found us where we now are at the close of 1863.

General McClellan, in the military policy he had marked out for himself, determined to strike at five strategic points, or rather he had in view five separate campaigns, any one of which would have inflicted a heavy blow upon the rebellion, but which, combined and successful, could hardly have failed to end it.    He first equipped an army with the object of capturing the rebel capital, not because of its strategic importance, but from the moral effect such capture would have produced both in the Confederacy and abroad.    He next designed and prepared for an expedition to capture Charleston, not on account of its strategic importance, but also for the moral effect which would result from the possession by the Union forces of that point where the rebellion originated.    In his instructions to General Buell, it will be found that he early appreciated the importance of immediately occupying East Tennessee, with a view of isolating the South Atlantic from the Gulf States, and getting possession of the range of mountains that jut into the rebel territory and permanently divide the region lying between the Atlantic and the Mississippi.    All his instructions and orders to General Buell had this object clearly in view.    The capture of the Tennessee valley, which was subsequently made, was no part of his plan, and, as we will presently show, was a questionable benefit to the Union cause.    Had East Tennessee been taken possession of in the spring of 1862, and the loyal people there relieved from the tyranny of the rebel government, the dreadful battles which have since drenched with blood the soil of Tennessee and Northern Georgia would never have been fought, nor would any of the many invasions of Kentucky by Bragg and Morgan have occurred.    The war, in fact,

would have been half ended before it had fairly begun.
Another of the strategic movements planned by General
McClellan will be found in his instructions to General Butler
previous to the capture of New Orleans. This document is
a marvel of military sagacity, and places its author among
the first cabinet strategists of the age. He did not desire
the capture of the city until General Butler had at least
twenty-eight thousand men under his command. He pre-
dicted that Forts St. Philip and Jackson were the only
impediments to the possession of the city, and the event
proved the correctness of his judgment. But the taking of
New Orleans was only a small part of the campaign he had
marked out. Butler was directed to seize, immediately on
entering the city, the avenues of approach to it; then so
much of Louisiana as was necessary to support New
Orleans and keep at a distance the rebel armies; after
which he was instructed to take possession of Natchez
and *Jackson, the capital of Mississippi.* This last instruction, as we see by what subsequently occurred at Vicksburg, Port Hudson, and all along Southern Mississippi,
was of supreme importance. Had General Butler been
able to obey orders and seize the capital of Mississippi,
our military annals might not have been made glorious by
the sieges of Vicksburg and Port Hudson; but within three
months after the capture of New Orleans the aspect of the
military map of the Southwest would have been as favorable as it now is, after the hideous waste of blood and treasure which it has cost to rescue that part of the country
from the grasp of the rebellion. General McClellan's final
object in the movements he contemplated, as will be seen
by his report, was the deliverance of the line of the Mississippi from the grasp of the rebel government.

    " But he was relieved from command prematurely. The
time had not arrived, nor had the preparations been made,
for moving the armies he had designed to act in concert

against the rebellion when Mr. Lincoln took from him the
supreme control of the army and administered military
affairs according to the ideas of leading members of the
administration. General McClellan did not design that
the grand campaign should commence till April, and his
judgment has been singularly confirmed by the history of
the war since then. All the movements of our armies in
the winter of 1861, and the early spring of the following
year were premature. Our victories, from the untimely
fruit they bore, were really disasters in disguise. Even
the capture of Donelson, and the army it contained, is to
be set down in our future annals as the most serious blow
the Union cause received in the early history of the war.
General McClellan's object in postponing the movements
of our armies until the early part of April was, that they
could all be simultaneous—that in one fell swoop General
Buell should capture East Tennessee; General Sherman,
Charleston; General Butler, New Orleans, Vicksburg, and
Jackson; General Halleck, the line of the Mississippi;
and himself the rebel capital. Had all these movements
been successful, which it would not have been unreason-
able to expect, there would have been no rebellion after
July 4th, 1862. Had any one of them been successful, it
would have been a cruel blow to the Confederacy. But
the opening of the campaign in the West in January and
February, the capture of Forts Henry and Donelson, and
the operations upon the upper Mississippi—all of which
were against the advice and in defiance of the plans of
the then commander-in-chief of the army—spoiled the
whole grand campaign. The rebellion was then a mere
shell. Davis subsequently acknowledged in his message
that he had attempted to guard too many points. The
Southern army was composed only of volunteers, and had
the attacks been simultaneous, the outer walls of the rebellion would have been broken down with comparative

ease.     he capture of Donelson spoiled every thing.   The Union armies in other quarters were in no condition for rapidly following up the blow.   The rebels became thoroughly alarmed.   The same February that saw the victory of Donelson, placed upon the legislative records of the Richmond government a stringent conscription law.   New lines of defence were taken up.   Every man that could be raised was pressed into the ranks.   Every thing was done that military science and the keen alarm of a ready-witted military people could suggest to make the Confederacy equal to the next emergency that should be forced upon it by the Union Government.

"The campaign against New Orleans also opened prematurely.   General Butler had barely enough troops to hold the city, and was unable to reap the fruits of his victory. Instead of capturing the best part of Louisiana, and occupying the capital of Mississippi, thus severing Texas from the Confederacy, he was hardly able to hold his own in New Orleans.   The story of the military blunders, resulting in the costly sieges of Vicksburg and Port Hudson, would never have had to be written had the plans suggested by General McClellan been executed.   It was found, too, when the movement was made upon Richmond, that the fatal blunder of the premature opening of the campaign in the West and in the Southwest had nerved the rebellion to put forth every effort to save its capital. Troops were hurried from all parts of the Confederacy to beat back the Union forces—and they succeeded.   Nor was any advantage gained from the operations along the Atlantic coast, except in perfecting the blockade.   It is in these points that history will justify General McClellan and condemn the administration for setting him aside at that critical period of the war.

"The limits of this article will not permit us to discuss at length the Peninsular campaign.   It is enough to say that it was under the general orders of Mr. Lincoln, and that it failed ; nor have we any thing to add touching the campaigns which followed the removal of General McClellan after the battle of Antietam. It is enough to know that, after the dreadful experiences of Fredericksburg, Chancellorville, and Gettysburg, General Meade is to-day where General McClellan was when removed from command of that army, and certainly in no better position. We make these remarks in no spirit of unkindness to the administration of Mr. Lincoln personally. We believe that the President acted from patriotic considerations, and did the best according to the light he had. Nor do we believe that the party who spurred him on to set aside the well-considered plans of the General-in-Chief, were animated by any other desire than a purpose to serve their country. Subsequent events have, however, placed them cruelly in the wrong, and they must accept the verdict which impartial military science will bestow upon them."

## GENERAL McCLELLAN'S LATEST SPEECH.

The most recent date upon which General McClellan appeared before the public, was on the eighteenth of February, 1864. An official reception was given on that day by the municipal authorities of the city of New York to the veterans of the First New York cavalry, and while the proceedings were progressing at Jefferson Market, one of the members of the regiment jumped upon a table and shouted, "Silence ; keep still a moment." The others, not understanding his purpose, cried, "Get down—keep still." "I won't keep still," he answered, in a stentorian voice : "Boys, General McClellan is coming in."

In an instant there was such a scene of enthusiasm as cannot be adequately described. Every one turned towards the door ; soldiers literally clambered over each other and the tables, cheering in the wildest manner. As the great commander passed through the room, they

caught him by the hands, and gathered about him so that
he could scarcely move.    Some of those about the sides
of the room caught the American flag that adorned the
windows and waved them, cheering in the most enthusiastic manner.    Hats were waved in the air in all directions, and there was one unanimous voice of glad greet-
ing.    When the general and a friend who came with him
had reached the officers, and been heartily welcomed by
them, Colonel McReynolds, the commanding officer of the
regiment, arose and requesting silence, spoke as follows:

### SPEECH OF COLONEL McREYNOLDS.

" SOLDIERS : But a short time ago the chairman of this
occasion did us the honor to refer to the fact that the First
New York cavalry were the last on the Chickahominy
and the first to reach the James river.    It was a proud
announcement, gentlemen, and it was true.    I now have
the honor, and the great pleasure, to announce to you that
the noble chieftain who led the Army of the Potomac on
that occasion, that matchless chieftain, General George B.
McClellan—(cheers lasting several minutes)—I do not
blame you for your enthusiasm—General George B.
McClellan, has honored you with his presence.    (Renewed
cheers.)    If you will keep still for a moment, I have no
doubt he will speak to you.    (Three cheers.)"

### SPEECH OF GENERAL McCLELLAN TO THE SOLDIERS.

The tumult of cheers subsided as General McClellan
arose, and the room became as quiet as if for a prayer.
He then spoke as follows:

" MY FRIENDS AND COMRADES : I came here not to make
a speech to you, but to welcome you home, and express to
you the pride I have always felt in watching your career,
not only when you were with me, but since I left the Army
of the Potomac, while you have been fighting battles under

others, and your old commander. I can tell you now, conscientiously and truly, I am proud of you in every respect. There is not one page of your record—not a line of it—of which you, your State and your country may not be proud. I congratulate you on the patriotism that so many of you have evinced in your desire to re-enter the service. I hope, I pray, and I know that your future career will be as glorious as your past. I have one other hope, and that is that we may yet serve together some day again."

The cheers that followed this speech were a repetition of the previous scene. Officers and men cried out, "We'll follow you anywhere, General!"

## SPEECH OF MAJOR HARKINS.

Major D. H. Harkins was introduced, and said : "Fellow-soldiers : I feel indeed proud that we have been so highly honored to-day, not only by the Common Council, the Mayor of New York, and by the people, but that we have had the distinguished honor of being addressed by the first chieftain of this age. (Loud cheers.) The man, who is not only the pride and glory of our country, but who has, in all its darkest hours, come forth as its saviour, and lifted us out of destruction, making victory once more to perch upon those banners that had been made to flee before the banners of rebellion. (Cheers.) The name of General George B. McClellan (renewed cheers), and his name only, could bring back those soldiers to discipline, and make them again an organization proud and glorious. (Great cheers, waving of flags and hats.) It may be that in the dark hour to come, if it is to come, General George B. McClellan will again, like another saviour, come, and bring victory and liberty to the whole United States. (Cheers.) I will say for the First New York cavalry, that though he has not been with us in the field, he has been in our hearts. (Renewed cheering.) It is a proud thing indeed for us to be assembled here, the first regiment of cavalry in the United States service, to see more than three-fourths of them, after their arduous duties, re-enlisted for the war. (A voice, "Under General McClellan." Cheers.)

## GENERAL McCLELLAN SPEAKS AGAIN.

General McClellan now arose to go. This caused another burst of cheers, which was succeeded by silence. The General said : "Gentlemen, now I shall have to say good-bye to you for the present, and in doing so, I shall propose the health of the First New York Cavalry." (Cheers. Three cheers for "Little Mac.")

With undiminished enthusiasm the soldiers crowded about him as he left the room; many followed him out to the street, their cheers re-echoing again and again.

In a similar manner, General McClellan is received, whenever he meets any of the soldiers of the old army of the Potomac. The enthusiasm extends to the new recruits also, and even to the soldiers of the Union generally.

THE END.

www.ingramcontent.com/pod-product-compliance
Lightning Source LLC
Chambersburg PA
CBHW020232030726
47497CB00009B/3052